The moon was full

Chloe smiled. As she let the brocade curtain drop, an odd scent struck her. She put her nose to the curtain. But the scent was in the air itself, not the fabric.

There was something familiar about it. Like rose petals. And then Chloe remembered. It was Amanda's favorite scent. Chloe recalled it because it had such a cloying quality. She had always wished Amanda would switch to another perfume. But she never had.

Chloe turned from the window and the snifter of cognac slipped from her hand. The liquor splattered and the glass shattered. Chloe barely noticed.

There in the entryway stood Amanda Emory, dressed in her billowy white robe with her luxurious blond hair flowing.

"Beware, Chloe. The devil wears many guises."

The singsong voice slithered into Chloe's mind—sharp, clear, insistent. She instinctively held her hands up, palms outward to ward off danger, and retreated until her back was pressed against the wall. There was no place to go.

ABOUT THE AUTHOR

Reading the works of such noted authors as
Barbara Michaels and Thomas Tryon
inspired Elise Title to try her own hand at
crafting a story that combined familiar
settings with occult elements. Elise found
creating the people of Thornhill so
fascinating that she soon realized there were
too many stories in the town to leave it
behind after *Shadow of the Moon*. She's
already hard at work on her second Thornhill
mystery, her upcoming Intrigue novel, *Stage
Whispers*. Like the residents of the fictional
town of Thornhill, Elise and her family live
in a small New England college town.

Books by Elise Title

HARLEQUIN INTRIGUE
97–CIRCLE OF DECEPTION
119–ALL THROUGH THE NIGHT
149–A FACE IN THE MIRROR

HARLEQUIN TEMPTATION
340–MAKING IT

HARLEQUIN AMERICAN ROMANCE
377–TILL THE END OF TIME

Shadow
of the Moon
Elise Title

Harlequin Books

TORONTO • NEW YORK • LONDON
AMSTERDAM • PARIS • SYDNEY • HAMBURG
STOCKHOLM • ATHENS • TOKYO • MILAN

With special thanks to my editor,
Sue Stone

Harlequin Intrigue edition published April 1991

ISBN 0-373-22160-6

SHADOW OF THE MOON

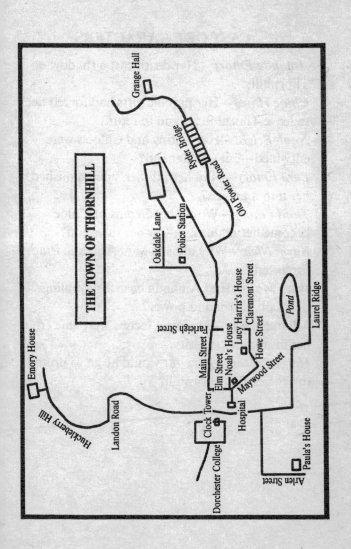

THE TOWN OF THORNHILL

CAST OF CHARACTERS

Amanda Emory—Her death cast a shadow on Thornhill.

Chloe Hayes—Her psychic gifts had forced her to leave Thornhill . . . and to return.

Noah Bright—His destiny and Chloe's were entwined—but to what end?

Lara Emory—Had her mother's death pushed her into madness?

Thad Emory—Would his dreams of Chloe become her nightmare—or her salvation?

Karin Niels—Why did she want Amanda Emory forgotten?

Peter Mott—Had Amanda been a stumbling block on his road to power?

Mildred Mead—No one's secrets were safe from her insatiable curiosity.

Harvey Mead—How far would he go to protect the citizens of Thornhill?

Prologue

Police Chief Harvey Mead stared down at the body, taking in the flowing robe, its snowy white color marred by a small circle of red blood around the hilt of a dagger. He studied the position of the body, then knelt down for a closer examination of the wound, careful not to touch anything.

George Denk, a tall, well-built, dark-haired officer came up to stand behind the chief. "The daughter found her. She's up at the house."

Mead nodded.

"There's a note."

Mead reached up a hand and Denk put the note in it.

"Looks like suicide—open and shut, like they say on TV."

Mead scowled, then read the note. There were only two lines. "I can't go on like this. I truly have no other choice." There was no signature.

Dr. Fischer, the wiry little physician with white hair and a pencil-thin mustache who doubled as the county medical examiner, came over and knelt down next to Mead. "I'll have to do an autopsy. But Denk is probably right. It looks like a self-inflicted stab wound. Right through the heart. I'd say death was nearly instantaneous. We'll know more after the autopsy."

"Anybody see anything?" Mead asked tersely.

It was Officer Denk who jumped in with an answer. "The daughter says her mother was out here conferring with the goddesses. I swear, Chief, that's what she said. Well, it's close to Halloween, and you know the rumors about Emory...that she's a witch and all. Must have been quite a kook."

"Dorchester College is full of kooks who don't kill themselves, Denk," Mead snarled.

Denk looked duly cowed as he glanced over at his fellow officer, Roy Filmore. Filmore, who'd been with Mead for over twenty years, had warned the newcomer, Denk, that the chief would be a bear over this death. Not that he'd said why. He wasn't one to spread rumors, especially not ones that involved his chief, and especially not ones that went back thirty years. What was then was then. What the heck, they'd all been young and foolish once upon a time.

Chapter One

At first glance it seemed very few things had changed in Thornhill in the seven years since Chloe Hayes had graduated from the ivy-covered sanctum of Dorchester College and left town. Although, she did notice that the college had added a much-needed low-rise dorm complex and a new gymnasium. And down along Main Street there were a couple of new banks and real estate offices. A hole-in-the-wall Chinese restaurant had taken the place of Penny's Pancake Emporium over on Arlen Street behind the bookstore. Chloe, not an afficionado of short-order chow mein, didn't see this as a change for the better. Then there was the new police station which had finally moved out of its cramped quarters in the town office building just off Main Street to a large but rather dreary two-story concrete slab building a mile from downtown.

Chloe had caught a brief glimpse of Police Chief Harvey Mead and his wife, Mildred, at Professor Emory's funeral that morning. She'd seen a lot of old familiar faces there—half the town and most of the college had turned out—and there'd been a few people she hadn't spotted. One in particular. One by the name of Noah Bright. Now Dr. Noah Bright.

She stopped along Main Street and glanced at the old clock tower. It was only a quarter past three in the afternoon, but the sky was darkening. A big storm was on the way. The late-autumn sunlight was all but blocked out, only a few rays escaping through the thick clouds and falling on the shops along Main Street, giving the whole scene a strange shimmering two-dimensional look.

A chill wind, already damp with the coming storm, tugged at Chloe's raincoat as she stared up and down the street and thought about the biggest change that had hit Thornhill since she'd left seven years ago. Professor Amanda Emory, Chairman of the Department of Anthropology, internationally acclaimed expert on witchcraft and magic through the ages, was dead. According to the *Thornhill Tab,* Professor Emory had committed suicide three days ago. Her body had been found in the glen behind her house. A ring of candles set in six-foot-high, wrought-iron candelabras had circled the supine body.

Just as when she'd first read of the tragedy, Chloe shivered, goosebumps spreading down her arms like a rash. Fragments of lines from the article flashed before her eyes—"rumors of witchcraft," "communing with the gods," "hysterical daughter swears mother was possessed," "an unusual double-edged knife pierced through her heart...."

"A double-edged dagger...unusual." Chloe felt clammy, and the street began to tilt as she thought about that dagger—a dagger she'd seen only twice in her life, each occasion making an everlasting impact on her.

Chloe first saw the dagger when Professor Emory brought it into the senior seminar she was giving on the history of witchcraft. The double-edged dagger had a black hilt on which magical symbols were engraved. Emory had called the dagger an atheme, explaining that it was a spiritual sword representing fire, one of the ancient elements needed to sanctify and ritually purify the magical space known as a circle within which witches gathered for their covens or spiritual meetings. The dagger had been passed around for the students to examine at close hand.

From the moment Emory displayed the atheme to the class, Chloe experienced a sense of heightened tension. Instinctively, she looked away from the glint of the blade. She felt foolish and embarrassed by her reaction, and when the atheme was passed around, she forced herself to take it in hand. As soon as she did, it was like wrapping her fingers around fire. A blackness surrounded her, and in that blackness she saw something white and flowing, a moving figure, a hooded phantom. It was coming toward her, the atheme raised—

The dagger clanked to the floor and all heads turned to Chloe who had gone suddenly white, her hands trembling. Professor Emory approached, picked up the atheme and passed it on to the next student. Emory took hold of Chloe's hand, the hand that only moments ago had felt on fire. Emory's touch was cooling, but her eyes, black as coal and all-knowing, stared hard into Chloe's eyes. Chloe's stomach knotted, ribbons of reds and purples seemed to smear and bleed together across the canvas of her mind, and she felt a terrible presentiment of doom drop over her like a thick blanket. The feeling only lifted after the professor drew her eyes away, removed her hand and returned to her lectures. Chloe excused herself to get some water, and could not bring herself to return to class that day.

It wasn't until a few days before graduation that she saw the atheme again. She'd been late finishing a paper for Emory and gotten an extension. As soon as she finished it, Chloe decided to bring it over to Professor Emory's house. It was just past dusk. Emory wasn't home. Her daughter

Lara, the same age as Chloe and once upon a time Chloe's friend, answered the door. Emory wasn't home but Lara said she'd take the paper and give it to her mother. Chloe didn't trust Lara and made some excuse about wanting to go over a few points with her mother. Lara shrugged, pointing to a path at the side of the house and told Chloe she'd find her mother out at the glen.

Chloe started down the path but never made it to the glen. Halfway along, a figure darted out from the woods and stood twenty feet in front of her blocking her way. It was a figure in white, flowing robe, the face hidden by a white hood. In the misty darkness the figure looked almost mystical.

Chloe froze on the spot, panic dancing like rain in her head. Fear swelled and crested, wave after wave, gathering momentum and power. Chloe called out Amanda's name, but there was no response. The white figure slowly raised a hand and then Chloe saw it—the atheme—the black-handled dagger, glinting in the shadow of the moon. The figure itself blurred before her as panic throbbed in her throat. Only the atheme maintained its sharp-edged clarity in Chloe's eyes. And then that, too, went through a metamorphosis as the white-robed figure started toward her, and the atheme became a tongue of flame. Chloe screamed as the lick of silver fire crossed her line of vision. And then she felt a searing pain jab into her chest and explode. Blackness descended.

Chloe awoke the next morning in the hospital feeling a bit dazed but in no pain. The nurse told her she'd been brought in after Professor Emory and her son, Thad, had found her unconscious on a path that ran behind their house.

Chloe remembered how her hand had gone to her chest expecting to find bandages from the knife wound. There was no bandage. She ripped open her hospital gown. No gash, no mark of any sort, not on her chest, not anywhere on her body.

As soon as she was released from the hospital, Chloe had raced back to her dorm and packed. She'd left Dorchester, left Thornhill, a day before graduation. And as she boarded the train for Boston she had made a vow never to return.

"Chloe? Chloe Hayes? Is it really you?"

Chloe started and turned at the sound of the voice. It was Mildred Mead, the police chief's wife, coming up behind her, a bag of groceries in her arms. Mildred had many claims to fame in Thornhill. Besides being what many considered the chief's right-hand woman, she was director of the community-based Doily Cart light opera company, she had a hand in a catering company called Pies to Go-Go, and perhaps most notable, she had a featured column called "What's What" in the daily *Thornhill Tab*.

At one time or another just about everyone in Thornhill had seen their name in print thanks to Mildred. Or no thanks to Mildred as was sometimes the case.

"Hello, Mrs. Mead."

The sprightly gray-haired woman looked up at Chloe over the top of her undersized wire-rimmed glasses. "Chloe Hayes, it is you."

Chloe smiled. "Yes, it's me all right."

The fifty-two-year-old reporter gripped Chloe's hand as she studied her more closely. "I thought that was you at the funeral this morning, but there were so many people there . . . quite a respectable turnout. I was pleased about that. Of course there would be, despite everything. Terrible business. Terrible business. Such a shock."

Chloe withdrew her hand from Mildred's firm, bony grip. "Yes . . . a shock."

"Her poor son, Thad, has taken it especially hard. He isn't one to hide his emotions. Not that I think there's anything wrong in that, mind you. And Lara's gone a bit over the edge, I think. Not that you can blame her. She was the one who found her mother...a terrible sight. My Harvey described it to me, of course. I don't know that it's the wisest thing for her to have moved back to her mother's house. I believe Amanda left it to her in her will. I imagine Amanda thought that once Thad went out to find fame and fortune on the West Coast, he'd settle there for good."

Chloe had thought so, too. She'd been surprised to read—in Mildred's column, of course—that he'd come back to Thornhill last year to take an appointment at Dorchester in the English department. Thad had been very involved in film studies as a student at Dorchester and had taken off for Hollywood four years ago with a briefcase full of screenplays that he'd written and full of high hopes for getting them sold. He'd stopped by to see her in Boston before catching his flight. It had been a somewhat awkward meeting, Thad making no attempt to disguise the torch he was still carrying for her, a torch he'd taken up at college.

"Students adore him," Mildred went on.

Chloe smiled. "I'm not surprised."

"I wouldn't be surprised if he isn't even more popular than his mother was. Of course it hurts to see her reputation being tarnished the way it is."

Chloe frowned. "What do you mean?"

"I hate to say it but Amanda brought some of the rumors on herself." She stopped short, not an easy feat for the loquacious small-town journalist. "All those silly secret rituals in the moonlight! Oh, she didn't advertise her little get-togethers, but in a town like this word gets around."

Chloe had to smile. Yes, word got around all right. Mostly due to Mildred.

"No disrespect intended, of course. I know you were fond of her. And she of you, of course."

"Yes..."

"She was very pleased that you got into all this hoodoo, voodoo yourself."

Chloe felt her anger surge. "I'm a researcher in parapsychology, Mrs. Mead. There's nothing hoodoo or voodoo about it. It's a perfectly respected field of experimental psychology." She didn't add that in her own way Amanda Emory had been influential in Chloe's choice of a career. She'd initially felt compelled to study parapsychology and psychic phenomena because of her own inexplicable experiences involving the atheme. Later, she came to find the subject fascinating in its own right. She'd even slowly come to accept that she did have vivid sensitivity when presented with certain types of stimuli. On a few occasions that sensitivity had even proved enormously helpful.

Mildred saw that the younger woman was irritated and on edge. "I'm only teasing you a little, Chloe. Why, I read in all the Boston papers, just last fall, about how you found that poor, lost child of your neighbor's. Using your psychic powers, so I read."

"Using common sense and having some luck," Chloe rebutted, not wanting to be quoted in tomorrow's *Tab* as a psychic kook.

"And wasn't there one other time...what was it I'd heard...?"

Chloe pulled her coat closed. "It looks like it's about to pour. We should both get going."

Mildred merely nodded, making no move to leave. Instead she eyed Chloe meditatively for some seconds, then spoke earnestly. "Do you believe Amanda killed herself?"

Chloe shouldn't have been surprised by the question. It had been the very one that had been troubling her ever since she'd read about Professor Emory's suicide. Troubling was too weak a word. And it had begun before she'd read the article in the *Tab*. The night before the article appeared she'd had a terrible dream. She'd seen Amanda Emory in the center of a circle of light, her arms uplifted, that mystifying, frightening atheme in hand. And then a voice, Chloe wasn't sure in her dream if it was Amanda's voice or someone else's. It had a strange warbly quality as it called out, "Come celestial goddess of the wind, come moon shadow of a thousand forms and look favorably on my sacrifice."

"Why, my dear, you're trembling," Mildred said softly taking hold of Chloe's hand. "I'm sorry. That was terribly insensitive of me."

Chloe shook her head. "No, no... really, I'm fine. It's just...well, it's such a terrible thing for someone to do..."

Mildred's nearsighted gaze was all consuming. "You don't believe it then, either. And I don't believe any more than you do that a strong-willed woman like Amanda would ever take her own life. Despite what Lara says about her mother going into a trance.

"The poor girl's convinced that Amanda habitually communed with goddesses and accidentally drew down the wrong goddess, an evil one. Lara thinks Amanda must have been trying to exorcise her and lost the battle. According to Lara it wasn't really her mother stabbing herself in the heart with that hideous dagger, but the evil goddess, you see."

Chloe's dark blue eyes narrowed. "Lara can't really believe that. She was always such a cynic about those rumors about her mother actually being involved in witchcraft. She knew it was pure scholarly interest on Amanda's part."

Mildred shrugged, dismissing the remark. "I suppose you know about Lara and Noah. The divorce, I mean."

Chloe winced inside. Seven years and Noah's name still hit a nerve.

"I continued my subscription to the *Tab*." Chloe had not only read about the divorce, she'd been kept informed about Noah's activities through frequent blurbs in Mildred's "What's What" column. Mildred seemed to have a particular fondness for Noah, his name popping up often in her articles—"Dr. Noah Bright has just been named head of the new neuropsychiatric unit at Dorchester Regional Medical Center." "Dr. Noah Bright has recently moved from Oakdale Lane to Maywood Street." "Dr. Noah Bright did a brilliant turn as the captain in the Doily Cart production of the *Pirates Of Penzance*." "Dr. Noah Bright cut quite a rug last night at the Christmas charity dance at St. Matthew's church."

"I don't suppose you were surprised."

Mildred's comment drew Chloe away from her wool-gathering. "Surprised?"

"You weren't, were you?"

Chloe knew Mildred was referring to Noah's and Lara's divorce, but that wasn't a subject she cared to discuss with Mildred or anyone else.

Mildred, it seemed, didn't require a response. "No," she said softly, "neither was I."

They parted then, Mildred heading up Main Street, Chloe heading south. She was staying at her old off-campus dorm that had since been converted to a bed and breakfast inn, still run by her old dorm mother, Lucy Harris.

There were two ways to get to Mrs. Harris's from Main Street. One way would take Chloe down Farleigh Street, past the old historic society and then down Clarmont. Mrs. Harris's whitewashed brick two-story colonial was on the corner of Clarmont and Howe Street, just behind Dorchester's Alumni Hall. The other route, the one Chloe didn't so much choose as find herself on, took her across Elm Street and down Maywood Street, which eventually curved into Howe at the end, three blocks away.

As she turned onto Maywood, Chloe did not have the conscious thought that this was the street Dr. Noah Bright had moved to nine months ago—after his divorce. She only realized it as she approached his house. How did she know this pale-gray-shingled cape with its dark gray shutters was Noah's house? Mildred hadn't noted Noah's exact address. Chloe could picture the item quite clearly. "Dr. Noah Bright has moved from Oakdale Lane to Maywood Street." Two years earlier Chloe had read all about the purchase of the old Morgan house on Oakdale Street. "The recently wed Dr. and Mrs. Noah Bright have great plans for renovating the old Morgan place," Mildred Mead had duly noted at the time.

Number seven Maywood. There was no name on the mailbox, just the ubiquitous green flag—Dorchester green dominated the little town—denoting a *Tab* subscriber. The car in the driveway was a nondescript dark blue sedan, no MD license plate.

Chloe's gaze swept over the tidy Cape Cod style house. She stopped, her breathing speeded up. This is silly, she told herself. There was no reason to believe this particular house was Noah's house. Really, it was such an ordinary little place. And there was nothing ordinary about Noah Bright.

Chloe literally jumped as the front door opened. Her breath caught in her throat until she saw the middle-aged woman in a print dress peer out.

"Can I help you?" The woman smiled pleasantly.

Chloe smiled back. After years in the big city it was nice to see friendly, unparanoid smiles as stranger greeted stranger. Chloe had always loved that about Thornhill, safety and tranquillity were so complete and so profound they permeated the air. And then, in a flash, she thought of Amanda Emory—pictured the professor lying lifeless in the glen, her mesmerizing dark eyes open but unseeing. No place was really safe.

"No thanks. I just stopped...to admire the house." Chloe forcibly pushed aside her painful visions.

"Well, isn't that nice. Thank you. I always have loved the place myself. Simple but homey."

Chloe felt foolish for having jumped to the false conclusion that this had to be Noah's house. She was also relieved to know her intuition could fail her on occasion.

"You've done a wonderful job on the landscaping, too," Chloe added.

"Oh, well, that's not my doing. I'm afraid I'm not the one with the green thumb. The doctor's the one—"

Chloe blinked rapidly. "The doctor?"

"Dr. Bright. I thought at first you might be looking for him. He's due home any minute. I was just making his lunch." The woman tsked. "Fine hour to be eating lunch. Nearly four in the afternoon. But he had an emergency at the hospital—doesn't he always? It's not easy to be a housekeeper to a physician, that's something I've learned. But this sweet little cottage would just fall apart around that poor man if someone didn't take charge."

All Chloe heard as the woman prattled on was that Noah lived here, Noah was due home any minute. All she could think was, I've got to move. I've got to get away....

If she moved, if she kept moving her pain might not catch up with her.

"I...better hurry. The storm..." Chloe left the housekeeper standing at the open door—Noah's open door—as she moved quickly away. Behind her she could hear a car turning onto Maywood. She didn't turn around. She didn't have to. It was Noah's car. Intuition. Damn her intuition. It was nearly always right.

The clouds yawned open and the rains came just as Chloe got to the spot where Maywood curved into Howe.

Noah Bright caught up with her at the curve. He'd been running, but he wasn't out of breath.

She'd known he was chasing her, that he was gaining on her, that there was no escape, but she'd kept walking briskly until he touched her arm. She turned. The rain was beating down on them.

They had first met during a storm....

Their faces were inches apart. Rain beaded on their skin and soaked into their clothes. Noah's wool tweed sport coat was no protection from the drenching downpour.

Chloe's heart quickened and an involuntary flush of desire swam through her.

Noah still looked much the same as he had when she'd met him eight years ago. His dark hair was thick and wavy, still in need of trimming. He remained lean but muscular, with an athlete's natural grace and energy. His features were sharply etched, strong, uncompromising and just short of being too good-looking. And his eyes were the same, too. Striking gray-green eyes, soul-searching eyes, bedroom eyes, eyes that could radiate so much warmth you could feel the heat seeping through your skin.

Even now, with the cold and the rain, Chloe could feel the heat. But at the same time she felt irritated. She thought of the nights she'd fallen prey to those eyes. She was a girl back then. But she was no longer a girl. With a curt move, she disengaged her arm.

"We need to talk. About Lara."

Chloe had to smile. Still as blunt as ever, too. No preambles for Dr. Noah Bright. And no chance that Lara

Emory Bright had faded from the picture. Even their divorce couldn't seem to accomplish that, Chloe thought.

"She wants to see you," Noah went on. "I don't think it's a good idea."

"Why?"

"Why does she want to see you or why don't I want you to?" Before she could answer, he took her arm again. "We're getting soaked. Come back to the house with me. We'll get out of these wet things. Shirley will put up a pot of tea for us. You still don't drink coffee, do you?"

He had a firm grip on her arm and he was guiding her back up the street toward his house. Still commanding as ever, too.

"I thought you'd leave Thornhill right after the funeral," he said tightly, his pace quickening.

Chloe gave him a sharp sideways glance. "I have some work to do in town. It sounds more like you hoped I'd leave."

He grinned. *Oh, that grin,* Chloe thought. It made his whole face light up with boyish charm. Thirty-two and still charming. That hadn't changed either.

"What's so funny?" she asked.

"Still reading minds, I see."

"Then I'm right," she said. "You are sorry to see that I'm still around."

His grin evaporated, his expression transformed from boyish charm to one of unnerving intensity. "It isn't safe for you here, Chloe."

"What are you talking about?"

"I'm talking about Lara. She showed up at the hospital. She was in such an irrational, disheveled state the intern on duty immediately shipped her up to the psychiatric ward. I just spent over an hour with her."

They were almost at Noah's house, but Chloe came to a stop, ignoring the quickening downpour. "What has Lara got to do with my being safe in Thornhill?"

"She's having vivid hallucinations and delusions. She's conjured up the belief that her mother's ghost has returned to their house. Lara is convinced that her mother's spirit spoke to her when she was alone in the house, told her that . . . you were next."

"Next?"

He grabbed hold of her shoulders. "Next to die, damn it."

Chloe stared at him incredulously. "And you're telling me you believe—"

He cut her off. "I believe that Lara is in a highly irrational state of mind right now and that she may well feel driven to make her hallucinations and delusions into a reality if she can."

Chloe stared at Noah almost in a trance. The air smelled slightly of ozone. Its very texture felt charged. Charged with danger. The danger seemed to clog the air around her, amplified, oozing from the clouds, raindrops tiny daggers . . .

Dagger. The atheme. The double-edged knife with the strange runes marking its hilt—the atheme, tiny red blood drops on its blade, flashing at her—the vision swarmed around her like attacking insects.

Chloe's eyes widened, a scream sliding along her throat. She stumbled forward, falling into Noah's arms. He held her tight, his embrace fierce and strong. Even the storm didn't seem able to penetrate his protective shield. Slowly she lifted her eyes to his. As their gazes locked and held, Chloe sensed the beginning of a new, uneasy alliance behind them. And even as she told herself that an alliance of any kind with the lover who'd betrayed her was the last thing she needed, she was unable to resist its compelling attraction, at least for the moment.

In the end she gathered up the strength to turn down Noah's invitation to dry off and chat, back at his house. She knew that would be a mistake. A premonition? No, this wasn't a case of premonition. It was a simple matter of common sense. She wasn't prepared for the intense flare-up of feelings that Noah had so quickly reignited in her. In himself, too, she thought. So she made up a lie about having an appointment with the chief of police. Noah had to know it was a lie, she'd been heading in the wrong direction to be going to the station house. But Chloe was relieved that he let the matter be.

Yet, once having told Noah the lie, she found herself thinking maybe she ought to go see Harvey Mead. She wasn't quite sure why. She wasn't even sure she wasn't simply trying to make good on her lie. Whatever the reason, she caught the free shuttle bus on the corner of Main Street and headed for the police station.

Chief Mead didn't seem surprised to see Chloe at his office door. Quite the contrary.

"I was expecting you."

Chloe gave him a disconcerted look.

Harvey Mead grinned. "I got a call from Mildred. She said she ran into you in town. Don't suppose I'll waste time asking what you two were talking about. Pretty sure I'll be reading all about it in tomorrow's *Tab*."

Chloe grinned back a little wryly. "I'd take book on it."

"Come on in and sit down, Chloe."

Chloe looked around the office. It was amazing how bright and homey it looked compared to the sterile structure of the building itself. On the chief's desk were framed photos of Mildred, his daughter Maggie with her ex-husband Rob, and their sons Leif and Mike. There was also a photo of Paula Dubois with her daughter, the chief's god-daughter Jessie. Bleached muslin curtains covered the windows, a bright multicolored rag rug the floor, and the walls were decorated with quaint Currier and Ives prints. Chloe was sure Mildred had taken a hand in the decorating. There was very little Mildred Mead didn't take a hand in.

Harvey Mead rose from his swivel chair to shake hands with Chloe as she stepped into the room. Only after he rose did she notice his chair bore a Dorchester crown insignia and the date 1956. Chloe remembered that Amanda Emory had graduated Dorchester that same year. She wondered if Amanda and the police chief had been friends.

"Haven't seen you in a long time, Chloe. We miss you at the old opera house. Mildred and I agree you were the finest soprano our little Doily Cart company ever had."

"Thanks, Chief Mead."

"Harvey. We're both all grown-up now."

Chloe smiled. "Thanks Harvey. I miss those days. I had a lot of fun doing those operettas. It was nice to get my nose out of a book on occasion."

Harvey motioned Chloe to a comfortable leather arm chair. After she sat down he pulled his swivel chair up closer and sat facing her. "Real pity about Amanda."

"Yes."

"Suppose that's what you came to see me about."

"Yes," Chloe said hesitantly. "Yes I suppose I just wanted to know..." What did she want to know?

She felt Harvey's watchful eyes on her. Slowly, she lifted her head. "I read in the *Tab*...she killed herself with a...dagger." Chloe's heart raced. "Amanda once showed us a dagger...in a witchcraft course. I wondered..."

"If it was the same dagger?" Harvey finished for her.

"Could I see it, Harvey?"

Harvey nodded, then rose from his seat, walked over to his safe and withdrew a sealed evidence bag. Inside the bag was a double-edged dagger.

Even as he carried the bag back over to Chloe, a pulse started to dance like rain inside her head. She tried to look away, to focus on Harvey's face but her eyes were riveted by the familiar-looking knife. The shape of the knife shifted and blurred...

She could see Amanda Emory in her flowing, white robe, her atheme raised, then descending....

"Chloe, Chloe are you all right?"

She heard Harvey's voice as though it were coming through a tunnel. Perspiration glistened on her face. Her skin tingled. Her chest throbbed. Her breathing was ragged.

Harvey Mead set the dagger down out of sight, and then knelt beside Chloe, lightly holding her clammy hand.

Slowly Chloe's heartbeat evened out, her vision cleared.

"I...I don't know what happened to me. Lack of sleep...I—"

"Maybe it's just too soon, Chloe. The strain. I understand. I know how much you liked Amanda. We all did. It's a shock. We're all feeling it. The whole town." He patted her hand as he spoke. "Why don't I have one of my boys drive you...where are you staying, Chloe?"

"What? Oh, at Mrs. Harris's."

Harvey smiled. "Well, that's nice. I bet Lucy Harris is glad to see you back. You were one of the few students she didn't see fit to report for 'dreadful carrying on' as she always put it. Her place is a lot quieter these days, now that she turned it into a guest house. But for all her telling me how much quieter and more pleasant it is now, I think old Lucy misses those hectic, crazy days."

Chloe sensed that Harvey was rambling to give her a few moments to regain her equilibrium, and she was grateful for it. She managed a weak smile. "I really am embarrassed."

"Nonsense. Why don't we have another little chat tomorrow? What do you say?" Harvey's grip on her hand was solid, far less bony than his wife, Mildred's. Comforting. Reviving.

A cloudiness still lingered in her head, but energy slowly flowed back into her body. Enough for her to rise. "Yes, tomorrow. Tomorrow would be better. I must be coming down with a bug. I never—almost never—have these attacks, Chief Mead...Harvey."

Harvey Mead couldn't help but notice that even though Chloe's complexion was very pale now, almost ashen, she had turned into quite an extraordinarily lovely woman. Lovely and curiously troubled. As he started to phone for a patrol car to take her home, Chloe insisted it wasn't necessary.

"I could use the walk. Fresh air will be just the thing...."

"But it's still raining pretty hard, Chloe."

"I'll be fine." But she didn't sound convincing, even to herself.

Chief Harvey Mead's smile wasn't particularly convincing, either, adding to her discomfort and tension. But even more disquieting was that black-handled knife that lay somewhere in its bag. Out of sight, but not out of mind. Would it ever be out of mind again?

"Chloe?"

Harvey's voice stopped her at the door. "Yes?"

"Was it the dagger Amanda had shown you in class?"

Her sweaty palm slipped on the doorknob. "I'm sorry Harvey...I'm just...not sure."

A puzzled frown etched Harvey's brow as he considered the ceremonial dagger, turned lethal. A few moments later he went to stand by his window and thoughtfully watched Chloe Hayes hurry down the path in the rain.

Chapter Two

There was a sharp rap on Chloe's door. Chloe was still in bed, but she wasn't asleep. Actually she'd been awake since seven. Normally she was an early riser, never one to lounge idly about. Not that she'd call these past three hours in bed lounging. What then? Deliberating? Yes, that seemed a fitting description.

"Chloe? Are you awake?"

Chloe got out of bed, threw on her white chenille robe and went to open the door.

"Good morning, Chloe," Lucy Harris said with a clear note of disapproval in her tone. The seventy-four-year-old widow did not abide people wasting their mornings in bed.

"Good morning, Mrs. Harris," Chloe replied politely, the corners of her mouth bearing faint traces of a smile. She knew from years past that old Mrs. Harris ran a tight ship. "I must have overslept."

"You aren't ill, are you, Chloe?" Lucy didn't really make exceptions for the sick, unless they were good and sick. There she was, after all, awake each morning at the crack of dawn, burdened with the heavy responsibility of running the house, and her suffering a terrible case of arthritis. Today was especially bad.

Chloe observed the flicker of pain across the old woman's face. "I'm fine, Mrs. Harris. But you don't look all that well, if you don't mind my saying."

"Old age is all," Lucy said in an oddly flat tone, smoothing back her white hair which she wore in a knobby bun on the top of her head. "The pain in my joints is something awful."

"You should see a doctor."

Lucy Harris waved her hand in a dismissive gesture. "All they do is give you pills to swallow. And pills don't do a thing. No, doctors can't help. Only the professor knew the proper medicine for me. And now she's taken it to her grave."

"Professor Emory gave you medicine?"

"Not medicine exactly," Lucy said cautiously. "A blend of herbs and such."

"A healing potion, you mean."

Lucy scowled. "Oh, I know there's some go on about the professor having been a witch, but that was stuff and nonsense. She was a brilliant woman and she…knew her herbs, is all."

Chloe had to smile. She'd once taken a fascinating anthropology course with Amanda called The Healing Magic of Witchcraft that had a unit on medicinal applications of witches' brews. The professor had even concocted a so-called love potion in class one day. All of the students had laughed about her claim that it had magical properties, but when Amanda had offered free samples, only a few students volunteered. Chloe hadn't been one of them.

Lucy Harris made a clucking sound with her tongue. "Here I am, talking about my aches and pains, and I almost forgot what I came up here for. She's here to see you."

Chloe started. *"She...?"* Given the fact that Lucy had just been discussing Amanda Emory, Chloe had a fleeting fantasy that Amanda's ghost was making a call.

"Lara Bright." Lucy tsked. "I suppose I should be calling her Emory again. She took back her maiden name after the divorce, you know. Not that I hold much with doctors, but Noah Bright's a good and decent man. He didn't deserve a wife who carried on behind his back."

Despite the warmth of the cozy room, Chloe felt a sudden chill. She ran her fingers nervously through her still-uncombed hair.

"She doesn't look at all well," Lucy commented. "Not that it's any wonder. Such a terrible shock. For all of us. Well...perhaps not all," Lucy added with a noticeable puckering of her lips.

"What do you mean?" Chloe asked with unmasked curiosity.

"Yes, Lucy, whatever do you mean?" came a husky voice from behind the garrulous woman.

Lucy emitted a little gasp as Lara Emory stepped into view. The tall, blond-haired woman, dressed in a pair of tight-fitting jeans, plaid flannel shirt and dungaree jacket, was smiling sardonically.

Lucy's hand went to her chest. "I'm sorry...Lara. I didn't mean...anything. I'm not one to gossip. Heaven knows I've never looked kindly on those that do. And there are certainly those in this town that make a habit of it. Some even make a profession... Well, I prefer to mind my own business." She quickly returned her gaze to Chloe, stuck her glasses back on, and gave the young woman a look of sharp disapproval. "You do realize that breakfast is served from seven to nine with no exceptions, Chloe. As it's nearly ten-thirty."

"It's all right, Mrs. Harris. I don't usually eat breakfast," Chloe said soothingly.

"We can always go over to Red's Coffee Shop, Chloe," Lara added, raising one finely shaped pale eyebrow in Lucy Harris's direction. "They serve breakfast till eleven. And, fortunately, they do make exceptions."

Lucy's mouth twitched and she clearly looked as if she regretted her few moments of sympathy for Lara Emory. Really, her expression said, the Emory girl had no manners at all, and certainly no respect for her elders.

As Lucy hurried off in a huff, Lara emitted a sharp, unpleasant laugh. "The stingy busybody," she muttered.

Chloe, still standing at her open door, observed her old schoolmate with a puzzled expression. Yesterday, Noah had led her to believe that Lara was on the edge, indeed, over the edge, of a nervous breakdown. Hallucinations, delusions, paranoia. And just a few moments ago, Lucy Harris had been commenting that Lara didn't look at all well. But at the moment Lara Emory looked just fine. It had been seven years and she'd hardly aged a bit. Still blatantly beautiful, with her long, lustrous blond hair, her provocative blue eyes, her aristocratic bone structure. And she was still as willful and acerbic as ever.

"You didn't come over to see me yesterday," Lara said with a mix of irritation and disappointment in her voice.

"You mean at the hospital?" Chloe asked, stepping back into her bed-sitting-room.

Lara followed her inside and closed the door.

At the sound of the lock turning, Chloe felt a spurt of alarm.

"I meant at the funeral. How did you know I was in the hospital?" Lara asked, her wide-set electric blue eyes narrowing in wariness.

Chloe sensed the heightened agitation and guardedness behind Lara's self-assured appearance. She hesitated before responding. "Noah—"

Lara cut her off with a sharp laugh that was none too pretty. "You didn't waste any time there, did you?"

Chloe felt her face heat up. "I didn't . . ." She stopped, irritated at herself for letting Lara make her feel guilty. That hadn't changed about Lara, either. She was still good at intimidation. But Chloe had changed. She was no longer easily intimidated. "I didn't seek Noah out, Lara. Not that it would be any of your business at this point if I did. As it was, we simply bumped into each other in the street." She saw no point in mentioning that she just happened to have been on Noah's street. Nor was she about to tell Lara that some inexplicable force had guided her right to his very house.

Lara's lips curved upward, but it wasn't exactly a smile. "Quite right." She gave Chloe a long, silent, assessing gaze. "You're looking good. I like your hair that way."

Instinctively Chloe smoothed back her thick tangle of uncombed auburn hair. She wore it shoulder-length now and let her curls have their way. Back in college she'd kept her hair short and was forever struggling to keep the curls at bay.

"Did Noah tell you why I was in the hospital?"

Lara's sudden switch threw Chloe off. "He said you were . . . distraught. It's certainly understandable."

"One thing about you hasn't changed, Chloe. You still don't lie very well."

Instead of becoming defensive, Chloe smiled. "You're right, Lara."

Lara smiled back. A real smile now. It softened all of the young woman's features, blunting the hard edge of her beauty, giving her an almost vulnerable look. It reminded

Chloe of why there'd been times when she'd honestly liked Lara Emory.

Lara flopped on Chloe's unmade bed. "I flipped out. That's what Noah told you."

"He didn't quite use that term, but basically, yes."

"And he told you that I was seeing things. Imagining things."

Chloe hesitated. "Yes."

Lara rolled over on her back and propped her head on Chloe's pillows. "I found her, you know."

The offhand way Lara said it made Chloe shiver. Her throat constricted as she said, "I read about it in the *Tab*. It must have been awful for you."

Lara sat up, pulling the blanket over her legs despite the fact she was fully clothed. Her vivid blue eyes held a wild glitter. "Awful, yes. But..." She crossed her arms over her chest and hugged her waist. Her look became distant and a strained smile played at her mouth.

"But what?" Chloe asked softly.

Slowly, Lara's eyes focused on Chloe. "He looks great, doesn't he?"

"Who?" she asked even though she was certain Lara was referring to Noah. Chloe wasn't sure if Lara was deliberately bouncing back and forth between topics to throw her off guard, or if under the controlled surface Lara really had flipped out.

When Lara made no response, Chloe said simply, "Noah looks the same. So do you." Chloe kept her tone light, pleasant, indifferent.

"He's changed. So have I." Lara impulsively flung off the covers and stretched, as if she were the one rising from a night's sleep in the bed. "So have you. Nothing ever stays the same."

Chloe shrugged. "I suppose that's true."

"You know it's true." There was a sharp edge to Lara's voice.

"What do you mean?"

Lara sprang athletically up from the bed and faced Chloe. "You knew she was going to die. You knew. Or at least you sensed it. You had a premonition. I know you did."

"Lara—"

"You always could sense things. That's what she told me."

"Who told you?"

"Amanda. My mother."

"When? When did she tell you?"

Lara's blue eyes burned with a bleak intensity. "Noah told you I saw her ghost. Mother's ghost. You think I'm crazy. That's what Noah wants you to think. He . . . hates me." Tears suddenly sprang from Lara's eyes. "He hates me, but it's mother he blames."

"Lara, what are you saying? What does Noah blame Amanda for?"

Lara's hands sprang out to grab Chloe. Instinctively Chloe recoiled.

Lara froze for several moments, and then abruptly let her hands fall to her sides. Her eyes were fixed on Chloe, her expression distraught. "He's turned you against me. I should have known."

Chloe felt a terrible wave of guilt as she watched Lara crumple into a heap on the floor, sobbing with her head in her hands.

Chloe knelt and gently squeezed Lara's shoulder. "If you mean Noah, he hasn't done any such thing. I'm not against you, Lara. I feel sorry for you. It's awful to lose a parent." Chloe pressed her lips together. "I know what it's like." She'd lost both her parents in a car crash. It had happened the summer before she'd started college. Her freshman year had been almost unbearable. She couldn't count the times she'd almost left school. Amanda Emory had been one of the people at the college who'd helped her through it. And now Chloe felt that she owed it to Amanda to reach out and help her daughter, Lara.

Chloe sat beside Lara on the floor, putting her arm around Lara's shoulder. "Give it some time, Lara. It's perfectly understandable to flip out a little. And it isn't true you have no one. You have me. You have Thad..."

Lara stopped crying and lifted her tearstained face, her expression grim. "My brother doesn't understand. He never did believe in witchcraft."

"You didn't either, did you?" Chloe asked gently.

"I was young. I wasn't... ready."

"What made you change your mind?"

Instead of answering Chloe's question, she asked one of her own. "Why did you leave before graduation, Chloe? Was it because of me and Noah?"

"No."

Slowly, Lara nodded her head. "Amanda didn't think it was that, either. Only Thad..." She stopped. "Unrequited love is such a drag."

Chloe couldn't help but smile. "It's not nearly as satisfying as the requited kind, that's for sure."

"Thad was heartbroken when you ran off. He blamed me. He thought I should have waited until after graduation to announce the engagement. Noah wasn't any too pleased, either, now that I think about it. Guilt, I suppose." She studied Chloe thoughtfully, almost clinically. "Or perhaps it was more than guilt. I rather think Noah would have liked to have had his cake and gotten to eat it, too."

"I didn't run away because of your announcement," Chloe said in a tight, strained voice.

"Run away?" Lara echoed. "That's an interesting way of putting it. What were you running away from, Chloe?"

Now Chloe was the one who wanted to change the subject. "Lara, I ran into Mildred Mead yesterday. You know how Mildred goes on. She told me that you're convinced your mother died during one of her rituals. That she...was possessed by an evil goddess and was trying to exorcise her with the...atheme."

Lara listened with a blank expression.

"Is that what you believe?" Chloe persisted. "Was your mother holding one of her rituals? Were you there? Who else...?"

Lara suddenly looked wary. "Noah is putting you up to this, isn't he?"

"What?" Chloe was incredulous.

"He'd like to see me committed. He tried his best yesterday. Had them send me right up to the psychiatric ward. If I were crazy, that would explain it, wouldn't it?"

"Explain what?" Chloe remained dumbfounded.

"Why I left him, of course. He can't stand the humiliation of it. It would be just punishment, wouldn't it?" Lara's eyes narrowed. "Or it could be Thad. Thad's always been jealous of me, you know."

"That's ridiculous."

"No, it's true. Because I've always gotten what I wanted. I wanted Noah and I got him. I wanted..." She stopped suddenly, her lips twisting in an unpleasant smile. "If I were committed, Thad would gain control of my half of the inheritance." She shrugged. "But it's not money Thad wants." Her moist eyes glistened. "It's retribution." She stared hard into Chloe's eyes. "Is that what you want, too? Is that why you've come back?"

"Lara," Chloe said sharply, giving the young woman's shoulders a firm shake, "if you don't want people thinking you're crazy then stop talking like that. I never wanted retribution. Neither does Thad. Or Noah, for that matter. We're all concerned about you."

Suddenly Lara flung her arms around Chloe in a desperate grip. "I didn't kill her, Chloe. I swear..."

Her release was as abrupt as her assault. But the look of desperation remained etched on Lara's face. "I need you, Chloe. I'm all alone. And...I'm so scared."

"Scared of what?" Chloe asked tremulously.

Lara's eyes burned into Chloe's, all of the color draining from her face. "You're scared, too."

Chapter Three

Chloe circled the college green, pulling her jacket closed against the wind. Yesterday's rain had left huge puddles and she carefully sidestepped them. There was no rain in sight today, the air was crisp and dry, the sun overhead a pale buttery yellow.

To the right of the green was a row of white brick buildings all dating back to the 1700s. These were Dorchester College's first structures: spare, immaculate Greek-Revival buildings fronted by sprawling lawns, bordered by lofty elm trees and sugar maples still bearing traces of vibrant fall foliage.

The other buildings on campus, while newer, were also classic in design so that the whole of the college bore an architectural integrity consistent with the original structures. All of the later buildings were brick, either white or red, many fitted with proud, thick Doric columns out front. Even the dormitories carried the Greek-Revival motif. Broad, solid structures with ivy creeping up the walls.

Chloe was strolling the campus, desperately trying to clear her head and clarify her plans. When she walked by Holderness House, she paused, staring at the building. Maybe, she decided, it would help to go inside and look around the building where she had spent so much of her time during her college days.

Holderness House, built in 1742, one of the original quartet of buildings at Dorchester College, housed the department of anthropology. For the past nine years, until her untimely death, Professor Amanda Emory, chairman of the anthropology department, had occupied a cozy book-lined corner office on the second floor.

"Yes, can I help you?" The young secretary looked up from the pile of mail on his cluttered metal desk. Just beyond him, the door to the chairman's office was slightly ajar.

Distracted by the sight of a figure moving about in that inner sanctum, Chloe didn't respond to the question.

"Did you want to see Dr. Mott?" the clerk asked.

Chloe started at the name, her eyes returned to the clerk. "Peter Mott?"

"Yes, he's acting chairman now that . . . we've lost Professor Emory," the young man said awkwardly.

So, Chloe thought ruefully, Mott finally made it to the top, at least temporarily. When she'd been a student at Dorchester, Peter Mott, the youngest professor ever to gain tenure at Dorchester, was considered the whiz kid of the anthropology department. He also had a justly deserved reputation for being supercilious, cutthroat, and seductive to female colleagues and students alike. Chloe had taken one course with him, Primitive Religion, only because it was a prerequisite for a course on the evolution of witchcraft that she wanted to take with Amanda Emory. It hadn't been a pleasant experience. Mott had made an overt pass at her during one of his mandatory office tête-à-têtes. Chloe had been so irate she'd not only rebuffed him, but she'd reported the incident to Emory, as the chairman of the department. Emory had called Mott on the carpet and threatened to have official charges lodged against him if he ever again made an advance to a student. From that point on, Emory and Mott, who'd never been exactly chummy, became bitter adversaries. But Mott did seem to take Emory's cautions seriously and eased up on his seductive behavior. Chloe wondered what would happen now that Emory was gone. One change had already taken place. Emory's chair wasn't even cold yet and Mott was already occupying it. Chloe's guess was he wouldn't give it up if he could help it.

"Excuse me, miss..."

The man's deep voice cut through Chloe's ruminations. "Oh, sorry. I was just...thinking."

"Would you like to make an appointment with Dr. Mott? I expect him around three this afternoon."

"Oh, I thought— Isn't he in his office right now?"

The clerk glanced over his shoulder at the door to the chairman's office. "No. That's just Professor Emory... cleaning out a few things."

A cold chill washed over Chloe. And then she realized. Not Amanda...Thad. Professor Thad Emory.

The clerk looked a bit perplexed but didn't say anything as Chloe walked past his desk to the chairman's office and gently pushed the door completely open.

"Hi," she said softly to the husky figure bent over a gray metal file cabinet.

Thad Emory straightened with a startled lurch. His expression was one of irritation until he recognized the intruder. Immediately a bright smile lifted his lips, giving his plain face an engaging look.

Smoothing back his brown hair, he shut the file drawer and hurried over to Chloe, giving her a warm, friendly embrace. "It's good to see you, Chloe."

His effusive tone and manner made Chloe a little uncomfortable, considering the cause for this reunion. "I'm so sorry about your mother, Thad."

He flushed. "Yes. For an instant there..." He shut his eyes. "I still can't believe she's really gone. Here I am, going through her things and yet—" He cleared his throat and opened his eyes, blinking away tears.

Chloe smiled gently. "Would you like some help?"

He took her hand. "What I'd really like is to get out of here for a while. How about letting me buy you some lunch?"

"I had breakfast just an hour ago. With Lara, as a matter of fact."

Thad stiffened visibly. "My sister?"

"She's in pretty bad shape, Thad."

"Can you blame her?" His whole expression darkened.

"Why, no. No, of course not. It must have been awful for her, finding your mother..."

"Now she'll be plagued, the same as mother was. No wonder she's in such a state." His expression darkened. "Bright's behind it. You can bet on it."

"Noah? Behind what?" Surely Thad couldn't have bought into Lara's paranoia about Noah wanting her committed.

"If Bright had his way, this would become another Salem."

"What are you talking about, Thad?" Had both the Emory heirs gone over the edge?

"I'm talking about witch-hunts, Chloe. First mother was persecuted and now it will be Lara's turn."

"Persecuted? How was your mother persecuted?"

"Let's just say it was a good thing she had tenure here at Dorchester or Noah and his cronies might have gotten her thrown out on her ear. What they'll do to Lara if she takes up where mother left off, I don't know. But it won't be pleasant. Poor Lara. I guess many of mother's followers expect my sister to carry on the tradition. And Noah and some others here in Thornhill aren't keen to have the tradition maintained.''

''Why would Noah care at this point?'' She hesitated. ''What Lara does now can't bear any reflection on him.''

Thad gave her a long, close look. ''My god, Chloe. You're not still carrying a torch for that bastard. After—''

''Don't be ridiculous, Thad. I may have had a schoolgirl crush on Noah, but I assure you, I'm not a schoolgirl any longer. I just think it's crazy to imagine that Noah or anyone else in Thornhill for that matter would start a witchhunt.''

Thad's frown made deep lines across his forehead and around his brown eyes. ''Oh, he's very clever about it. Keeps a low profile. Lets others do the...dirty work.'' His voice was low and ominous.

''What do you mean? What are you saying?'' Chloe murmured, but even as she spoke the words, that muted terror erupted inside of her again. She was staring at Thad, but suddenly she saw Mildred Mead again. *''You don't think Amanda killed herself either, do you, Chloe?''* No. No, Chloe didn't believe it. Amanda was too full of life, too strong willed for suicide. Besides, what reason would she have had? Chloe didn't believe in Lara's black magic theory. But if Amanda hadn't committed suicide...

Chloe had a sudden wild, luminous vision of a figure in a flowing, white robe, arms extended. And then a strange pleading voice, *''Come celestial goddess of the wind, come moon shadow...''*

The arms were clasping her shoulders, shaking her. ''Chloe. Chloe, are you all right?''

A muffled cry escaped Chloe's lips as her eyes focused on Thad. He put his arms around her. "Don't be scared, Chloe. I'm here," he murmured. "I won't let anything happen to you."

Chloe drew away abruptly and pulled herself together. "Why should anything happen to me?"

"I just thought . . . maybe Lara . . . frightened you."

Chloe's back stiffened. "Why is everyone suddenly so worried about me? You, Lara, Noah . . ."

"Noah?" Thad gave a harsh laugh. "The only person Noah's ever worried about is Noah. He broke your heart and then he broke my sister's."

Chloe remembered Lucy Harris's remark about Lara carrying on behind Noah's back during their marriage. If that was the case, wasn't it Lara who'd broken Noah's heart? Was Noah still carrying a torch for Lara? Was he seeking retribution?

"I've got to go, Thad." She hoped he couldn't detect the edge of panic in her voice. "I didn't realize how late it was getting. I have a meeting with Chief Mead."

"Chief Mead?" Thad cocked his head. "Why would you be meeting with the chief?"

For some inexplicable reason she lied. "Just to reminisce. About our old Doily Cart days together. I have a feeling the chief hopes I'll stick around for a while and take part in their upcoming production."

Thad leaned a little closer to her. "Will you stay around for a while, Chloe?"

Chloe met his gaze. She couldn't tell if he hoped her answer would be yes or no. "I'm still considering it, Thad."

A heaviness hung in the air as Thad took her response with a faint nod. Chloe bid a quick good-bye and hurried out of the office.

Once outside Holderness House, she took a long, steadying breath. Then she reached in her purse for the shuttle bus schedule. While she was checking it, a car pulled up at the curb about thirty yards from where she stood. Chloe looked up just as Peter Mott stepped out of the idling car. A moment later a woman popped out of the driver's door.

"Peter, you forgot this." She was waving an envelope at Mott. He came hurrying back, took the envelope and then gave the woman a brief but passionate kiss.

Chloe stared in sharp surprise at the woman in Mott's arms. It was none other than Lara Emory.

"They make a nice looking couple, don't they?"

At the sound of the familiar voice behind her, Chloe spun around. Noah Bright smiled. A decidedly cynical smile.

"Revisiting old haunts?" Noah asked. Though he was smiling, there was a measure of coolness in his tone. He guided Chloe away from the walk leading from Holderness House to the street. Chloe guessed Noah didn't wish to cross paths with Peter Mott who was heading up the path to the building. At the moment, neither did she.

"I was just...taking a stroll," she said, keeping her tone light.

"And visiting old chums," he added. "I just came from Amanda's office. Thad said you'd been there. He seems delighted you're back."

"I'm taking advantage of my trip back to do some research at the college. It shouldn't take long." Chloe gave Noah a sharp look, then turned and walked away across the campus lawn. She had no intention of discussing her work with Noah Bright.

Noah caught her arm before she'd gone more than a few steps. His gray-green eyes flickered with concern. "Don't get tangled up with the Emorys again, Chloe. For your own good.''

Chloe extricated her arm from Noah's grip. She faced him, her auburn head even with his jaw so that she had to tilt her chin up to meet his gaze. "I don't see where you come off knowing what's in my best interest, Noah. Why don't you just . . . leave me alone?''

"Lara visited you this morning.''

"Are you spying on me?''

"I went by Lucy's to invite you to lunch. She told me you'd just taken off with Lara.''

Was that a flicker of alarm she saw in Noah's gray-green eyes? "What of it?''

He sighed, his expression softening. "Maybe it's just as well that the two of you got together. You always used to have a settling effect on Lara. She's heading for disaster if she doesn't pull herself together.''

For all her own jumble of feelings, Chloe felt a wave of sympathy for Noah. He obviously still cared about Lara. While he sounded more disgruntled than concerned, she sensed this was just a cover-up. She'd often been able to perceive people's inner feelings even if they tried to shield them from view.

Out of the corner of her eye she caught sight of Mott entering Holderness House. "How long has Lara been seeing—?''

"Mott?'' he broke in firmly. "For a while.''

"Is it . . . serious, then?'' she asked, and then regretted the question realizing Noah might think it tactless.

A harsh laugh escaped his lips. "It's intense. Is that the same thing?''

Chloe didn't think it was, but she didn't say so. She headed for the street, intent on catching the next shuttle bus across the campus. Noah kept pace with her and for a few moments neither of them spoke.

The sun cast a mellow glow over the fading autumn landscape. The air held a crisp purity, the soft blue sky shining over the surrounding rolling hills. "I used to think Thornhill was the most idyllic town there ever was," Chloe mused.

"And what do you think now?" Noah asked softly.

She stopped abruptly and stared grimly at Noah. "I feel as if Amanda Emory's death has cast a dark shadow over everything here in Thornhill. Over...everyone. Noah, do you think Amanda killed herself?"

His jaw muscle twitched. "Do you mean, do I believe Lara's theory that by a twist of black magic or some such nonsense, an evil goddess invaded Amanda's body and she sought to exorcise it?"

Chloe quirked a brow. "Obviously, you don't believe that."

"Come on, Chloe. Oh I know you're into parapsychology and such, but surely you don't buy all that tripe about supplicants prancing naked in the fields, creating cones of power, offering sacrifices to the goddesses? White magic, black magic...it's just plain foolishness. And maybe worse. It could be dangerous."

"Dangerous?"

"That kind of superstition can prey on people's minds, delude them into believing that they have some kind of secret mystical powers, work them up into a frenzy. You'd be amazed, Chloe, at some of the supposedly sane folk here in Thornhill who've bought into this hokum."

"Like who?"

"Lara, for one. And Mott."

"Peter Mott?"

"I think he just likes being around a bevy of naked women." Noah gave a wry grin. "Oh, yes, Lara dragged me to a few of Amanda's circles. Of course, Amanda was always careful to call her little get-togethers academic recreations of the covens of old. Strictly educational." Slowly he shook his head. "Amanda may have been a brilliant anthropologist and an expert on the study of witchcraft, but at some point along the way, she lost her scholarly perspective. And she had herself quite an illustrious group of followers."

"And an equally illustrious opposition group virtually up in arms?" The corners of Chloe's mouth tightened. Was Thad right? Was Noah part of a group of witch-hunters?

That frustratingly enigmatic smile reappeared on Noah's face. "No town is really idyllic, Chloe. Not once you peek below the surface."

"I realize that all too well," she responded, fixing her gaze on Noah.

He seemed unperturbed by her close scrutiny. "And the answer to your earlier question is no. I don't think Amanda Emory died because she was exorcising an evil goddess."

"Then you think it was a simple case of suicide?" Her voice was breathy and sounded oddly unlike her own.

Noah gave Chloe a long, appraising stare. "Is anything in life...or death...ever simple?"

Chapter Four

"Was that Noah Bright who dropped you off out front?"
Chief Mead asked, stepping away from his window as
Chloe entered his office.

Chloe shrugged. She didn't want people in Thornhill
thinking that she and Noah were an item again. "I bumped
into him on campus and he offered to give me a lift."

Harvey Mead smiled good-naturedly. "He's a good man,
Bright."

"There are some who agree with you," Chloe muttered,
recalling Lucy Harris's comment. *"He's a good and decent man."* Of course there were some who disagreed. Like
Thad and Lara Emory to name two. Chloe was doing her
best to suspend judgment, to remain neutral where Noah
Bright was concerned. Fat chance, she thought ruefully.

"You don't still hold a grudge against Noah, do you,
Chloe?"

"Really, Harvey, I didn't drop by to discuss my feelings
for or against Noah Bright."

"No, of course you didn't," Harvey agreed amiably,
motioning for her to take a seat.

She gave a nervous look around the room, especially
scrutinizing Harvey's desk.

"The dagger's not here," the chief said softly.

"What . . . ?" She felt her cheeks warm. "I guess seeing that atheme yesterday . . . just made it all so . . . real." The image of the dagger flashed before her eyes and once again she felt a wave of dizziness, but forced it away. "It's so horrible," she whispered.

"Yes, I agree, Chloe."

"Chief . . . Harvey, I have to ask you something," Chloe said, unable to mask the note of desperation in her voice.

"Please. Sit down first."

Chloe wondered if the chief was afraid she'd have another "spell." She sat down, trying to look cool and composed. But, of course, it was impossible. "Was it really suicide, Chief Mead? Is there any question of . . . ?"

"Foul play?"

She gave a humorless smile. "At least you didn't say witchcraft."

He smiled back with a touch of tenderness, but the smile winked out as he said, "It looks like suicide, Chloe. But I've been in this business long enough to know that looks can be deceiving." He pulled up a chair and sat down across from her. "You saw Lara Emory this morning. What did . . . ?"

"How did you know I saw Lara? My god, I know news travels fast in small towns, but really, this is too much." And then she looked at the chief with alarm. "You aren't having me . . . watched?"

"Lucy Harris called me." He grinned. "Lucy Harris calls me every day. Either there's a car illegally parked outside her house, or she thinks her rear door might have been tampered with, or some newcomer staying at her place for the night seems suspicious. Or just to pass on gossip for that matter."

"I get the picture."

Harvey chuckled. "Mildred thinks Lucy's got a crush on me. But she doesn't mind as long as I pass the gossip on to her. Mildred can't be in all places at all times, and nobody hates missing a scoop more than my Milly."

He was clearly hoping to niggle a smile out of Chloe, but she wasn't in a mood for levity.

"So, Lucy told you Lara came to see me. What of it?" There was a challenging note in Chloe's voice.

"When you left Thornhill you and Lara weren't on the best of terms."

"That was a long time ago, Harvey."

"And when Mildred and I were at Amanda's funeral the other day, I...uh...noticed that you didn't go over to Lara to pay your respects."

"There were so many other people gathering round both Lara and Thad, I just thought I'd...wait for another time."

"It was a big turnout," Harvey commented. After a brief pause, he asked, "When Lara dropped by today, did she tell you her theory about how her mother died?"

"No." Chloe hesitated. "She did say it was awful finding her mother's body."

"Yes. When we arrived on the scene, Lara was in pretty bad shape. She told some wild tale about her mother being invaded by an evil goddess."

"Yes, I know. Your wife told me about it."

Harvey smiled. "I can always rely on Milly to spread the word, which is why I haven't told her I questioned Lara again yesterday..."

"Yesterday?"

"Before she showed up at the hospital."

"There really are no secrets in a small town," Chloe reflected.

Harvey sighed. "Well now, if that were entirely true, my job would be a lot easier."

Before Chloe could ask him what he meant, he returned to the subject of Lara. "What she told me yesterday morning was that her mother was holding one of her circles that night. Lara usually attended, but she said she wasn't feeling well and decided to stay up at the house and lie down. She claims she had a bad headache."

"She did suffer from migraines in college," Chloe confirmed, then wondered why she felt the need to support Lara's claim. And then she remembered Lara's words that morning. *I didn't kill her... I didn't...*"

If her expression gave away her upset, Harvey didn't seem to notice. "Anyway, Lara never saw her mother alive again after Amanda went off to the meadow for her little... get-together."

"Who was at this... get-together?" Chloe asked. "Did Lara know?"

"She gave us the names of the ones she thought would have been there. We checked them out. They all say the meeting ended by 10:00 p.m. Everyone also confirms that Amanda stayed behind for some... private communion with the spirits." He smiled. "If anyone could... how did Lara put it...? Oh yes, draw down a goddess... well, I'd put my money on Amanda Emory. However, Lara's theory about Amanda drawing down the wrong goddess during her communion is blatant conjecture. Pure fantasy. It looks like Lara's a chip off the old block." He slowly shook his head.

"You think Lara's theory is groundless?"

Harvey held up his hand. "Let's say I'm not ruling out a connection between the power of suggestion and Amanda's death. As my Milly says, you just never know. But one thing I'm sure of. When I talked to Lara Emory the first time, she was understandably dazed and in shock. When I talked to her yesterday morning, I got the distinct impression she was real scared." His eyes fixed on Chloe. "What was your impression when you saw her?"

Chloe felt her chest constrict. "Why would she be scared? You don't think she had anything to do with..." She couldn't finish the sentence. It was too awful.

Harvey leaned way forward in his seat so that he was practically nose to nose with Chloe. "I think she knows more than she's telling me. Maybe she felt safer opening up to you."

Chloe shook her head slowly. "You were right before. I wasn't on the best of terms with Lara before I left Thornhill. And, to be honest, I'm not sure how I'd define our relationship now. I'm not sure how I feel toward Lara, nor how she feels toward me."

"She sought you out."

"She knows I had a...special bond with her mother."

"Noah called me yesterday. Just a few minutes after you left here as a matter of fact."

"So, he was the one who told you Lara went to the hospital."

Harvey nodded. "He also told me about Lara imagining she'd seen her mother's ghost and that business of her believing you'd be next."

"She didn't say anything about that to me this morning, Harvey. I think she was just...very upset...yesterday. Possibly having to go over everything again with you..."

"You think I drove her over the edge?"

Chloe blushed. "Oh no. Of course not. You were just...doing your job." She hesitated, then went on. "Why did you question Lara again? Don't you think it was suicide?"

Harvey didn't answer immediately. "Amanda left a note."

"A suicide note?" Chloe's skin prickled.

Harvey Mead shrugged. "Could be interpreted that way." His brow furrowed and he rubbed at the creases. "It was just a couple of lines. 'I can't go on like this. I truly have no other choice.'" He left off rubbing his forehead and rubbed his hands together instead. "That was it."

Chloe experienced a mix of trepidation and anticipation. "Can I . . . see the note?"

He gave her a curious, thoughtful look. "Yes, I suppose so. As soon as it comes back from the state police. Sent it down to their lab for handwriting analysis and such."

A bubble of panic swelled in Chloe's chest. "Then you don't think it was suicide?"

Harvey Mead stood up abruptly and stared solemnly down at Chloe. "I'll tell you, Chloe. I knew Amanda Emory for over forty years. We were in college together. But what I'm saying here is, Amanda didn't change much over the years. Kept her looks, her flamboyance, her zest for life. I think that, of all the women I ever knew, Amanda Emory was the least likely to kill herself. Would you agree?"

He snapped the question out at her and Chloe answered immediately and with conviction, "Yes, I agree." She closed her eyes, a shadowy image in white gliding across the fabric of her mind. And then a soft, hollow moan. Instantly she opened her eyes.

Harvey was studying her closely. "The way I see it, Chloe, if we're right and she didn't stab herself to death," he said in a low, tight voice, "then there's only one other alternative. Somebody else stabbed her to death. It's as simple as that."

"Nothing's ever as simple as it seems," Chloe murmured so low that Harvey didn't hear.

THERE WAS A LETTER waiting for Chloe when she returned to Mrs. Harris's. Chloe took it up to her room to read. The note was neatly typewritten.

Dear Ms. Hayes,

You probably don't remember me, but I'm the reference librarian at the Thornhill Library. I was one of Professor Emory's most ardent followers. My heart is deeply troubled and I write you out of desperation, knowing no one else to turn to. Would you meet me this evening at the old Grange Hall just past the Ryder Bridge? I'll be there at 9:00 p.m. Please, please, be there.

Yours very truly,
Alice J. Donovan

Chloe set down the note. Alice J. Donovan. Chloe did remember Alice. Not only had she chatted with her on a few occasions while using the town library, but everyone in the town knew that Alice Donovan was one of Amanda Emory's devout fans. Rumor was that Alice had even finagled a recipe for one of Amanda's love potions, which she whipped up and drank with regularity. Chloe wondered if it had done the spinster librarian any good. She also wondered what it was Alice wanted to see her about. She'd have to go to find out.

Lucy Harris's head popped out of the front parlor. "Where are you off to at this late hour, Chloe?"

"It's not very late, Mrs. Harris. It's only a little past eight-thirty."

Lucy Harris gave her a shrewd look. "I see you rented a car for yourself this afternoon."

"The shuttle bus service doesn't operate past 8:00 p.m."

"Not to mention that it doesn't cover all areas of the town. The outskirts and such."

Chloe gave Mrs. Harris a sharp look. The old Grange Hall where she was heading to meet Alice Donovan was located on the outskirts of town. And the shuttle bus didn't cross the Ryder Bridge. Had the old busybody, as Lara had called Mrs. Harris, actually managed to read her note?

"I'd be careful, if I were you, Chloe," Lucy said, peering over her spectacles.

"What do you mean?" Chloe retorted, not masking her irritation. Yes, she felt certain that Lucy had read that note.

"Thornhill isn't the same place it was when you were a student here all those years back."

"You make it sound like a century ago, Mrs. Harris. It's only been seven years."

"A lot has changed in seven years. You don't know."

"Well, thanks for your concern, Mrs. Harris, but I'm sure I'll be just fine." Chloe took a firm hold of the knob on the front door.

"Will you be back by ten? I lock the doors at ten o'clock sharp. Used to be a time when no one here in Thornhill locked their doors, but like I said, things change. People aren't safe anymore...."

"I'm not sure when I'll be back, Mrs. Harris. But I believe the key to my room also unlocks the front door."

"Well...yes."

"Then there's no problem," Chloe said, opening the door.

As she shut it after herself, she heard Lucy Harris's last words. "Oh, there are problems aplenty..."

IT WAS STILL DUSK as Chloe started for the Grange, but as she drove, night took over by degrees so that by the time she turned onto the Old Fowler Road, ten miles past the downtown area of Thornhill, darkness had descended. Along with the night came the winds. They were strong enough to buffet the minicompact Chloe had rented. The moon was shrouded in clouds tonight, shedding an eerie slant of light on a landscape otherwise swathed in blackness. There were no street lamps on the Old Fowler Road.

The car tires beat a rumbling tune over the wooden planks of the Ryder Bridge that traversed the long-ago dried-up stream. Beneath the planks was nothing more than a deep rock- and bottle-strewn gully that kids from Thornhill and neighboring Mill Creek were forever being warned against messing about in. As Chloe got to the center of the bridge, she could feel the wind slam hard against the car. She slowed down for better control. Off in the distance, about one hundred yards or so, she saw a flickering light and guessed it was coming from the Grange. Alice Donovan must have arrived.

Why had Alice chosen such a deserted spot for their little meeting? Chloe wondered with no small amount of anxiety. Until this moment, she'd been so irritated at Lucy Harris for snooping into her mail that she hadn't given much thought to Alice's motives for such a secret out-of-the-way meeting. More to still her mounting anxiety than out of common sense, Chloe decided that Alice simply didn't want everyone in Thornhill knowing her business. Well, neither did Chloe.

The landscape at the other end of the Ryder Bridge was flat meadowland and cornfields. So the gusting wind, with no trees or buildings to temper it, picked up force. As Chloe rounded the bend and caught sight of the old deserted Grange Hall, she realized that there was no light now. Perhaps she'd just caught the flash of Alice's car lights as she'd pulled up to the Grange. There was a car parked out front. Chloe felt a bit better seeing it there. What with the wind and the desolation and the darkness it was easy enough to get a bit spooked.

Just as Chloe was pulling up to the Grange, a streak of blue lightning flashed across the sky, casting a sickly green light upon the small wooden building and the hill just behind it.

Chloe's foot jerked on the brake as she saw, silhouetted in that flash of electricity, a figure on the top of the hill. Ghastly, eerie, the figure was cloaked in a long, white, hooded robe, arms outstretched, the material flapping like wings in the wind, a filmy, silvery shape . . . like some apparition risen from the dead.

The bloodcurdling scream from inside the Grange was probably all that kept Chloe from screaming in panic and terror herself. Leaving the engine running, Chloe leaped out of the car. No sooner had she started for the open door of the Grange than the vision disappeared, as if, in the tradition of ghosts, dematerializing. Chloe froze, her eyes searching the darkness. And then she darted into the Grange Hall.

"Alice," Chloe called out, her voice little more than a croak. "Alice, are you here? It's me. Chloe Hayes. Alice?"

There was no response. Had poor Alice Donovan caught sight of the apparition from one of the Grange windows and taken off out the side door? Chloe felt about for a light switch. When she found one and switched it on, nothing happened. No surprise. The old Grange hadn't been used for a good ten years. No reason to have kept the electricity hooked up.

Chloe took a step back toward the front door, convinced that Alice must have fled and resolving to do the same. But then she remembered that Alice's car was still parked out front. If it was Alice's car . . .

As Chloe got to the door, her foot came into contact with something hard and cold. She let out a low cry of alarm. Just then another flash of lightning streaked across the sky shedding a momentary burst of light inside the Grange.

The cold object Chloe had come into contact with was a flashlight. She stooped and picked it up. She let out a sigh of relief as she switched it on and a beam of light shone.

Chloe's own ragged breathing rasped in her ears as she aimed the light around the large barren room with its rows of empty benches.

"Alice," she called again in a croaking voice. Cautiously, she took a few steps forward, angling the light toward the stage at the far end of the room. "Alice..."

And then she saw her. "Alice..." Chloe's voice trembled as she came to a heart-stopping halt. And then she lurched forward down the aisle toward the stage.

Alice Donovan lay flat on her back, eyes closed, arms clutching her chest, hands balled into tight fists. Chloe dropped to her knees beside the librarian. Her hand trembled as she pressed two fingers to the pulse point beneath Alice's jaw. The woman's pulse was weak, but at least she was alive.

Chloe flashed the light on the reed-thin woman whose complexion was a ghostly white. There was no overt sign of injury, but Chloe knew it was best not to move her. Just as she made up her mind to leave Alice and drive to the nearest house to phone for help, the prone woman moaned and began to stir.

"Alice? Don't move. I'm going to get help," Chloe said soothingly, but as she reached out to give the librarian a reassuring stroke, Alice Donovan let out a bloodcurdling shriek.

"No, no," she screamed. "Please, please don't take me. Please, please..."

"Alice, Alice, calm down. It's me. Chloe Hayes."

It took several moments for the words to penetrate, and when they did Alice Donovan gave Chloe a dazed look. And then she clutched at Chloe, her thin face suffused with panic. "She's back. She's come back. I . . . saw her."

"What are you saying?" Chloe asked feeling a tight knot in her stomach.

Alice's trembling hand pointed to a back window. "There . . . there on the hill. She was calling to me. She was . . . beckoning me . . . to the great beyond. The high priestess . . ."

"The high priestess?" Chloe's voice quivered.

"Professor Emory. Amanda Emory."

When Alice said the name, Chloe felt a coldness invade her body. She, too, had thought immediately of Amanda when she'd witnessed that ghostly figure on the mount, glowing against the lurid sky. Chloe may have accepted that she, herself, had a certain psychic sensitivity to stimuli, but she had never believed in ghosts. At this moment, however, a trace of doubt surfaced. What was it Mildred Mead had told her husband? *"You just never know . . ."*

Suddenly, trembling hands were clutching at Chloe again. Alice was speaking in a hoarse whisper. "She's . . . back . . ."

Chloe started to soothe the petrified woman who was staring past her. Alice's face had gone white, and her eyes were glazed with a manic terror.

Chloe didn't understand why, until she saw the shadow looming on the wall. She stared in horror as the shadow grew.

Chapter Five

The wind sighed through the porous window frames of the old Grange Hall as the shadow stretched. Alice Donovan sought refuge in another dead faint. Chloe, kneeling beside the prone woman, felt her breath clog and stop in her throat.

"Chloe?"

Chloe's breath came out in a whoosh of relief as she recognized the voice. "Thad? Is that you?" She aimed the flashlight in the direction of the sound of his cautiously approaching footsteps.

The sudden burst of light in Thad's face made him shield his eyes. "What's going on?"

"I need help, Thad. Alice Donovan's fainted." She did her best to guide him with the beam of her flashlight.

Thad, dressed in brown cords and a maroon Dorchester College windbreaker, smoothed back his windblown hair as he hurried up the aisle.

"I don't think she's injured. Just . . . scared. You scared us both to death, Thad Emory," she scolded, now that relief had flooded her with courage.

"I scared you? I was scared as hell, myself," Thad retorted, but he was smiling as he bent beside Chloe.

"What are you doing here, anyway? I don't seem to be able to make a move in this town without everyone knowing where I am."

Ignoring her question, Thad carefully lifted the limp Alice in his arms, his burly frame managing her weight without apparent effort. "Aim the light. We'll put Alice in my car and I'll drive her home."

"Maybe you should bring her over to the hospital," Chloe suggested, picking up Alice's black leather purse. "She's had quite a scare. More than one."

Tad cast her a puzzled look.

"She thought she saw a ghost," Chloe said, deliberately keeping her tone light. "Once just as I was arriving. And then again when you showed up."

"Alice thought I was a ghost?"

"You weren't strolling up on the hill behind the Grange Hall about ten minutes ago by any chance?"

"What would I do that for?"

"I can't imagine."

Chloe held the front door of the Grange open for Thad as he carried Alice out.

"What in heaven's name were you and Alice Donovan doing here?" Thad asked as Chloe opened the back door of his sedan, and he gently slid Alice inside.

"Surely, Lucy told you," Chloe challenged, guessing that her landlady had been the one to direct Thad to the Grange.

Thad grinned. "Actually she was trying to track down Harvey Mead when I showed up to see if you wanted to take in a movie or something. Poor Lucy was in a state. She insisted she'd had a premonition of something terrible happening. When she couldn't get hold of Harvey, she finally told me she was worried sick about you going off for a secret meeting with the town librarian. She felt certain you were in some sort of danger."

"And so she sent you after me?"

Thad smiled. "I volunteered." He hesitated, then went on. "What did Alice want to talk to you about that she had to meet you here in this godforsaken spot?"

Chloe shrugged. "I guess I won't know that until Alice comes to." She shivered as the cold wind bit into her skin. "Why don't I follow you back to the hospital. I'll stay with Alice there and make sure she's all right."

Thad nodded, but before Chloe headed for her car, she took his hand and held on to it for a moment, as if to ground herself. "Thanks for coming out to find me, Thad."

He smiled tenderly. "Come on. Let's get away from here, or pretty soon I'll start imagining I'm seeing ghosts, too."

Chloe laughed, but her laugh had a hollow sound.

ALTHOUGH THORNHILL'S Harriet Michner Hospital was situated in a sleepy little college town with a population of not quite ten thousand, it was one of the most prestigious and well-equipped medical centers in northern New England, thanks to its affiliation with Dorchester Medical School. As Chloe followed Thad's car to the emergency entrance of the hospital, she noticed that a new wing had been added and the hospital as a whole had undergone a sprucing up.

Alice Donovan, who'd revived during the drive back from the Grange, continued to act disoriented and frightened as Thad helped her out of the car.

At the sight of Chloe, the frightened librarian sprang free of Thad and rushed to her side. Except for the poor woman's palpable fear, Chloe guessed that Alice probably was no longer in need of medical attention, but she encouraged her to have a doctor examine her just to play it safe.

Alice was too distraught to argue, but she insisted that Chloe come inside the hospital with her.

"Of course, Alice," Chloe agreed with a reassuring smile.

Thad, who stood on Alice's other side, added, "We'll both keep you company."

Chloe thought she detected a flicker of a frown on Alice's face at Thad's suggestion that he join them, but the librarian allowed each of them to take an arm and escort her inside.

It was a slow night in the emergency room and Alice did not have a long wait before a young, pretty, blond resident guided her into one of the curtained cubicles. Chloe and Thad took a seat on a padded bench in the waiting area. It was close to ten o'clock. Over the hum of the hospital's cadence, Chloe could still hear the roar of the wind, swollen with night noises, in her head. Her eyes darted nervously over to the curtained cubicle where Alice was being examined.

"I'm sure she'll be fine," Thad said, catching Chloe's anxious look. "Ghosts. Visions. Premonitions." He shook his head sadly. "My sister, Alice Donovan, Lucy Harris, and who can guess how many more of mother's little fan club, are all starting to freak out. 'Ding dong the witch is dead,'" he said, "and now what will become of them all?"

"The witch is dead..." Chloe echoed in a low whisper.

Thad gave her a contrite smile. "Sorry. I didn't mean to sound so callous. It's just..." His eyes got watery. "It's so hard to accept that my mother...actually took her own life. It makes it even worse to have all these ridiculous rumors running rampant about witchcraft and evil spirits."

"Why would she kill herself, Thad? Was she depressed? Was she...in trouble?"

"Trouble?" He blinked several times. "Amanda was never one to confide in others. Not even in her family. I don't know what was wrong. But...something was the matter with mother. She...wasn't herself. Oh, she'd always gotten a kick out of this high priestess business. Mother was always so colorful and theatrical. But, in the past few months she became obsessed with the belief that a secret coven dedicated to...black magic...had been formed in Thornhill. She was convinced that this group was engaged in dark deeds, macabre rituals... And she managed to convince quite a few of her followers that they had to engage in battle with this evil force. Lara could tell you more about it. The idea of fighting black magic with white magic struck Lara's fancy. She was all juiced up about it."

A ribbon of anxiety suddenly stiffened the muscles along Chloe's lower spine. She flashed back on the old Grange Hall, seeing it again across the surface of her mind. Only she didn't picture it as she'd left it, all dark and desolate. In her vision, a faint glow of light appeared. First one candle, then another and another. A figure in a long black robe stood on the stage. Only the stage resembled an altar now. The figure genuflected, then poured a steamy hot liquid out of a pitcher into a wide-mouthed basin. The steam rose and with it a vile, acrid stench. The people sitting on the benches began to chant. In the dull candlelight it was hard to tell who they were or even how many. Maybe six or eight... The chanting was low and hypnotic. And then, abruptly, above the hum of the chant came a loud piercing scream...no, more a screech. Not human...

"Chloe, are you okay?"

Thad's voice broke through her vision and she flushed as she saw his critical survey.

She smoothed her hair away from her face. "I was just...thinking. I'm fine." But she could hear the uncertainty in her voice, the prick of fear. She turned to give Thad a reassuring smile, as much to reassure herself as him, but the smile froze on her face as she saw a flash of white approaching.

Not a ghost. No. But still a figure who kept managing to evoke a myriad of emotions.

He looked different tonight. Perhaps it was the setting. Perhaps it was the white lab coat with the stethoscope dangling conspicuously from his left pocket that gave him an especially vivid aura of authority and assurance. Or perhaps it was simply that Noah Bright had the kind of face that was constantly reflecting different aspects of his personality.

She watched his steps quicken as he spotted her on the bench. Chloe couldn't help the flurry of pleasure she experienced as she saw the look of concern sweep across his handsome face.

"What are you doing here?" Noah asked her anxiously, immediately taking hold of her wrist.

"You've got the wrong woman, Bright. Chloe's not the one in need of your attention," Thad said a little snidely.

Noah shot Thad a hard, cold look. There was no love lost between the two men. Even back in college it had been that way.

Chloe tried to take deeper breaths in an effort to release the knot of anxiety in her stomach. "Thad and I brought Alice Donovan in." Chloe hesitated. "She fainted."

"You look white as a ghost, Chloe," Noah said, still gripping her wrist, checking her pulse now, his expression a study in concentration.

Noah was bending so close Chloe could spot a tiny dot of dried blood on his jaw where he must have nicked himself shaving. She felt a rush of arousal as she thought of the times, years ago, when she would have kissed that spot *to make the pain go away.* Noah had always used to tease her about having magical powers. A magical touch. Magical kisses . . .

Thad was giving Noah the evil eye. "There's nothing the matter, medically, with Chloe, Noah. You can cut the Dr. Kildare routine."

Noah gave Thad a dismissive glance. "Your pulse is racing, Chloe. And your color is poor. Come into one of the exam rooms and let me . . ."

"No," she said so sharply that everyone in the hallway stared curiously in Chloe's direction.

Noah released Chloe's wrist. In a low voice that bore an edge of embarrassment, he said, "I'll call in Dave Leeds. He's the head resident on duty. He can check you out."

Chloe was taken aback to see the reflection of hurt in Noah's eyes. "I'm sorry," she said. "It's just that . . . I don't need an exam. I'm really all right. I just had a bit of a scare."

"A scare? What do you mean?" Noah probed.

Chloe hesitated. Should she be telling other people about Alice's plea to speak with her out at the old Grange? Then again, with Lucy Harris knowing about the meeting, surely by tomorrow word would have spread all through Thornhill. So she told Noah, leaving out the part about the ghostly vision both she and Alice had witnessed on the hill behind the Grange.

At the mention of the old Grange Hall, Noah's features darkened. "Why would she want to meet you out there of all places?" His gray-green eyes reflected puzzlement and a definite glint of alarm.

Out of the corner of her eye Chloe noticed that Thad looked uneasy. But as soon as she turned to give him a closer look, he smiled. "The latest scuttlebutt around town is that evil goings-on have been afoot at the old Grange,"

Thad said, his smile now decidedly forced-looking. "I'm afraid my mother was to blame for getting the rumor going."

Noah explained. "About three months ago, Amanda's cat turned up at the old Grange Hall. Dead."

The air stalled in Chloe's lungs, and once again she heard that piercing screech. An animal. A terrified cat... "Dantes?" There was a look of panic in her eyes.

Thad nodded, taking Chloe's hand. "The cat must have been at least sixteen. It was practically blind, it limped, the tip of one ear was missing. Dantes certainly lived a full, rich life."

"Someone had cut the poor animal's throat," Noah said in a low voice.

"Kids," Thad was quick to say. "An ugly prank. Kids are always fooling around on the rocks below the Ryder Bridge. Dantes must have wandered by them, they chased him into the Grange and..."

But Chloe wasn't listening. Her heart was racing even faster. An impression of Amanda's cat, Dantes, took shape in her head like a holograph. Again she heard its piercing screech, this time seeing the large silver cat, frozen in place, on the stage of the old Grange Hall, his back hunched in abject terror, his hair standing on end as a hand gripped the scruff of his neck. And then came a flash of silver. A silver blade... double-edged, the hilt of the handle etched... an atheme. The black clad figure began chanting, *"Come moon shadow of a thousand forms and look favorably on my sacrifice..."*

"Chloe...?"

She heard her name being called as if through a tunnel. She started to rise, but the floor seemed to shift like sand under her feet. The hospital corridor tilted and she started to topple....

"CHLOE?"

Her eyes fluttered open. When she saw Noah looking down at her, she gave him a puzzled frown. "What happened?"

"You . . . fainted."

She closed her eyes again. "No," she whispered. "I didn't faint. Things didn't go blank. I was . . . there."

"Where?" Noah asked, taking her hand.

"At the Grange. I saw . . ."

"Yes, Chloe. You were at the Grange earlier. And you saw Alice Donovan . . ."

"No. Dantes. I saw . . . Dantes." She struggled to sit up. "Where . . . am I?"

"One of the examining rooms at the hospital. I'd like to admit you."

"No."

"Just for the night. You're overwrought, Chloe. It's no wonder."

"Where's Thad?"

"I told him I was admitting you for tests, then booted him out. He insisted he'd come to see you first thing tomorrow morning."

"And Alice? Where's Alice?"

"She went home with a prescription for some tranquilizers. She was still pretty worked up but there was no reason to keep her in the hospital." He started to say something else, but hesitated. Chloe saw the pinch of tension and fatigue at the corners of his gray-green eyes.

"What is it?" she asked warily.

"Chloe, you told me earlier that Alice sent you a note to meet her at the old Grange."

"Yes. That's right."

"Do you . . . have the note?"

Chloe gave him a puzzled look then reached for her purse on the bedside table. After rummaging through it, she shrugged. "I must have left it at home. Back at Lucy Harris's." She saw the questioning look in Noah's eyes. "There was a note. Ask Lucy Harris. She snuck a peek at it, I'm certain she did. Anyway, why all this interest in Alice's note?"

"Alice claims she never sent you a note, Chloe. She says you were the one who wrote her and asked her to meet you at the old Grange Hall."

Chloe's eyes narrowed. "That's ridiculous. Why would I want to meet with Alice Donovan? And why the Grange of all places?"

Noah looked uncomfortable. "Alice claims you had something very important to give her."

"*I* had something to give Alice Donovan? What?"

A redness crept up Noah's neck. "She wouldn't say at first, but she was still so distraught she finally broke down. She claims you had a potion for her."

"You mean a love potion?" Chloe asked, astonished. "Why, in heaven's name would she think I..."

He smiled. Noah, like everyone else in Thornhill, knew about Alice Donovan and her love potions. "No, not a love potion."

Chloe was truly puzzled. "Then what?"

"Something to protect her...to ward off evil spirits. You see, Alice Donovan believes Lara's theory that an evil spirit entered Amanda's body and caused her death. Alice claims you were offering her some sort of...psychic antiseptic...that would prevent a similar invasion from happening to her."

"That's crazy," Chloe declared.

Noah threw up his hands. "This whole affair is getting completely out of hand. It all escalated with Dantes's death.

Amanda claimed that the cat was killed during some sort of—''

"Sacrificial ritual." The words escaped Chloe's lips, unbidden.

Noah gave her a sharp look. "Yes."

Chloe swallowed hard. The texture of the air in the room changed. It was suddenly too still, too warm.

Noah rubbed a hand over his face. "Did you know that Amanda was convinced you were a...clairvoyant, Chloe?"

His question elicited a tense smile. "She always insisted I had a...special gift. She never put a label on it for me."

Noah didn't meet her gaze. "I guess the fact that you went into the field of parapsychology after you left Thornhill, coupled with those articles about you in the Boston papers, convinced Amanda that special gift of yours was very potent. According to the papers you did help the police track down a missing child. And then there was that other time—" he hesitated "—when you were instrumental in bringing a murderer to justice."

"Hunches," Chloe stated. The hard, skeptical side of her truly believed that. But then again that same side also believed there was no such thing as ghosts. "The papers made far too much of my involvement in both incidents," Chloe added brusquely, hoping her tone would discourage any further discussion of the matter.

But it wasn't her tone of voice that ended discussion of the matter. It was the arrival of Harvey Mead.

The instant Chloe saw the chief of police standing at her open door she knew something terrible had happened. And her intuition had nothing to do with clairvoyance.

Noah saw it, too. It was written all over Harvey's face. "Chloe," Harvey addressed her with sharp concern. "How are you feeling?"

"I'm okay," she muttered tensely.

"What happened?" It was Noah who managed the question.

"It's Alice Donovan," Harvey said solemnly. "She's dead."

Noah's hand shot out to the wall to steady himself. "She was fine when she left here."

Harvey gave him a puzzled look. "Alice was here earlier?"

Noah looked at Chloe. "Yes," she confirmed. "Alice sent me a note asking me to meet her tonight out at the Grange Hall past the Ryder Bridge. When I got there...she'd passed out cold. Then Thad Emory showed up...Lucy Harris told him where I was. And we brought Alice to the hospital to make sure she was all right."

"And she was fine," Noah was quick to add. "I spoke with her and with the resident who checked her. There were no indications of—"

"Exactly when did she leave the hospital?" Harvey interrupted.

Noah checked his watch. "Close to two hours ago. And like I said, she was perfectly fine when she left."

"How did she...die, Harvey?" Chloe's voice was a hoarse whisper.

Harvey slid his hands into the pockets of his windbreaker. "Have to wait for the coroner's report before we can say for sure, but I can give you my opinion."

"Yes?" Noah's voice held an edge of impatience.

"I'd say it was poison."

"Poison?" A heavy cloud settled over Chloe's spirits.

"Just before Alice lost consciousness," Harvey went on, "she managed to phone 911. Orvie Mathers took the call. Seems Alice said she'd just drunk some kind of drink...she called it a potion...and she was feeling real queasy."

Chloe and Noah shared a quick look. Not too quick for Harvey to spot. "You know something about this potion?"

Blood rushed into Chloe's head, drummed in her ears. Once again, she looked at Noah, then lowered her gaze.

"Everyone knows about Alice and her love potions," Noah said, his voice huskier than usual. "She must have whipped up some concoction...."

"I don't think so, Noah," Harvey said, each of his words bearing a momentous weight. "I think someone sent her this drink. There was some wrapping in the trash. Looked to me like the bottle had been packed in it."

"Who sent it?" Chloe hardly recognized her own voice.

Harvey stared at Chloe for several moments before answering. "Your name was typed on the upper left-hand side of the wrapping."

Chloe's hand darted out instinctively for Noah, and he immediately put a reassuring arm around her.

"I never sent Alice Donovan anything. Not a package, not a letter...not anything," Chloe insisted.

"Anyone could have typed Chloe's name on that wrapper, Harvey," Noah challenged.

Harvey nodded slowly. "I agree. Fact is, I think someone did just that."

"What do you mean?" Chloe asked, confused but relieved.

"After I picked up that wrapper at Alice's place. I stopped by Lucy's to have a word with you. She heard you were in the hospital."

"I suppose Thad Emory told her?" Chloe guessed.

Harvey shook his head. "No, it was little Kelly Davis who works in the emergency room who phoned her. Kelly's Lucy's niece." He hesitated. "Anyway, while I was there at Lucy's, I...uh...asked her if she happened to have any typewriters around the place.''

"And?" Chloe asked in a tight, controlled voice.

"She showed me the only one she had, in her office." A glimmer of a smile showed on Harvey's lips. "Type's altogether different from the one on that wrapping. My boys will be checking around for the right typewriter, but it may be like looking for a needle in a haystack. Anyway, even if we find it, it's not exactly gonna be hard evidence since no one in Thornhill locks their doors, meaning anyone who wanted could have access to more than half the typewriters in town."

Harvey's smile deepened. "Relax, Noah. I have no reason to believe Chloe here would want to do poor Alice Donovan any harm. I think the reason her name was there was simply to make Alice believe Chloe'd sent it, so that she would drink it."

Noah wasn't aware of the sigh of relief that escaped his lips until both Harvey's and Chloe's eyes fell on him. He flushed. "I knew it all the time," he muttered.

"Just a hunch, but so did I." Harvey winked at Chloe, but then his eyes narrowed. "I guess," he said, rubbing his hands together, his features again solemn, "that leaves us with the question of who did send that potion to poor Alice that sent her to her grave?"

After much discussion, Noah agreed that Chloe could leave the hospital, but only if she'd stay at his place overnight where he'd be on hand in case of further dizzy spells. The puzzle of Alice Donovan's death pursued Chloe like a hovering shadow. She slipped out of her bed in Noah's guest room and walked over to the window. It was almost midnight.

The winds had died down and the promised storm had never materialized. It was, Chloe realized, the night before

Halloween. Perhaps that explained the ghostly vision she'd seen on the hill. Just some teenager in costume—dress rehearsal for the night to come.

Poor, desperate, lonely Alice. And that meeting tonight that each of them had thought the other had instigated. Who had sent those notes? And why? Chloe shivered. The same person who set up the meeting at the Grange must have sent Alice that psychic antiseptic. Why? Why did someone want Alice dead? And then a voice inside Chloe's head answered, *Because she knew too much. She knew who killed Amanda Emory.*

At the sound of footsteps behind her, Chloe spun around, panic sweeping her face.

"I'm sorry. I didn't mean to frighten you, Chloe. I was just coming in to check on you."

Noah looked truly alarmed by her response to his arrival, but once she realized who it was, some of her panic bled away. Not the sorrow, though.

"Oh Noah, Amanda Emory had to have been murdered," she said in a pained whisper. "And I think Alice must have known who murdered her."

Noah came closer to her, and Chloe had a premonition. In a moment, she saw, she would be in his arms. Not a wise move, that voice inside her whispered cynically. But Chloe knew, in this instance, she wasn't going to heed her inner voice. Even though she knew how unwise it was to ignore it.

Noah drew her against him without a word. The starchy scent of his shirt mingled appealingly with his lemony after-shave. His mouth moved along her neck, against her throat. She pressed into the heat and safety of his skin. His mouth brushed against her lips. Instantly her lips parted and they kissed deeply, his tongue dancing with hers.

When finally she drew back from him, her breath heated, her pulse racing, her forehead damp with perspiration, she saw that he was smiling.

"You knew this was going to happen, didn't you, Chloe?"

She didn't lie.

Noah's smile deepened. "Maybe there's a little of the psychic in me, as well. I knew this was going to happen, too."

Chapter Six

The socially elite women of the Thornhill Improvement Society were in a dither. Mildred Mead, chairwoman of the society, tried to bring the agitated group to order.

"Please ladies, you sound like a gaggle of geese. Let's settle down and discuss the situation in a reasonable and rational fashion."

Elaine Mayhew, the town's celebrated interior decorator and member of the school board, snickered. "Reasonable? Rational? You should talk, Mildred Mead—'Which Witch is Next?' Really, with a headline like that on the front page of the *Tab,* is it any wonder the few sane people left among us are alarmed and deeply distressed? Why, my Jonathan says everyone at the college is carrying on. Peter Mott is organizing a special seminar on the resurrection of the Craft. I wouldn't be surprised if every citizen in Thornhill didn't start hanging garlic cloves around their necks next."

"Whose neck next?" Lydia Powell, the elegant and alluring owner of Eva Fashions, said wryly.

"I don't feel this is any time for levity," scolded dowdy but monied Jane Morgan, wife of the minister of St. Paul Episcopal Church. "Two of our own are dead. And I, for one, certainly don't believe either poor Alice or our dear

Amanda were victims of . . . sorcery. And, furthermore, I think it blasphemous, Mildred, that you participate in a journalistic enterprise that would in any way support such hogwash. I plan to cancel my subscription to the *Tab*." She hesitated. "Or at least write a scathing letter to the editor."

"I didn't write that headline, Jane," Mildred said with a persnickety glare. "But I, for one, happen to think there is something to this witchcraft business."

Mildred's statement produced the hush she desired among the group. They all stared at her, duly shocked.

Mildred, who always enjoyed taking center stage, smiled at the group as she rose from her seat at the end of the large conference table. "Or let's say that I, for one, believe in the extraordinary power of suggestion. Why else would poor Alice have gulped down a vile-smelling, sickly green solution without so much as a pause? Well, of course I don't actually know if she paused. But I do know that she drank it down. And, I have it from a good source that she believed that potion had magic properties that would protect her from harm."

"Is it true, Mildred, that your husband now suspects that Amanda's death wasn't . . . ordinary suicide?" This from Paula Dubois, caterer of Pies to Go-Go, a flourishing business which Mildred had helped to get off the ground.

Paula had always been one of Amanda Emory's most devout followers. Ever since Amanda's death, Paula had been in a constant state of fear and agitation. If anyone in Thornhill was going to start wearing garlic garlands around their necks, Paula was likely to be the first.

"Harvey's keeping very mum about all this," Mildred said, obviously none too pleased by her husband's closed-mouth policy. "All I know is that Amanda's death is still under investigation. And, of course, there's Alice's death now. Harvey isn't saying much, but I don't think we need to be policewomen or sorcerers to conclude that Alice Donovan's death was murder.''

Paula blanched. "Murder...or black magic."

"Now, now, Paula," Mildred soothed. "I doubt the sender of that poisoned brew is in cahoots with the devil. No, there's got to be some other explanation."

"Whatever the reason, no one is safe," Paula concluded.

Mildred felt sorry for Paula. The shy but pretty young woman had grown up in Thornhill, the only child of a strict, arch-conservative French Canadian couple. In her senior year in high school, Paula had gotten pregnant. People in Thornhill were shocked, especially as Paula had always been so quiet and reserved, not to mention that her parents had forbidden her to date. Rumor had it that innocent young Paula had been seduced by an older man...someone with enough clout to dissuade Paula from ever revealing his name. Paula's parents had booted her out of the house and Mildred had ended up taking her into her own home.

The timing for Mildred couldn't have been better. Her only child, Maggie, had just gone off to graduate school and both she and Harvey were feeling lonely. Harvey had his work, but Mildred's maternal instincts were sorely in need of expression. And if ever there was someone in need of a little tender but firm mothering it was Paula. Mildred had not only seen to it that Paula got her high school diploma, and taught her how to cope with being a single parent to little Jessica, she'd even helped her start the catering business that Paula had turned into one of Thornhill's most successful enterprises.

"It's all too horrible," Mary McKensey, co-owner of McKensey Auto, exclaimed. "Murder in Thornhill. It's positively gruesome."

"Who would do it? That's what I'd like to know. And why?" Elaine Mayhew mused. "Of course, I've been hearing rumors for months now—ever since that cat of Amanda's got slaughtered down at the old Grange Hall."

"Black magic," Paula whispered nervously. "That's what's behind this. And now that Amanda is…gone, we're just not equipped to fight such a powerful force."

"I don't believe in this black magic nonsense for one moment," Lydia announced disdainfully. "But, there could be a madman on the loose. A psychotic who thinks he's in cahoots with the devil."

Paula gasped, all the color draining from her face. "Oh yes. A devil worshipper."

"I don't think it's a psychotic killer or a devil worshipper," Jane declared, praying that her husband never found out she'd participated in this blasphemous discussion. "If you want my opinion I'd say it's a witch-hunter, out to put a stop to all this hocus-pocus Amanda was promulgating. That's what happens when mortals dabble in sacrilegious rituals," the minister's wife concluded.

"It wasn't sacrilege," Paula argued, some of the color coming back into her face. "Amanda always used to say that paganism had nothing to do with decadence or satanism. Paganism's a perfectly legitimate spiritual movement, begun in ancient times, that preaches living in harmony with nature. What's wrong with that?"

"I certainly don't believe in black magic or white magic," Mary announced, "but every one of us has heard the rumors of devil worship meetings going on in the dark of night down at the Grange."

"Didn't the paper say that Alice was down there at the Grange last night?" Elaine mused. "With…what was that woman's name?" She looked around the table.

"Chloe Hayes," Lydia offered. "You know who she is, don't you?"

"She's a clairvoyant," Paula said with awe.

"She's an old student of Amanda's who came up for the funeral," Mildred stated.

"Oh, now I know who she is. She's the psychic from Boston," Elaine exclaimed, turning eagerly to Mildred. "Is that why she's here? Is she working on the case with Harvey?"

"Psychic, my foot," Jane muttered disdainfully as she helped herself to a piece of apple pie, courtesy of Pies to Go-Go.

"A psychic's exactly what's needed," Paula declared. "I mean Lara Emory would like to step into her mother's shoes, but really I don't think she has the calling."

"I heard she was the last to see Alice Donovan alive," Lydia said, helping herself to a slice of pie, too.

"Who? Lara?"

"No, no. This Chloe Hayes."

"Is this Hayes woman on the case then, Mildred?" Mary asked.

Mildred gave an enigmatic smile. "I can't imagine my Harvey actually employing the assistance of a psychic. But I suppose stranger things have been known to happen."

"I want to go on record in opposition," announced the voluptuous Karin Niels, who up to this moment had been the one nonparticipating member of the group. She gazed at the ladies of the oval table with righteous indignation, before continuing with her statement.

Elaine Mayhew, who was the secretary of the society, sat with brow raised and pen poised.

"I strenuously object," continued Karin in a haughty tone of voice, "to our spending the society's time and energy on such pointless gossip. This kind of rumormongering is precisely how so many innocent people in this town get hurt. As to the facts, as far as I know, the cause of Alice Donovan's death has not yet been determined. And as for Amanda—" Karin faltered "—I happen to know that Amanda was deeply troubled about something. And let's not forget, ladies, that she did leave a suicide note."

"How did you know about the suicide note?" Mildred inquired. Harvey had made sure there'd been no mention of the note in the *Tab*.

"George Denk mentioned it to me," Karin said airily. "He happens to be a neighbor."

Mildred bristled. She would have to report this to Harvey. He wouldn't be at all pleased to know that one of his junior officers was blabbing police business around town.

"The point is," Karin said brusquely, "I, for one, am not the least bit surprised Amanda...killed herself." With that, Karin Niels rose and made a very dramatic exit.

"That's just like her," Mary observed. "Drop a bomb and take off."

"What do you suppose she meant about Amanda being troubled?" Elaine pondered.

"I don't see how she would know about Amanda's troubles," Paula commented snidely. "They haven't spoken to each other in months."

"Yes," Lydia piped in, "I heard they had a terrible falling-out."

While none of the ladies knew the cause of the breach, speculations were, nonetheless, rife.

Paula had a theory. Rivalry. Karin had been a member of Amanda's circle for a while. Paula was certain Karin envied Amanda's role of high priestess and couldn't stand not being the one in the limelight.

"Well, I'm certainly not one to spread rumors," Jane said piously, "but I wouldn't be surprised if Amanda simply didn't care for the way that young woman conducted herself. For all I may have thought about Amanda's witchcraft nonsense, the professor was always a lady and wouldn't have condoned . . . wanton behavior."

Elaine Mayhew grinned. "Karin is a terrible flirt. Everyone in Thornhill knows that."

"Let's face it, ladies," Lydia said, "Lawrence Niels is a perfectly nice man, and certainly well-heeled, but he's also a good thirty years older than Karin. My hunch is she's been doing more than flirting."

"I know I shouldn't say anything," Mary said, her blue eyes sparkling, "but a couple of months ago, when my mother-in-law came to visit, I took her on a country drive. I'm almost positive I saw Karin at a motel in Marion. I mean, that little red sports car of hers is so distinctive. And how many willowy brunettes with a figure to die for drive around in a car like that up here in the country?"

"Get to the good part, already," Elaine said impatiently. "Who was she with?"

"Now ladies, remember, without my glasses I can't absolutely swear to this, but he looked awfully like Professor Peter Mott," Mary said with a sly smile.

"Peter Mott? I thought he was dating Lara Emory," Elaine commented.

"Well, well, well," Mildred mused. "Our Professor Mott certainly gets around."

"How ARE YOU feeling this morning?" Noah asked Chloe. He wasn't wearing his white doctor's coat today, as this was his day off.

Chloe had just come downstairs. She gave Noah a nervous glance. "Better than last night. I...I wasn't...myself last night, Noah. I really wasn't."

He knew what she was referring to and he had the good graces not to smile.

"I thought you might want to skip my bachelor cooking. How about letting me take you out for a big stack of blueberry pancakes? Do you still love blueberry pancakes?"

"Well, I...don't eat them much anymore." Her gaze shifted around the room, covering every spot except the one where Noah was standing.

"Remember how you used to devour those blueberry pancakes over at Polly's? It never ceased to amaze me how one slender young woman could eat that many pancakes in one sitting."

Chloe remembered, all right. She remembered rolling over in Noah's bed on a chilly Sunday morning; she remembered how he had screamed playfully as she ran her cold feet along his thigh and then pulled her onto him with hungry abandon; she remembered how after lingering in bed, they had raced, seeing who could get dressed quicker. She remembered walking hand in hand into Polly's Pancake Emporium, laughing, kissing, making bets on who could eat more pancakes. Oh yes, she remembered it all.

"That was ages ago," she said out loud. "I really don't remember..."

"Polly's moved."

"Oh. I thought it had gone out of business."

He did smile then.

"I couldn't help but notice...all the changes in Thornhill," she mumbled defensively.

"Yeah," he said softly, "there have been a lot of changes. Then again there are things about Thornhill that remain the same."

Chloe didn't respond.

"It moved over to Mason Road, just behind the high school."

"Huh?"

"Polly's."

"Oh."

"Still make the best blueberry pancakes this side of the Connecticut River."

"I . . . can't, Noah."

"Why not?"

"Well . . . Thad said he was coming to see me this morning, didn't he?"

Again Noah smiled, this time sheepishly. "He already stopped by the hospital."

Chloe gave Noah a stern look.

A faint redness crept up over the collar of Noah's blue pullover shirt. "I . . . uh . . . had the nurse on duty tell him that . . . you were having some . . . tests run this morning. And you wouldn't be released until noon."

"Why did you do that?"

He took a step closer to her. "I think it should be obvious, especially for a woman with . . . your special gifts."

"Please don't do this, Noah." She couldn't hide the note of desperation in her voice.

"Can't we simply go have breakfast together . . . and talk? Can't we talk, Chloe?"

"There's nothing to talk about."

"In the past seven years, I've been down to Boston twelve, thirteen times. And I think . . . no, I know, that every single time I was there, I longed to call you . . . to talk to you." Nervously, Noah combed his fingers through his dark hair and Chloe couldn't help remembering how those fingers had once incited passion in her blood.

"The past is over, Noah. Why don't we let it be?" she whispered.

"It isn't over, Chloe. It's hanging over us. It's haunting us."

"Maybe you. Not me."

"You never were very good at lying."

Chloe laughed sharply. "Lara said that same thing to me the other day."

At her mention of his ex-wife's name Noah's face closed. Where before, when Lara's name came up, Chloe had seen pity, perhaps even love in his expression, today she saw nothing. But she sensed...hostility. And something more...despair. Chloe experienced a surge of sympathetic pain.

"Are the pancakes really still as good?" The question just tumbled out of her.

Noah smiled. The smile lit up his whole face. He had been, and remained, the most appealing man she had ever known. Was it psychic powers that told her no one else was going to edge him out of that position in the future?

"Want to bet, Miss Hayes, that I can eat more stacks than you?"

THE NEW Polly's Pancake Emporium was all slicked up and shiny. Gone were the cracked walls, the rickety wooden chairs, the overhead fans. But Noah, true to his word, had been right about the blueberry pancakes. They were as good as ever. Clearly the best pancakes this side of the Connecticut River.

"Hey, you don't have as big an appetite as you used to," Noah said, observing the half-eaten stack of cakes she was pushing away from the edge of the table.

"How did I ever eat so much back in college?" Chloe said, laughing.

"And where did you ever put it?" He slid his own empty plate out of the way and leaned forward, his gray-green eyes amused. "You really do look wonderful, Chloe. I guess Boston agrees with you."

"And Thornhill agrees with you."

"Today it does," he said softly.

She fiddled with her paper napkin. "I keep trying to push what happened last night out of my mind..." She raised her eyes to Noah's face. "I mean... Alice."

Noah reached across the table and took Chloe's hand. She didn't protest. His touch was too comforting.

"You should never have gone out to the Grange alone," Noah said in a worried voice.

"It was spooky, all right." She thought again about the ghost on the hill. "I wish I knew who sent me that note. And who sent one to Alice. And why?"

"Don't you have any... idea?"

She slipped her hand out from under Noah's. "I'm not getting any psychic messages, if that's what you mean," she said tightly.

"I wasn't mocking you, Chloe."

"Well, that is a change."

"Whoever coined the phrase, the older you get the wiser, didn't know what he or she was talking about. The older I get, the less I seem to know, the more I'm willing to believe anything's possible."

"Even... ghosts?"

The morning sunlight streaming through the glass front of Polly's burned across one side of Noah's face and left the other side in shadow. Once again he looked different, more mysterious, more alluring than ever. "Let's say, as for ghosts in particular, I'm skeptical. But," he smiled faintly, "a skeptic's better than a cynic, isn't it?"

She slid into the corner of the booth, her own shadow deepening. Being with Noah made it hard for her to breathe. "I shouldn't have come back," she murmured.

"I'm glad you did."

It wasn't only what he said, it was the way he said it, that excited her. With the arousal, though, came a huge ache, an ache she'd been fighting for years, an ache she felt she had to keep fighting desperately, for her own protection. "You weren't glad I came back...that first day."

"I was frightened for you. I still am."

"I can look after myself."

"Then you're going to stay awhile?"

She wished she could read him better. What did he want? Maybe she wished she could read herself better. What did she want?

"For a few days at least. I'm working on a research paper. The library at Dorchester has a collection of papers that I need to use. I...thought I'd spend...a little time...checking it out."

"I've read a few of your publications. You're good, Chloe. You're finally getting to do what you always wanted." There was a wistful note in Noah's voice that surprised her.

"I was pretty determined, I guess."

He smiled. "You guess? You were the most driven person I'd ever come across. And the most independent. You were so tough, Chloe."

"Is that what you thought, Noah?"

"Amanda always used to say it came from having lost your parents. Some people turn desperate and needy, she said, and others build a tough shell and vow never to be weak, never to get hurt like that again."

"You talked to Amanda about me?"

"You were so close to her. She seemed to understand you. And . . . I wanted to understand you better. You always baffled me, Chloe."

"*I* baffled *you*?" She was incredulous.

"You were so damned elusive, so secretive . . ."

She started to protest, but suddenly she realized that what Noah was saying was true. All of it. Her fierce independence, her drive, and yes, even, her elusiveness. And Amanda was right about that protective wall. Only Noah had pierced that wall. She'd let herself love him. But had she ever let herself trust him? Would things have ended as they had if she had? Was it possible she'd actually driven Noah away, driven him into the waiting arms of a woman who reached out to him, made a great show of needing him? Chloe remembered Noah telling her in exasperation that it just wasn't going to work for them. They'd broken up then, and less than a week later Lara was hanging on Noah's arm. Could she have been wrong about Noah all this time? Had he merely turned to Lara on the rebound, because Lara made him feel needed and she hadn't?

Tears stung Chloe's eyes and she suddenly felt desperate to get out of the restaurant.

Noah noticed her distress, plunked some bills on the table, took her arm and led her out the door.

They'd left Chloe's rental car at the hospital parking lot the night before, so Noah drove her over there to pick it up. He pulled up beside it and turned off the engine. He turned slightly in his seat so that their shoulders touched. An erotic charge spread across Chloe's skin. They stared at each other in silence. Noah's hand moved to the back of her neck, slipping under her thick curly auburn hair. He shifted in his seat as he kissed her, a light, chaste kiss on the cheek that just caught the edge of her mouth. "Thanks for letting me take you to breakfast. How about letting me take you to lunch and dinner?''

She didn't trust her voice so she just shook her head. Her chest tightened with a now familiar anxiety.

"Just dinner then." He didn't ask, he announced. "Rosco's. Go on. Ask me if they still make the best steaks this side of the Connecticut River."

A ball of emotion rose in Chloe's throat. She closed her eyes and breathed deeply until the black dots before her lids evaporated. "I don't want to relive old times. I don't want to revisit old haunts with you, Noah. I do believe in ghosts." Her blue eyes took on a hard, defensive edge.

"What do ghosts have to do with it?"

"Not all ghosts are ephemeral, Noah. Lara . . ."

He looked away and she knew she didn't have to finish the sentence. Instead, she opened the car door. "Thanks for the breakfast, Noah. The pancakes were as good as ever. I guess it's me that's changed."

She hurried over to her own car, wanting to drive off as fast as possible. She was glad she hadn't locked her car door. Her hands were trembling so badly it would have been hard to work the lock. She was aware that Noah hadn't started up the engine in his car again. He was just sitting there. Her back was to him but she knew he was watching her.

She slid into the driver's seat and slammed the door shut. The pounding of her heart filled the heavy silence inside the mini compact. Her eyes fell to a black object on the floor. A gasp escaped her lips. Alice Donovan's purse. She'd picked it up at the Grange Hall last night and then forgotten all about it. Only in a town like Thornhill, would a bag in an unlocked car not get stolen. Chloe stared at the bag, her fingers twitching, her pulse racing. The innocent handbag drew her eyes like a magnet. A wicked presence seemed to emanate from it, whispering, "Ha, ha, I'll get you, too."

She felt the dark twist of ghostly hands, felt a sharp searing pain in her chest. An invisible stab, just like that time seven years ago when she'd been on the path behind Amanda's house. Back then she'd blacked out with the pain and the fear. But this time she fought the terror. Her eyes remained fixed on Alice's purse. She grabbed it and wrenched the latch open.

A sob slipped past her clenched lips as she pulled out a small clay figurine from the top of the purse. It was a slender doll, carefully detailed with blue eyes and curly, shoulder-length auburn hair. The costume, a simple blue dress, was a replica of the one Chloe had worn at Amanda's funeral. It wasn't only the likeness that terrified Chloe and made the inside of her mouth taste thick and sour. It was the miniature knife sticking into the chest of the figurine. Into the heart. And not an ordinary knife. Someone had taken the painstaking effort to carve symbols on its black hit so that it bore a striking similarity to Amanda Emory's atheme.

A whoosh of fresh air across her face saved her from passing out. Noah was bending toward her.

"Chloe, what's wrong? What is it?" Then his eyes dropped to her lap and he saw the figurine. He grabbed it and flung it from the car. The ghastly figurine bounced off the cold concrete ground, jarring the knife loose from the clay chest.

And then Chloe was in Noah's arms.

"It's okay, Chloe. I won't let anything happen to you. It's okay." He was breathing the reassuring words into her. Her lungs filled with the words, and slowly she stopped trembling.

Chapter Seven

Harvey Mead carefully encased the clay figurine and the tiny dagger in separate evidence bags. Then he looked across his desk at Chloe and Noah.

"I'm glad, once you pulled yourselves together, you thought to bring this—whatever you call it—in."

"It's called an image," Chloe said, amazed at her own sense of calm. The calm after the storm, for a change. Or was there a new storm brewing? "It's a form of sympathetic magic," she went on, in a lecturing tone of voice that reminded her of Amanda. Maybe, by distancing herself emotionally, she'd be able to prove to herself that she wasn't still so frightened. "It's most effective if the image maker can get actual locks of hair or nail parings or some such bodily part from the victim." Chloe felt a tiny crack in her calm. "I did take a second look at the image. And...there were some actual strands of auburn hair mixed in with man-made fibers from a wig. I have a feeling, when your people check it out, they'll discover it was...my hair."

Noah's mouth plunged at the corners. "How would someone get strands of your hair?"

"From my hairbrush," Chloe guessed. "Either back at my room at Mrs. Harris's or from the brush in my purse. There were plenty of opportunities."

"And plenty enough suspects," Harvey interrupted. "Mrs. Harris for one. And then there's Lara. She visited you the other day. Or, perhaps, someone who had access to your purse at the hospital."

"Like Thad Emory," Noah said tersely.

Chloe gave Noah a sharp look. Harvey regarded Noah, too, but his expression reflected curiosity. "What about Thad?" the chief asked.

"He had plenty of access to Chloe's purse over at the hospital last night. And he was back at the hospital this morning before coming over to my place. He could easily have stopped by Chloe's car to plant that doll—"

"That's crazy," Chloe protested.

"Why is it crazy?" Harvey asked.

Chloe frowned. "For one thing, whoever made that image must have believed in its...powers. Thad's certainly the last person to set any store by sympathetic magic."

Harvey's expression was pensive. "Well, now, the way I see it, it isn't so much that the maker of that image had to believe in sympathetic magic. Just that . . . you did."

"I . . . don't," Chloe said tensely. "Not really."

"It's okay, Chloe," Noah soothed. "I think all Harvey is saying is that the image was meant to frighten you. And . . . well, it did."

Chloe was glad now she hadn't told Noah about the chest pains she'd experienced in her car right before she'd seen the image. Or how those pains had disappeared the moment that tiny dagger had been dislodged from the chest of the clay figure. "It was in Alice's purse. It could have been there all the time. Maybe she . . ."

"If Alice had meant to frighten you off, why was she . . . murdered?" Noah clearly didn't buy that possibility. "No. I still say Thad—"

"Do you realize what you're suggesting, Noah?" Chloe asked harshly. "If Thad put that image in Alice's purse, then he had to have been the one who..." She couldn't finish the sentence.

Harvey crossed over to the window. "Not necessarily," the chief reflected, having completed Chloe's thought in his mind. "It's possible he's protecting someone else."

"Someone else?" Chloe said. Who would Thad protect? One name came immediately to mind. His sister, Lara.

Harvey sighed. "We don't want to jump the gun here. First thing we've got to do is ask ourselves why Alice was murdered. I think one conclusion we've all been skirting is that Alice knew too much. Too much about what? Too much about the circumstances of Amanda Emory's death."

"You're saying Amanda's death wasn't suicide?" Noah asked tightly. "What about the note you found? Lara told me..."

"Did Amanda write the note?" Chloe asked, remembering that Harvey was having it checked for authenticity.

"She wrote the note, all right. Her handwriting checks out," Harvey said. "And, I have it from a local source that Amanda was very upset about something for a while prior to her death. I plan to do some digging to find out what that something was."

"Then it definitely was suicide." Noah said, a hint of relief in his voice.

Harvey smoothed his hand over his thinning gray hair. Slowly, he strolled back over to his desk and sat down. "I just got back the final autopsy report on Amanda. Her death was a result of a stab wound to the heart. That much was pretty well established on the site. The autopsy concludes, from all evidence, that the wound could have been self-inflicted." He stopped, but both Chloe and Noah sensed there was more to come. They stared at the chief of police in tense silence.

Harvey cracked his knuckles. There was more to the story, all right. "But something...odd...showed up in Amanda's blood analysis. There were faint traces of a substance known as hyoscine."

"Hyoscine? Is it a poison?" Chloe asked puzzled.

"Not in small doses," Noah offered. "It's a natural sedative. Produces a sort of light sleep or trance state. No one uses it anymore..."

"Correction, Noah," Harvey broke in. "Someone did. Possibly Amanda herself. Or somebody administered it to her."

"It sounds just like Amanda. She was always whipping up these weird ceremonial concoctions," Noah said.

"Is there any kept around the hospital?" Harvey asked casually.

"No," Noah answered succinctly. "And it's not the sort of thing they carry in drug stores these days, either. My bet is, you'll find the only hyoscine around these parts right where Amanda kept all her herbs and potion ingredients."

"Which means," Harvey said, "anyone who cared to, could have filched some of the drug from Amanda's place, seeing as how people were always coming and going from there."

"Why would anyone else...?"

A burst of sudden awareness flashed through Chloe's brain. Her breath caught and goosebumps sprang up on her arms. "To put Amanda in a trance. The power of suggestion," she said thickly, blinking at first Noah's face and then Harvey's, blurred out of focus. "I think Lara was right," Chloe breathed.

"What? That Amanda was possessed by an evil spirit?" Noah remained cynical.

"No," Chloe whispered, tears in her eyes. "All she had to do was *believe* she was possessed by an evil spirit."

Both Noah and Harvey stared at Chloe in tense silence. It was Harvey who spoke first. "Are you saying that you think someone drugged Amanda and then convinced her that she was possessed?"

Chloe's pulse throbbed in the hollow of her throat. "It's just a . . . hunch, Harvey."

Harvey leaned forward. "Can you go on with that hunch, Chloe? Any ideas who . . . ?"

"No." The word was a bare whisper.

Noah gave Harvey a fierce look. "This business has nothing to do with Chloe. She hardly knew Alice Donovan and she hasn't had any contact with Amanda for years. I really think you should leave her out of this."

Harvey shrugged. "She seems to be involved, whether she, you, or I like it or not, Noah." The chief stood up, pressing the palms of his hands on his desk. "Someone sent Chloe that phony note to get her out to the Grange and someone, most likely that same someone, or an accomplice, planted that doll. What I'm saying is someone here in Thornhill seems intent on putting a real scare into Chloe."

"Why, though?" Noah asked sharply.

The chief smiled thinly. "My hunch is someone's scared of her. Scared enough to want to frighten her off."

"That doesn't make any sense," Noah insisted. He looked to Chloe for confirmation, but she sat silent and rigid.

"Everyone in town knows about Chloe's . . . experiences . . . down in Boston. The papers called her a psychic. It was big news in Thornhill. Oh, of course plenty of people scoffed. But there are those who didn't. Who still don't."

Noah frowned. "You're not going to tell me, chief, that Amanda's murderer is afraid that Chloe will *psychically* track him down?"

"Like I said," Harvey answered laconically, "according to the papers, she's done it before."

"It didn't really happen the way the media presented it," Chloe protested. "It just made better copy and sold more papers to call me psychic. Labels are all too easy to stick on someone."

"And hard to unstick, Chloe. The word's spreading like a barn fire that a clairvoyant tracker has come to town. It's generating a lot of excitement. And a lot of anxiety. I'm not just talking about the people who might be involved in this ugly business I'm investigating. You know how these things spill over. Those who believe you've got special powers could be working themselves into a panic, afraid that you'll find out all their wicked secrets, their varied sins."

"Maybe the best solution is for me to simply hop the next bus back to Boston," Chloe said quietly. Neither man responded. Chloe stared at them each in turn. Something flickered in her eyes. "But I hightailed it away from Thornhill once and I regretted it. This time I won't be scared off. I won't turn my back and run. I won't leave Thornhill until I'm good and ready."

A tight silence hung in the air, broken after several moments by the shrill sound of Noah's hospital beeper. He used Harvey's phone. There was an emergency at the hospital that he had to attend to.

Harvey noticed Noah's reluctance to leave Chloe. "Don't worry, Doc. I'll look after her."

Noah still hesitated for a few moments, long enough to cup Chloe's chin, tilt her head up and touch his thumb to her lips.

When Noah left, Chloe nervously wondered if the heat of those few moments showed on her face. When she looked over at Harvey, she saw it did.

"It's not what you think," she felt compelled to say.

Harvey smiled. "And what was I thinking, Chloe?"

"It doesn't matter, anyway, Harvey. Noah's still in love with Lara."

"Oh? Is that what he told you?"

Chloe's mouth quirked in a wry smile. "Call it a hunch."

Harvey sighed. "I worry about Lara. She's a very troubled woman."

"She just...lost her mother. And they were...very close."

"It's a messy situation," Harvey muttered. "But then murder usually is. Not that I've had many murders here in Thornhill, knock on wood." He rapped his desk. "No question that it was murder as far as Alice Donovan is concerned. But I'm still going to have to go with a verdict of suicide for Amanda, even though you and I have our hunches to the contrary."

"But the hyoscine?"

Harvey shrugged. "There's no evidence to indicate that someone else administered it to Amanda. And I can just see myself trying to convince the attorney general that the drug was used to hypnotize Amanda, then convince her she was possessed and, to top it off, served to get her to stab herself in the chest as a means of exorcising the demon." He quirked a brow. "I doubt anyone's ever been successfully convicted on a charge of murder by power of suggestion."

"But...I have a strong intuition that's precisely what it was," Chloe whispered.

"I don't know about that, Chloe. But I do know that a person can be driven to take his or her own life. If he—or she—is scared enough. And if someone else is deliberately doing the scaring," Harvey said, smiling thinly, "then I'd call it murder in my book. Problem is, it can rarely be proven. I'm afraid the only way we're ever going to bring Amanda's murderer to justice is to track down the person who killed Alice. Alice either knew something about Amanda's murder, or someone believed she did. Believed it enough to silence her permanently. When you saw Alice at the Grange, did she say anything at all?"

"She was out cold. When she did come to, that first time, she was terrified. But all she would say is...she's back. Alice was convinced she'd seen Amanda's...ghost." Chloe hesitated, deliberating as to whether to tell Harvey about the eerie figure she'd spotted on the hill. While she was still trying to make up her mind, Harvey asked her an altogether different question.

"How would you like to put some of those hunches of yours to the test, Chloe?"

Chloe gave him a wary look. "What do you mean?"

"What I said before about someone wanting to frighten you off because they're scared of you, scared of what you might know...or what you might sense. Well, maybe you can use that fear of theirs to our advantage. When people are scared they do dumb things. They can slip up, panic, say things they don't mean to say."

Chloe stared at the chief of police for several long moments. "You want me to deceive people, encourage them to believe I have some sort of supernatural power."

"People are going to believe what they want to believe, Chloe. All I'm asking you to do is...help me bring a murderer to justice."

Murderer. Someone in Thornhill was a murderer. Someone she might know. Someone she might care about.

"Of course," Harvey said in a low voice, "you've got plenty of reason to be scared yourself. And I'm not saying you wouldn't be at risk. Maybe the smartest thing would be for you to go right over to the inn and catch that next bus to Boston. No one would think any the less of you, Chloe."

Chloe looked up sharply. "That's not true, Harvey. I would." She took a deep steadying breath. "I admit I'm scared, Harvey. Whether we believe in witchcraft, in psychic phenomenon, or in the supernatural, we all have our own private demons. I really do need to face my demons or I think they're going to haunt me all my life."

"Demons," Harvey echoed, a play of emotions coloring his voice. "Yes, I suppose we do all have them." His attention drifted for a moment and Chloe felt a powerful wave of sadness emanating from the chief. At first, she didn't understand, and then, inexplicably, as had happened at certain times before, she knew.

"You loved her," she murmured. "You loved Amanda."

Tears glistened in Harvey's eyes. "It was a long time ago, Chloe. She was so vibrant, so very beautiful. She was my first love. There's something magical about a first love. For some, no other love ever quite matches it," he admitted.

Oh, how well Chloe knew that. Noah was her first love.

Harvey pulled out a red bandana and blew his nose. He shrugged and affected a crooked smile. "Don't get me wrong, Chloe. I'm a happily married man. Have been for close to thirty-two years now. I was lucky to find Mildred. Sometimes I'm not so easy to put up with."

Chloe smiled, but an edge of tension and something else, something she couldn't quite put her finger on, remained.

Harvey tucked his hanky into his back pocket. "So what do you say, Chloe? Will you help me?"

This elicited a sigh from Chloe. "I don't know, Harvey."

Harvey seemed to take that as a yes. "The way I see it, accepting that this case revolves around Amanda's death, the first question is—who stands to gain from her dying?"

His gaze slipped away from Chloe. "For starters there's ... Thad and Lara."

A prickle of apprehension chilled the back of Chloe' neck. "What do they gain?"

"About a quarter of a million apiece. And Lara gc Amanda's house. She'd been sharing it with Amanda eve since her ... divorce. Thad already owns a place over o Bucks Rock. And, from what Lara told me, he never muc liked Amanda's house."

Again, Chloe could hear Lara's voice. *"I didn't kill he I swear..."*

"They're close, those two. Thad and Lara," Harvey wa saying. "Even though they're as different as night and da; Not that that's surprising since Thad was adopted."

"Adopted?" Chloe did a double-take. So much for h supposed clairvoyance. It had never crossed her mind tha Thad wasn't Amanda's natural-born child. Oh, it was ce tainly obvious that Thad bore no physical resemblance either Amanda or Lara, whose own similarity in looks w quite extraordinary. But Chloe had simply assumed th Thad must have looked more like his father, Ben Emor who had died shortly after Lara was born.

"I'm not revealing any secret here," Harvey con mented. "Amanda told Thad he was adopted as soon as I was old enough to understand what the word meant. Sl certainly always treated him like her own. And, as I sa Lara and Thad were as close as any natural siblings." I gave a little chuckle. "I've known plenty of natural si lings who fought like cats and dogs."

Chloe managed a weak smile. She was herself an on child and had grown up wishing fervently for a sibling.

Harvey sobered up fast. "Not that I'm pointing my fi ger, necessarily, at Thad or Lara, mind you. Money is on one motive for murder, after all. There's plenty of othe

Jealousy, revenge." He hesitated. "Then there's the possibility that Amanda acquired some distressing knowledge about someone in town..."

Chloe didn't hear the rest of Harvey's sentence. All at once she received a brilliant flicker of realization. "Harvey, Amanda's note. The...note you found by her...body. Is it back from the lab? Can I see it?" Her voice was a choked whisper. An odd, knowing silence filled her eyes.

Harvey gave her a curious look. Then, without a word, he went to the safe and got the note. He extended it toward Chloe, observing that the hand that took it was trembling badly.

Chloe stared at the note in silence for several moments. Then her eyelids flickered closed and she recited from memory, in a husky voice, "'I can't go on like this. I truly have no other choice.'" Slowly, she opened her eyes. First she looked down at the note again, and then she lifted her gaze to Harvey's face, as though the effort pained her. "This is no suicide note."

"What is it, then?" Harvey asked, his voice strained.

She lay the note in her lap and pressed the palm of her hand on top of it. "I believe it's...a threat."

"CHLOE. Chloe, wait."

Chloe was just about to cross Main Street on her way to the pharmacy to pick up some toiletries when she heard her name being called. She turned to see Lara Emory, long blond hair flying, black raincoat flapping, running toward her. Lara's features were taut, her violet eyes as wide as an owl's. The fine alabaster skin now had a pasty texture, its color like powdered sugar. She looked, thought Chloe, just like a woman who had seen a ghost.

"Oh, I'm so glad...I found you. I...looked everywhere...for you. I called Noah. He said...last he saw you...you were at the...police station. But you left there...hours ago." Lara spoke in a voice that was both halting and pained.

"I've been doing errands in town," Chloe said calmly. "Why the desperate search for me?"

"I've heard you're not going right back to Boston. You're planning to stay in Thornhill."

Chloe winced. So Noah was still confiding in his ex-wife. "Not permanently, Lara. The college has some materials I need for a research project I'm doing..."

"You aren't going to continue staying at that old busy-body's place, are you? I don't like Lucy Harris. Not that she cares for me, either. It was mother she adored."

Chloe disengaged her arm from Lara's grasp. "I have to admit I'm not overly fond of Lucy Harris at the moment myself." She was still quite angry at Lucy for reading her mail. On the other hand, if Lucy hadn't read it and sent Thad off to find her, something terrible might have happened. Chloe knew she was not imagining the aura of danger she'd experienced down at the Grange.

A car whizzed by, too close to the curb, and Chloe drew back, pulling Lara with her.

"College kids," Lara muttered. "They're so reckless." She turned to Chloe with an enigmatic look. "We never think at that age that we'll have to pay for our sins." The dull look in Lara's eyes alarmed Chloe. She wondered if Lara might be on drugs of some sort. That would explain her odd behavior, her disconnected thoughts and statements. But would it explain her terror? There was no doubt in Chloe's mind that Lara was frightened.

"I'm not going to be here in Thornhill for very long," Chloe said. "Mrs. Harris's place is clean, convenient and cheap. Anyway, Thornhill has no dearth of busybodies."

She smiled, hoping to elicit a smile from Lara, but she failed.

Lara's expression grew more desperate. "Please, stay with me, Chloe. Mother would want that. And...I'll mind my own business. I swear. Please...Chloe."

"Lara," Chloe said soothingly, "if you're scared to stay in your mother's house, why don't you stay with Thad for a while. I'm sure he'd be pleased to have you."

"Thad? No. No, Thad doesn't understand, Chloe. No one else understands but you."

"Lara, you've got me wrong." Chloe stopped, remembering something Harvey had said earlier. *"People will believe what they want to believe."*

"I've got my car. You will come home with me, Chloe. You must. You can have my old room. It's bright and cheerful. You remember. I'm staying in...mother's room now. It's better that way."

Better for whom, Chloe wondered.

Suddenly, the dullness left Lara's eyes. "Are you scared, Chloe? Because of what mother told me? That...that you were next?"

"Listen to me, Lara..."

"You don't have to be scared. You see, mother came back again. She told me that you had the power to fight a psychic attack. And that you would protect me."

"Lara—"

"My car's parked right in front of the bookstore. Can you drive? I seem to be trembling like a leaf. I'm afraid...to drive myself." Despite the chill in the air, perspiration beaded on Lara's face.

"Look Lara, maybe in a few days...if I end up staying in Thornhill that long."

Lara blinked, the expression on her face poignantly childlike. "Oh Chloe, you've got to come now. You've got to be with me tonight. Especially tonight."

"Why especially tonight?"

Lara's expression seemed haunted. "It's . . . Halloween. Tonight's Halloween."

"Lara—"

"You've got to stay with me tonight, Chloe. Please. Please."

Chloe was tempted to ask Lara why she didn't invite Peter Mott over to ward off the ghosts and goblins of Halloween. Maybe she had and Mott had other plans. Or maybe Lara had a good reason not to ask him. Chloe had to admit he'd be the last person she'd ask for protection against danger of any sort, real or imagined.

Chloe hesitated. Her conversation with Harvey Mead hugged her like a shadow. Lara was a suspect. A frightened suspect who just might open up to her. Or slip up around her, as Harvey had suggested. Then again, if Lara was involved in either her mother's death or Alice's, she could be dangerous. Chloe certainly was witness to Lara's instability, her rapid mood swings. Noah had warned her about Lara's hallucinations and delusions. And he'd seemed frightened that Lara might be driven to act on those hallucinations. Or had he just used that as an excuse to encourage her to leave Thornhill. He was certainly giving her mixed messages.

"I know the keys are in here somewhere." Lara had begun a frantic search in her large leather tote bag. After several agitated moments, she finally pulled out a jangle of keys along with a pack of cigarettes. "I gave up smoking last week," she said, tapping out a cigarette and popping it into her mouth. "Maybe it wasn't a good time." She was once again rummaging in her bag. "Do you have any matches?"

Chloe shook her head. "I don't smoke."

All of Lara's motions and her pattern of speech had a manic energy. Chloe thought it the kind of energy that fed off panic and terror. *Like a vampire fed off blood.* Having such a silly thought made Chloe jeer at herself. Halloween, indeed.

Lara finally found a book of matches, but the wind kept blowing them out before she could manage to get her cigarette lit. She gave it up, tossed the cigarette back in her tote and plunked the keys in Chloe's hand. For a moment, her violet eyes fixed on something—or someone—beyond Chloe.

Instinctively Chloe glanced over her shoulder. She saw a striking brunette coming up Main Street. The woman wasn't only beautiful, she radiated a cool elegance and haughty sophistication that was rare in Thornhill, even given that the town was relatively cosmopolitan, thanks to the college and the medical school.

Chloe didn't recognize the woman, and wasn't even sure that she was the target of Lara's tense glance. She had already started to turn back to Lara when the woman's gaze fell upon her. Chloe gasped. Never could she recall anyone, certainly not a perfect stranger, regarding her with such open animosity. No, more than animosity. A palpable hatred. A sudden warning sounded in Chloe's head. *She's a bad one. She's out for blood.* A harsh laugh escaped Chloe's lips.

"Chloe?"

Chloe jerked round to face Lara.

There was a glint in Lara's violet eyes. "She thinks she's better than us. Well, she'll find out—"

"Who?"

"Karin Niels," Lara said in a low, vengeful tone. "That bitch who just gave you the evil eye."

Chapter Eight

Amanda Emory's house was situated on a knoll in a section of Thornhill called Honeysuckle Hill, about three miles north of the heart of the town. It was one of Thornhill's oldest established residential areas. Back in the seventeen hundreds, when Dorchester College was in its youth, Honeysuckle Hill was all farmland. Little by little some of the more affluent members of the college began buying out the locals. Pretty soon, Honeysuckle Hill became the exclusive domain of Dorchester College's monied, intellectual elite. It had remained so to this day.

As for the Emory homestead, it was one of the oldest structures in Thornhill and afforded a panoramic view of Mt. Ascutney. On a clear day you could even see the snow-capped peaks of the Green Mountains. Save for the glorious views, however, the house itself lacked any sign of architectural merit. It was a huge, gloomy, ramshackle structure. Its leaded windows dimmed the light entering the house, and the kitchen and baths hadn't been updated since Amanda Emory bought the property nearly thirty years ago. The floors creaked, the paint was peeling inside and out, and the whole building could have done with shoring up. The original structure was brick, but over the years different families had haphazardly tacked on wooden additions, porches and storage spaces. They were not always up to code, and all too often showed no thought had been given to design or style.

Back in college, when Chloe and Lara had been friends, Chloe used to visit the old dilapidated house quite often. There was a time when she'd slept there with more frequency than she'd slept in her dorm. She'd always wondered why the house was kept in such disrepair, since it was common knowledge that the residents of Honeysuckle Hill had plenty of money. Chloe had concluded that Amanda must have been the exception and simply didn't have the funds to remodel or renovate the house. Having learned from Harvey today that Thad and Lara had inherited a cool half million from their mother's estate, Chloe had to assume now that Amanda simply hadn't cared about such mundane enterprises as home maintenance and repair. Her interests had been, till the end, far more ethereal.

It had been seven years since Chloe'd been to the Emory homestead. And the memory of her last visit remained indelibly imprinted on her brain. She hadn't even gone into the house itself. She'd merely walked down the path to the glen in search of Amanda. Instead, she'd come upon a ghostly vision in white, atheme raised.

As she drove up the narrow winding road leading to the Emory house, an intangible fear curled through Chloe. She fought to dispel it. Having agreed, for a jumble of reasons, to keep Lara company tonight, Chloe refused to let her anxiety get the best of her.

Lara sat in gloomy silence throughout the ride, not helping Chloe's morbid mood any. Chloe glanced at the pale blond woman as they neared the house. "I can only spend the night," Chloe reiterated. "Since I need to work at the library every day it doesn't make sense for me to be way out here when Lucy's place is only a five-minute walk from the college. That reminds me. Tomorrow, first thing, my rental car is due back.'' Chloe wouldn't admit it, even to herself, but having found that image in the rental car had spooked her enough to want to be well rid of the vehicle.

In response to Chloe's statement, Lara merely nodded and continued to stare vacantly out the car window.

"We should have picked up some candy. Didn't the neighborhood children usually ring your doorbell at Halloween?''

Lara didn't answer, and Chloe asked the question once again.

"This is my first Halloween here in…a long time,'' Lara muttered.

That's right, Chloe thought with an unbidden flicker of jealousy. For several years, Lara had been in her own home on Oakdale Lane, the bright, cheerful, carefully restored home she'd shared with her husband—Noah Bright. They'd spent Halloween together, Thanksgiving, Christmas….

Shaking off her thoughts about Noah Bright, and her continued apprehension about spending the night at the Emory homestead—now, according to Lara, haunted by an Emory ghost—Chloe again resolved to make the best of a tense situation. She turned the car onto the gravel driveway.

At the end of the driveway was an attached garage. Chloe brought the car to a halt in front of its closed and lopsided hinged wooden doors. "Do you want to run out and open the doors so I can pull your car inside?'' she asked Lara.

"What? Oh, no. We never use the garage. It's…filled with old tools, cartons, and cast-off furniture.''

Chloe shut off the ignition and handed Lara the car keys.

"Thanks,'' Lara muttered, dropping the keys absently into her tote. There was a lengthy pause. Finally Lara looked over at Chloe. She studied her closely for several moments before saying, "Mother was a true witch, you know. Or if you prefer, a high priestess. Mother preferred that term." Slowly she turned in her seat to face Chloe. There was a faint smile on Lara's lips. The dullness in her violet eyes had again vanished. Gone, too, was that hint of madness. At the moment Lara looked remarkably sane.

"Most of my mother's followers didn't really believe she was a witch. For a long time I certainly didn't. We participated in her rituals because they had a romantic, mysterious appeal, a touch of the macabre, an illicit sense of daring as we chanted and danced naked in the meadow, our bodies shadowed by moonlight and candlelight." Another long pause. "Mother always said you had the calling, but you were afraid of your own powers. I used to be very jealous of you. There was a time . . . I hated you, Chloe."

Fear tickled Chloe's spine. "And now?"

"I need you," she answered simply.

Lara's response in no way comforted Chloe since she was well aware that need didn't necessarily obliterate hatred.

Quashing her reluctance to actually go into the Emory house, Chloe resolutely opened the car door and stepped out. Staring at the house, she felt an odd twinge in the pit of her stomach that she quickly attributed to hunger. "I hope you have some food in the house for supper," she said to Lara.

By way of an answer, Lara said, "I'm vegetarian."

Chloe, determined to be upbeat, said, "Great. We can make a big salad. I'm a whiz at vinaigrette dressing."

They started for the house. Neither woman walked with what one might call a sprightly step. Their pace was more suitable to a funeral march. So much for being upbeat.

"Are you going to keep the house, or sell?" Chloe asked with a deliberately light tone.

"I won't sell," Lara said firmly. "Thad thinks I'm crazy. Of course, he would."

"Why do you say that?"

Lara turned a blank gaze to Chloe, but her verbal response was quite cogent and tinged with cynicism. "I could probably get three hundred grand or more for the property. If I did sell, the stipulation in my mother's will calls for Thad and me to split the proceeds. I already have a very interested buyer."

"Someone from the college?"

"Of course," Lara said with a laugh. "I'd be strung up by the residents of Honeysuckle Hill if I so much as considered an offer from an outsider."

Chloe's brow puckered. "Is that really still such an issue up here?"

Lara grimaced. "There'd be civil war, honey chile. We must uphold tradition here in idyllic Thornhill," she uttered sarcastically.

"So, who's the interested buyer?" Chloe asked as they walked up the rickety porch to the front door of the house.

Lara came to an abrupt halt, her eyes fixed on Chloe's face. "Peter Mott." She shrugged questioningly. "You remember Peter, don't you?"

"Yes. Quite well," Chloe said in a desultory voice.

Lara laughed. There was a definite hint of maliciousness in that laugh. "Peter remembers you, too. You singlehandedly almost ruined his career. Well, I should include mother in that effort, too."

Chloe felt a flare-up of rage. "If anyone almost ruined that lecher's career it was Peter Mott, himself. And I wasn't the only student who suffered his sexual advances."

Lara smiled provocatively. "Oh, I know, Chloe. Only I don't know that I'd personally use the word *suffered*."

Chloe stared at Lara with a stunned expression. "You and Mott? Back in college?"

Lara laughed. "I think mother suspected something was going on. But we were very discreet. You can imagine what she might have done if she'd found out. She never did like Peter's interest in pretty young girls."

"Did . . . Noah know?" Chloe asked in a strained voice.

"About me and Peter? You're the psychic, Chloe. You tell me."

Chloe's blue eyes flickered with disgust. "Then you were involved with Mott while you and Noah—"

Lara stared at Chloe; her violet eyes were as hard and cold as a North Country winter sky. "If Noah had wanted someone who was perfect, who had no weaknesses, no faults, I never would have managed to lure him away from you." She looked away, an oddly pensive expression on her face. "Then again, maybe I never really did."

Her mood shifting dramatically, Lara turned back to Chloe, gave her a warm, girlish smile colored with good-hearted mischief and grabbed her hand. "This is going to be fun, Chloe. Just like old times."

Just like old times . . .

THEY HAD DINNER—a vegetable-laden Greek salad—in the front parlor. It was a large, chilly room with high ceilings, overstuffed, unfashionable furnishings and a Persian rug that had seen better days. There were no plants in the room and only a few faded prints on the walls. A musty scent permeated the air, but this was the case all through the house. The house had a silent, hollow tone. With Amanda gone, it felt to Chloe like the house itself was lifeless.

Their dinner was interrupted a couple of times by trick or treaters, but the secluded location of the house kept the Halloween callers at a minimum. The thought also crossed

Chloe's mind that the children of Thornhill might deliberately avoid a *witch's* house on Halloween. Even a dead one's. Maybe, especially a dead one's.

After dinner Lara insisted Chloe stay put and relax while she went off to the kitchen to clean up. About a half hour later, Lara returned with a big bag of marshmallows and made a fire. For a woman who'd seemed so terrified only hours before, Lara was now bright and bubbly. Chloe was just the opposite. She stared morosely at the fire, her mood clouded by the pervasive gloominess of the house and by her earlier disturbing conversation with Lara. Especially the part about Noah.

"So," Lara said, settling down beside Chloe on the floor in front of the fire, "shall we tell ghost stories? It's only fitting." Her eyes sparkled. "After all, it is Halloween."

Being with Lara was like being on a roller coaster ride in the dark, Chloe thought. You never knew what to expect, but you were constantly in for a surprise twist or turn.

"I'd have thought," Chloe said wonderingly, "that telling scary tales would be the last thing you'd want to do."

Lara smiled ingenuously. "Not as long as you're here with me, Chloe."

Chloe didn't even think Lara's new affability was bogus. The woman was baffling with her mercurial shifts of mood. Was it mental instability? Was it drugs? Or was she . . . bewitched?

"Tell me about that woman we saw in town this afternoon," Chloe said, having no interest in fictitious ghost stories. Lately the truth was proving far more fascinating.

"Which woman?" Lara asked coyly.

"Karin Niels."

Lara giggled. "Why, that's no ghost, Chloe. That's our very own devil worshipper."

"What?"

"Peter calls her the Princess of Darkness. They had a thing going for a while."

"She and Mott had an affair? My, he certainly gets around."

"Peter likes to flatter himself that no woman can resist him," Lara said, smiling slyly. "But, if you want to know the truth, Chloe, Karin was only trying to get her husband jealous."

"Her husband?"

"The very rich, very distinguished-looking Lawrence Niels, president of the Savings and Loan."

"Niels," Chloe mused, the name now ringing a bell. "Is that the Niels who owns that fabulous mansion up on Laurel Ridge?" Those prominent citizens of Thornhill not connected to the college had developed their own select enclave, Laurel Ridge, located, as its name indicated, on a ridge overlooking a Currier and Ives pond just south of town.

Laura confirmed Chloe's guess.

"Now I remember," Chloe reflected. "I met Lawrence Niels over here once, back in college. Your mother had him to dinner. With his wife. But she was a plain-looking woman who was forty-five if she was a day."

"That was his first wife, Ellen. She . . . died."

Chloe caught the hesitation in Lara's voice. "How did she die?"

Lara stared into the fire. "Suicide."

Chloe felt a sharp jab in her chest.

Lara looked over at Chloe, an eerie smile on her lips. "Don't you want to know how she killed herself?"

Chloe fixed her gaze on the fire. She felt her skin crawl and a palpable aura of blood and flashing silver enveloped her. She wanted to say no. No, she didn't want to know how Ellen had died. But she knew already.

"She stole Mother's atheme. And stabbed herself right in the heart," Laura said, watching Chloe.

"The atheme...?" Chloe's voice was barely a whisper. "Why did she kill herself?"

"She found out about her husband's affair. Really, don't you think the older generation takes fidelity too much to heart?"

Chloe experienced another wave of disgust, but she felt compelled to pursue the subject of Ellen Niels's suicide. "Who was her husband having an affair with? Karin?"

"No. He didn't even know Karin then. She isn't from Thornhill. Guess again," Lara said with impish glee.

Chloe stared coldly at Lara. "With you?"

Lara laughed. "Larry and me? Why, he's not at all my type. I don't know, Chloe. Maybe you aren't the psychic you're reputed to be."

And then, whether it was psychic ability, intuition, or simply the look in Lara's eyes, Chloe did know. "Your mother. Lawrence Niels was having an affair with Amanda." Amanda Emory. Chloe was truly disappointed. She had greatly admired Amanda, who had helped and guided her during her troubled college years. Why, Amanda had even offered solace to Chloe when Lara had taken the man Chloe loved. This same lovely, caring woman had not only had a sordid affair with a married man, but had been in some way responsible for the death of that man's wife. And then an even more awful thought assailed her.

"Was there any question—? It was suicide?" Chloe asked nervously.

Lara's gaze was hooded. "I'm sure Harvey Mead had some doubts at first, especially as how the weapon belonged to Mother." She paused, her features strained. "Do you think Mother's death by the same weapon was...retribution, Chloe?''

Chloe shivered, but she made no response.

Lara pulled herself together. "Harvey Mead ruled out homicide. Ellen left a note. Unlike Mother's, Ellen's left no room for doubt. Not that there wasn't a thorough investigation anyway. Both dear old Lawrence and Mother had to account for their whereabouts and such.''

"Was your mother in love with Lawrence?" Chloe asked softly.

Lara studied Chloe with amusement. "You're still a romantic, Chloe. Oh, Mother fully intended to be the second Mrs. Niels, but it had less to do with passion than with position in the community. With Niels as a husband, Mother would have bridged the town-gown gap. That appealed to her. Unfortunately, Larry took a business trip to Boston and met the young, vivacious and wickedly beautiful Karin. Mother wasn't all that pleased when Larry arrived back in Thornhill with a new wife in tow." Lara's eyes sparkled. "But Mother eventually evened the score."

Chloe gave Lara a puzzled look.

"One day, a few months back, the snooty Mrs. Niels number two spotted her hubby's car here in Mother's driveway. She pulled in and went up to the house to find out what her husband was doing here." Lara grinned lasciviously. "She found out."

"What did Karin do?" Chloe asked, a tight band of tension squeezing her temples.

"For one thing, she seduced dear Peter, wanting to show her husband that two could play the same game. For another, she quit Mother's circle and started up her own coven."

"What kind of coven?"

"It's all very hush-hush. Secret meetings in the dark of night. Secret membership. I've heard that all of her converts wear black robes and black hoods covering their faces so they can't be identified even amongst themselves. There are rumors of Black Masses and Devil worship. I've heard they hold their little get-togethers down at the old Grange Hall." Lara didn't even glance at Chloe. She seemed intent on the roasting of a marshmallow. "You remember Mother's old cat, don't you, Chloe? Dantes."

"Yes," Chloe said, her throat dry. "I remember the cat."

"Mother's *familiar*," Lara smiled brightly at Chloe. "Any witch worth her salt has to have her own personal little demon to help carry out her magic, be it white or black."

"What about the cat?"

"Mother accused Karin Niels of slaughtering it."

"As a sacrifice to the Devil?"

Lara smiled icily. "That's what Karin would have liked Mother to believe. From what I hear, there are those here in Thornhill who are more gullible than Mother. They believe Karin's a legitimate Satanist. But Mother had Karin's number. Vengeance be thine..."

Chloe shivered. Had Karin Niels's vengeance only been the killing of Amanda's cat? Or, had Dantes's blood not been vengeance enough? Had Karin sought further retribution against Amanda? And one more question pulsated in Chloe's mind. She voiced it aloud. "Why was Karin Niels giving me the evil eye this afternoon?"

Lara seemed surprised by the question. "Don't you know? Why, now you're the one she must do battle with, Chloe. Black versus white. Good versus evil. And may the best witch win."

SHADOWS OF NIGHT were stretching over Thornhill as Noah Bright walked into Ali's Café, an upscale restaurant and bar that exuded collegiate charm, but was pricey enough to eliminate a noisy college crowd. Noah headed for the bar and took a stool at the far end.

He'd just come from the lab where he'd been analyzing the "potion" that had killed Alice Donovan. The lab workers hadn't been able to identify the actual poisonous element in the drink, and Noah had persuaded them to let him run his own tests. His persistence and intuition had paid off. Noah had believed that, like the hyoscine, the potion was likely a plant extract, one that in small doses might even be used medicinally. And he'd been right. The poison in that potion had turned out to be an extract of the water hemlock, a lethally poisonous plant. They'd found hyoscine on Amanda Emory's herbal shelves, and Noah was willing to bet they'd find water hemlock extract there as well. He'd called Harvey Mead from the lab, and Harvey had agreed to arrange to confiscate all of Amanda's remaining collection of herbs. He'd no doubt check for hemlock.

When Jeannie, the pretty, dark-haired bar girl, sauntered over to Noah, she was wearing a skimpy black cat costume. He gave her a curious look. "What's with the getup, kid?"

"Boy, Doc, where have you been? Up on Mars? Get with it. It's Halloween." She wiped off the bar space in front of him. "Aren't you going trick or treating tonight, Doc?"

Noah smiled wryly. "I could dress up as a doctor."

Jeannie laughed. "What'll you have?"

"A beer and a roast beef on rye. Easy on the mayo."

"Make it the same for me," said a voice from behind him.

Thad Emory came around and slipped onto the bar stool next to Noah. "So, how'd those tests pan out?" He arched an eyebrow at Noah ever so slightly.

"What tests?" Noah asked tersely.

"The tests that were run on Chloe this morning."

Jeannie brought the beers. Thad gave a broad wink of approval at her costume.

"There were no tests," Noah admitted.

"No, I didn't really think there were." Thad's smile was slow and humorless. He eased out of his jacket and threw it on the empty stool to his left. Just a casual gesture, Noah wondered, or was Thad trying to ensure a private conversation?

Noah took a sip of his beer. He wasn't in the mood for conversing. Even if he had been, Thad Emory would be the last man in town he'd choose to talk to.

"Chloe looks terrific, doesn't she, Bright?"

Noah laughed dryly. "Terrific? She sure as hell didn't look too terrific last night in the emergency room. Just what went on down there at the Grange Hall?"

Thad shrugged. "Don't ask me. When I arrived, Alice was out cold and Chloe looked like she'd just seen a ghost. I did my best to assure her I was flesh and blood." He glanced over at Noah. "How was she this morning?"

Noah looked suspiciously over at Thad. "How should she have been?"

Thad cocked his head. "I figured she must have heard about Alice Donovan's death. Not that they were close or anything, but there must have been something between them. Otherwise what were they doing getting together in the dark of night down at the old Grange?"

The sandwiches arrived, but Noah had lost his appetite. Thad didn't seem all that hungry, either.

"Harvey Mead stopped over at the school to tell me about poor Alice," Thad said. "I think Harvey believes her death is somehow connected to my mother's suicide."

"Is that what he said?" Noah asked.

Thad shrugged. "Maybe I have ESP."

"Do you think there's a connection between your mother's death and Alice's?"

Thad took a bite of his sandwich and chewed slowly. Then he glanced over at Noah. "I don't know about that. But I do find it fascinating that both women came to bad ends over serious cases of unrequited love."

Thad's words were a chill breeze. "Who were they each in love with?"

"Oddly enough, they were both in love with the same man," Thad finished off one half of his sandwich.

Noah had a pretty good idea about the identity of the man. A few years back, there'd been another suicide in Thornhill. Ellen Niels, first wife of the eminent Lawrence Niels, had stabbed herself to death. Noah remembered, with a lurch, that she'd actually done it with Amanda's dagger. And for months afterward rumors had been rife that Ellen had killed herself after discovering her husband and Amanda Emory were having an affair. Ironically, after Ellen's death, Niels had ended up marrying Karin, a beautiful young woman with no ties to Thornhill

Thad downed the last remnants of his beer. Jeannie came over and gave him a Cheshire cat smile. "Want another, Professor Emory?"

"No thanks, Jeannie. I'm heading out to my sister's. Halloween always spooks her so I thought I'd keep her and her house guest company." Thad reached in his pocket for his wallet.

"House guest?" Noah asked warily as he watched Thad pull out a few bills.

Thad gave Noah a taunting grin. "That isn't jealousy I hear, is it?"

"No," Noah said coolly. "It certainly isn't."

Thad gave Noah's shoulder a squeeze. It was a little too rough to be mistaken for a friendly gesture. "Well, don't worry, Noah. Your ex-wife isn't entertaining a male friend. Does that make you breathe easier?" Thad said, with a smile.

But it didn't make Noah Bright breathe any easier at all. He read the smile on Thad's face accurately and it bothered him. Lara's house guest was Chloe. Why after all he'd told Chloe about Lara's unstable state of mind, she'd spend an evening alone with Lara, Noah couldn't fathom. Suppressing a swell of anger, he plunked money down on the counter to cover his bill and said, "Think I'll ride on up to Lara's with you." He didn't ask permission, not wanting to give Thad the opportunity to refuse. To Noah's surprise, however, Thad merely shrugged, albeit begrudgingly. "Sure," he said laconically. "We'll have ourselves a little Halloween party."

"How about some music?" Lara suggested. "I've still got a bunch of old LPs up in my bedroom."

"Sure, music would be great," Chloe said. Anything to fill the heavy silence.

Lara popped up from her crossed-legged position on the floor in front of the fire. "I'll pick some out."

Chloe watched Lara skip off, again marveling at the woman's constant flip-flops of mood. She took a sip of cognac, liking the way it warmed her insides. Rising, she stoked the fire a bit then walked over to one of the draped windows. Pulling the heavy curtain aside, she looked out. Again, it was quite breezy. The tips of the trees curved with the wind. The moon was full. Chloe smiled. How appropriate.

As she let the brocade curtain drop, an odd scent struck her. Something faintly sweet mingled with the musty air. She put her nose to the curtain. But the scent was in the air itself not the fabric. Was it a new smell, or had she simply not detected it earlier?

There was something subtly familiar about the scent. Like rose petals. And then Chloe remembered. It was Amanda's favorite scent. Chloe recalled it because it had such a cloying quality. She had always wished Amanda would switch to another perfume. But she never had.

Chloe turned from the window, and the snifter of cognac slipped from her hand. The liquor splattered and the glass shattered.

Chloe barely noticed. She stood frozen in place, a solitary sob escaping her stiff lips.

There in the entryway of the parlor stood Amanda Emory dressed in her billowy, white robe, with her luxurious blond hair flowing. She wore a look of worry on her ethereal face.

"Beware Chloe. The devil wears many guises."

The singsong voice slithered into Chloe's mind—sharp, clear, insistent. Chloe instinctively held her hands up, palms outward, to ward off danger while a sick sense of dread worked at her stomach.

"Beware..." Amanda urged, coming toward her. Chloe retreated until her back was pressed against the wall. There was no place to go.

Chapter Nine

Chloe's scream shoved its way up her throat but caught there as she saw yet more visions in the entryway. Only these, thank God, were flesh and blood.

"Chloe, are you okay?" Noah asked anxiously as he saw her pressed against the wall, the shattered goblet at her feet.

She stared first at Noah and then at Thad. "I just saw a...ghost."

Thad laughed good-naturedly. "No surprise, Chloe. It's Halloween. Noah and I saw a couple of ghosts on the road, ourselves."

"Beware. The devil wears many guises," Amanda's warning reverberated in her head. She stared at both men. Their eyes were like darkened mirrors, reflecting nothing, revealing nothing. Lara appeared behind them, carrying a handful of record albums. Chloe observed her carefully. Lara didn't seem the least bit surprised by the arrival of their visitors. Had she invited them, phoned either or both when she was in the kitchen cleaning up the dinner dishes? Just like old times...

"The devil wears many guises..."

Chloe's gaze swept over all of them. Who are you? she thought. Who are any of you?

Chloe, Lara, Thad, and Noah sat together in the front parlor of the Emory homestead. It was a strained and rather bizarre Halloween gathering, to say the least. At eleven-fifteen, long after the last of the trick or treaters had any business making house calls, the doorbell jingled. Lara started, but Thad was the one who rose from his seat.

"I'll take care of it," he said firmly.

Noah started to pace.

Chloe watched Noah out of the corner of her eye. She was still badly shaken from the vision of Amanda she'd seen, but she continued to fight off the temptation to break down.

Lara, sitting alone on the overstuffed, worn, flowered chintz sofa, also watched Noah pace. "You'll wear out the carpet, darling," she said coyly. "If you must expel nervous energy, why don't we dance?" Not waiting for a response from her ex-husband, Lara scurried over to the old phonograph and pulled a Frank Sinatra LP from its jacket. Just as she was setting it on the spindle, Thad returned. He wasn't alone.

"Well, well, well. You didn't tell me there was a party going on tonight, Lara. How come I wasn't invited?"

Lara laughed gaily, not at all put off by her uninvited guest's arrival. Quite the contrary, she smiled with delight. "Your invitation must have gotten lost in the mail. I can't imagine what other explanation there could be."

Sleek and mocking, Professor Peter Mott studied the group with a daunting classier-than-thou insouciance. He was dressed impeccably in a deep gray linen jacket, creamy beige sport shirt, silk designer tie and pale gray twill trousers. He looked far more like a suave high-roller than an underpaid college professor. The glint of gold from the Rolex watch on his wrist and his large diamond pinky ring only reinforced the successful man-about-town image.

Chloe took in the changes in Mott's appearance with a heightened degree of wariness and curiosity. Mott had always attempted to mimic the wealthier, more sophisticated residents of Thornhill. Seven years ago he hadn't quite succeeded. He'd lacked the necessary funds to pull it off. Now, either he was choosing to live beyond his means, Chloe thought, or there'd been a substantial change in his financial situation. Chloe wondered what had altered Mott's situation. An inheritance? Some very lucky investments? Or was there something more insidious and corrupt about Mott's newfound wealth?

While Chloe continued to observe Mott, Lara was giving him a too bright smile and an overzealous hug of welcome. "We were just about to dance. I promised the first slow one to Noah, but I'm sure you'll enjoy dancing with Chloe. You remember Chloe Hayes, darling. Doesn't she look wonderful? She's got this marvelous aura radiating from her. Don't you all feel it?" There was an edge of hysteria in Lara's voice, her mannerisms jerky and exaggerated.

Noah was scrutinizing his ex-wife closely, a look of consternation on his face. "Lara, I don't think any of us are in a dancing mood. How about if we—?"

"Damn you, Noah," Lara said pouting. "You always were a party pooper. You never have liked me to have any fun. You're always standing nearby with a straitjacket at the ready. Well, I have news for you, Doctor Noah Bright, there is nothing crazy about wanting to have a little fun." She stamped her foot. "And since you're being such a drag, I won't give you the first dance after all."

Peter Mott draped his arm around Lara and smiled slyly at Noah. "That moves me up on the list then."

Lara pivoted, lost her balance and fell heavily against Peter. Chloe thought Lara looked and sounded as if she'd had too much to drink, but she'd only had one glass of wine with dinner and then part of one snifter of cognac afterward. Chloe had had nearly the same amount to drink and she was far from intoxicated.

But Chloe had to admit she'd been feeling oddly off kilter all evening. Lara's mercurial mood swings were certainly in part to blame. But Chloe's intuition hinted there was more to it than that.

As Lara continued her temper tantrum, Chloe's eyes wandered to the wet patch on the rug left by her spilled cognac. The broken shards of glass were gone, Thad having swept them up.

Chloe recalled how her fingers had suddenly gone numb as she'd turned away from the window. All of her attention had been absorbed by that eerie vision in white standing in the doorway. Amanda. Correction, Amanda's ghost.

Chloe found herself drawn more intently to that stain of cognac on the rug. It was as though there was a message hidden there for her to discover. The trick, she knew, was to ground herself, erase all extraneous noises in her head, let herself sink into a place where she could detect sensations, impressions that might otherwise be overlooked or go unnoticed. The noises around her vanished, the people themselves fading away. Slowly, Chloe shifted her gaze away from the spilled drink to the opposite end of the room. She started to move with the pace of a somnambulist. Her steps took her to the bar where a decanter of cognac sat on a silver tray. There were two crystal snifters still on the tray.

Chloe poured cognac into one of the snifters and lifted it slowly. She breathed in deeply. Nothing unusual. She stared at the drink in the goblet. Hunch, instinct, clairvoyance? Whatever it was, Chloe felt sure that the cognac had been tampered with. Possibly some kind of tasteless but potent hallucinatory drug. LSD would have done the trick. It would explain at least some of Lara's bizarre behavior this evening. And, Chloe realized with a start, it could also explain the ghost she'd seen. Or thought she'd seen. She resolved that first thing tomorrow, she would bring a sample of the cognac over to Harvey for testing.

"I don't think you should have anything more to drink. Come on. I'm taking you home."

Chloe heard Noah's voice as if it were coming from a long way off.

He took the snifter from her hand.

"Please, Chloe," Noah coaxed.

Thad came over. "What's gotten into everyone tonight? Lara's completely off the wall. Mott's twirling her around the floor like Fred Astaire. Chloe here is behaving like she's in some kind of a trance. What gives?"

Chloe felt a rush of fear and confusion. She managed to master the sensations but was miserably aware that Noah, experienced as he was in matters of the human psyche, sensed her undercurrent of agitation.

"I'm driving Chloe home," Noah stated emphatically.

Thad grinned. "You drove up here with me in my car, so if there's any driving to be done, I'm the one who'll be doing it."

"I'm not going home," Chloe stated. "I'm spending the night here with Lara."

Noah glanced over his shoulder at his ex-wife and Mott. The couple was dancing now to a dreamy Sinatra tune, but their pace had slowed considerably and their movements were far more suggestive and erotic. "I don't think," Noah said sarcastically, "that Lara will want for company tonight, Chloe."

Chloe's gaze had followed Noah's. She had to agree with his observation. But if she left now, what about the cognac? She meant to bring in a sample for testing. Did she want everyone in the room to know that was what she was doing? No, that wouldn't be wise. But she was going to feel more than a little awkward and uncomfortable spending the night here if Mott meant to stay as well. Chloe felt a flash of fury, as the question she'd asked herself earlier came to mind. Why hadn't Lara simply invited Mott to spend the night with her in the first place?

This time Chloe had an answer. Not a very comforting answer at that. Maybe Lara had had a hidden purpose in luring her here. Maybe Lara had spiked the cognac herself. Maybe it was Lara's doing that Chloe had seen the ghost of Amanda Emory. What was it Noah had said to her that first day? *"I believe that Lara is in a highly irrational state of mind right now and that she may well feel driven to make her hallucinations and delusions into a reality if she can. . . ."*

When the song ended, Lara tried to induce Noah to dance with her. After a frigid refusal, she looked around for Peter, but he'd slipped out of the room.

Lara sighed. "Come on Thaddy. It looks like it's you and me. Come dance with your little sister. I promise not to say a word about your having two left feet, Thaddy."

It was a cruel remark, Chloe thought, but to her surprise Thad merely laughed good-naturedly and swept his sister into his arms. "Why is it always two left feet?" he asked teasingly. "Why not two right feet?"

"Or two wrong feet?" Lara said with a giggle. Then, immediately, she pressed her mouth against Thad's shoulder, her own shoulders heaving. "Oh Thaddy. Poor Momma. How she loved to dance. Remember?" With effort, she lifted her head. "We should have been nicer to her, Thaddy. We shouldn't have argued with her. Children should respect their mothers. Especially if their mothers are witches.''

"It's okay, Lara," Thad said tenderly as they danced. "All children argue with their mothers. Even if their mothers are witches."

Tears trickled down Lara's face. "I did love her, Thaddy. Even if she didn't love me.''

"Of course she loved you, Lara."

"No. We had an awful fight that night, Thaddy. That's why I didn't go to the coven meeting. It wasn't a headache. We said some terrible things to each other. She called me awful names, Thaddy. Vile names. And I called her a jealous shrew, an ugly witch. Oh Thaddy…I'm so dizzy…" Lara tripped and then fell into her brother's arms.

Thad lifted her up. Lara giggled. "You're so good, Thad. Whenever I stumble you're always there to catch me." She yawned. "I'm so tired, Thaddy. The fun's just started, but I'm so sleepy." She dropped her head to his shoulder, yawned again, and closed her eyes.

"I'll carry you upstairs and tuck you in," Thad said softly, but Lara was already asleep. As he started from the room Peter sauntered back in, munching on an apple.

"What happened to Lara?" he asked. His concern seemed forced at best.

Chloe really did find the man despicable. Even if she'd never had that unpleasant encounter with him in his office seven years back, the unctuous Peter Mott would have made her skin crawl now.

"It's all been too much for her. She's beat. I'm taking her up to her room," Thad said.

Peter shrugged. "I guess I'll be off then," he said with bland indifference. His eyes strayed to Chloe, his gaze seductively bold and positively fiendish.

"Beware Chloe, the devil wears many guises…"

"Sorry we didn't get to have that dance," Mott said glibly. "Lara was right though, Chloe. You do look . . . radiant." Having said his little piece, he turned on his heel and exited.

As soon as the front door shut, Chloe muttered, "That man gives me the creeps."

"I'll second that," Noah said in a harsh, ugly voice.

Chloe looked at Noah. His hatred of Mott showed in his face and he made no effort to mask it. Why should he? Chloe thought. Noah had every reason to hate the man. And why wouldn't he choose to put the blame on Mott rather than on his weak ex-wife, replete with all her lovable faults?

Chloe, herself, felt more at ease focusing on Mott rather than on Lara. For a variety of troubling reasons. "Mott's certainly come up in the world, it seems. Diamonds, Rolex watch, designer clothes. Did he win the lottery or something?"

"Or something," Noah muttered.

She gave him a look that encouraged his being a bit more specific, and Noah obliged. "A few months back he bought up about a hundred acres of supposedly worthless property over on the east end of town about a mile from the hospital. Only it turns out it wasn't so worthless after all. Seems Dorchester College and the Thornhill Savings and Loan were working up a deal to buy that acreage. They'd already succeeded in tying up an adjoining three-hundred-acre site for a high-tech industrial park. Mott's acreage was crucial to the development. They ended up having to pay him a pretty penny for it."

Chloe raised a brow. "And Mott bought it for a steal, no doubt."

"Old Herb Wilman owned that land. He had no idea what it would end up being worth. He thought it was useless, and probably figured Mott was a fool."

"A mighty lucky fool," Chloe said cynically.

"Luck? If you ask me..." Noah paused, reticent about making unfounded accusations.

But Chloe prodded. "I am asking you."

Noah's features hardened. "I think Peter Mott's utterly unscrupulous. Somehow or other he got an inside scoop on that proposed land deal. Someone at the college must have leaked it."

Or someone at the bank, Chloe thought. Lawrence Niels was the president of the Savings and Loan. Lawrence Niels's wife and Peter Mott had a brief affair. In bed, lovers might reveal almost anything....

As Chloe tossed those thoughts around, Noah suddenly disappeared from the room. For a moment there, Chloe was afraid he'd vanished into thin air. The next moment her fear took a more concrete turn. What if he'd just up and left the house? She felt a stab of panic. *Don't desert me again, Noah...*

Before she'd completed the thought, he was back. He had his coat on. Her coat was draped over his arm. "Come on. I'm getting you out of here."

"How?" She began, instead of making even a vague attempt at a protest.

He smiled wryly, holding up the keys that he'd swiped from Thad's coat pocket. "Let big brother stay and look after Lara tonight. That's what families are for."

He held out Chloe's coat for her. She slipped it on. He took her arm.

"Wait."

Noah frowned, clearly anxious to get away.

Chloe rushed into the kitchen, grabbed a small empty jar, rushed back into the living room and filled her container with cognac from the decanter.

Noah observed her actions in curious silence. Only when they were outside did he say anything. "We could have stopped at a bar if you wanted something more to drink. You didn't have to bring booze with you."

"I don't plan to drink it," she said succinctly.

He opened the front passenger door for her. She slid in. He hurried round the car, got in behind the wheel, turned on the ignition and beat a hasty retreat down the driveway before Thad could come running out to stop them.

"Thad isn't going to be happy," Chloe mused. Nor was Lara, she thought. But the likelihood was that Lara had duped her into coming for the night for the specific purpose of drugging her, and heaven only knew what else. So Chloe was not in the least concerned about Lara's unhappiness at her desertion.

As soon as Noah turned onto the road back to town, he glanced at Chloe. "You think there's something else in that jar besides cognac?"

Chloe hesitated. "Yes." Another pause. "It's just a hunch."

"A hunch?"

"Yes."

"So you deliberately broke that snifter just before Thad and I arrived."

"No. I didn't realize there was anything wrong with the cognac then."

He glanced at her, but her face was in shadow.

"I think there might be some kind of hallucinogenic drug in the cognac," Chloe said in a low voice. "I think I had a hallucination. Just before you showed up I saw Amanda's ... ghost ... framed in the doorway." She took a deep breath. "It was probably a combination of several things; the spiked drink, the power of suggestion—Lara had been talking about seeing her mother's ghost—and my own heightened state of anxiety."

Noah's hands gripped the wheel tighter. "You think Lara spiked the drink?"

Like Noah, Chloe wasn't particularly keen on making unfounded accusations. She hesitated, thinking how best to answer. "She had the opportunity. But then so did anyone who's visited her recently, I suppose." Chloe knew she sounded less than convinced that anyone other than Lara had tampered with the liquor. All of the pieces were slowly, irrevocably stacking together for Chloe, pointing to Lara as the murderer. Lara could have drugged her mother, hypnotized her into believing she was possessed. It was her theory, after all. She admitted having fought bitterly with her mother that night. She had means, motive, and she was now a quarter of a million dollars richer, not to mention owning a piece of prime Thornhill property. And Lara could have done all the rest to protect herself. She could have thought Alice was on to her. And Chloe knew that Lara believed her to be psychic. If so, it made all the sense in the world that Lara would do anything in her power to scare her off.

"Did Lara drink any of the cognac?" Noah asked, cutting through Chloe's distressing thoughts.

"Yes. She had a glass after dinner."

Noah frowned. "If she'd spiked it, why would she drink it herself?"

"Maybe she wants to be in a drugged state," Chloe said cautiously. If Noah was still in love with Lara, the last thing he'd ever accept was the idea that she was a murderer.

She was surprised when he said, "You may be right." But then he clarified. "The pain of losing her mother may be too much for her. Lara never was one to deal well with her emotions. She always preferred to act them out." There was a profusion of feelings in Noah's voice: confusion, betrayal, hurt, anger.

"I'm sorry." The words simply came out of Chloe.

"Are you?" A pause. "You would say that," he said softly. "I don't deserve your sympathy, Chloe. I did all the wrong things for all the wrong reasons."

Chloe didn't know what to say in response to that. Noah's tone and the remark itself made her feel oddly uneasy and disturbingly aroused. She quickly shifted her attention to another thought pressing on her mind. "When Thad and Lara were dancing, she said something about having had a fight with her mother on the night Amanda died. Do you know what they fought about?"

"No." He paused. "Until Amanda's death, I hardly saw Lara. We both made a point of keeping our distance." He cleared his throat. "But when Lara and I were married, she and her mother used to argue fairly often." He paused again. "No, that's not exactly true. Lara was usually the one who did the arguing. Amanda seemed to take her daughter's frequent emotional outbursts in stride."

"Lara said she'd called her mother a jealous shrew that night. Why *jealous*? Why would Amanda be jealous of her daughter? What did Lara have that Amanda would have wanted?" Chloe wondered.

"I don't know. Jealousy was more Lara's department I would have thought. Lara has always seemed to want whatever someone else possessed and valued."

Chloe felt her cheeks suffuse with warmth. Noah looked over at her. They were driving along Main Street, the street lamps lighting their faces. Chloe saw that Noah wore a cynical smile, but his captivating eyes were giving off another message, one that Chloe couldn't quite interpret. Or perhaps she was merely afraid to decipher it.

A couple of minutes later, Noah spelled it out by pulling into the driveway of his sweet little Cape Cod style house, instead of dropping her off at Mrs. Harris's.

He turned, and then she turned. Their eyes locked. Noah made the first move. His hand slid under her hair, warm and sensuous on the back of her neck. Time slowed. Thoughts evaporated. Desire licked at Chloe's skin. Hunger shadowed her features. Noah leaned closer and Chloe tilted her head just enough so their mouths fit perfectly. Her hands were clenched in tight, scared fists in her lap, but her lips parted against his.

A slow heat spread through her bones. No one kissed like Noah. His kiss was a private, unique language that only he could speak, only she could intuitively translate.

His fingers tangled in her hair, the pressure of his mouth intensified, his tongue sliding across her teeth, then deep into her mouth. She moaned, and then was ashamed, quickly blaming her uninhibited response on the spiked cognac. She was a jumble of pain, pleasure, panic, desperation, hunger, all of them, none of them, she didn't know....

She pulled away from him, cheeks burning with embarrassment. Was she no better than Lara? Was she afraid to cope with her feelings, simply acting them out so as not to own up to them and deal with them in a rational way?

Her hands moved in quick, jerky motions over her hair, smoothing the slightly tousled strands into place.

She met Noah's gaze. She was suddenly grateful for the shadowy darkness. "Please, Noah..." she whispered, not entirely certain what she was going to ask for. Maybe for everything to revert back to the past. To seven years ago, before she'd driven him into Lara's arms.

"Stay the night, Chloe. You shouldn't be alone to-night." He hesitated. "You can stay in the spare room again. I'll be...close by if you need me." A pause. "Please, Chloe...I need you, too."

Chapter Ten

The phone was ringing when Noah and Chloe walked into Noah's house. "That's probably either my service or Thad calling to chew me out," Noah said, grabbing the receiver.

But it wasn't Thad. Nor was it Noah's service. The caller was Harvey Mead's wife, Mildred.

"I'm sorry to bother you at such a late hour, Noah, but, well...I'm looking for...Chloe Hayes." Before Noah could say anything, Mildred rushed on. "You see, when I phoned her at Lucy's, Lucy told me Chloe had called her earlier from Amanda's house—oh dear, I should say Lara's house now—to say that she was spending the night with Lara. I do think, considering everything—well, you do know what I mean—that it was rather magnanimous of Chloe to be with Lara in her...her time of need. But when I called at Lara's, her brother Thad answered the phone. And I don't mind telling you, Noah, the man was quite surly. Not at all like the Thad Emory I used to know. Always was so soft-spoken and well-mannered. Of course, there were those screenplays of his. All blood and gore from what I hear. But then, Hollywood seems to thrive on those sorts of films. If the truth be known, poor Thad's work probably wasn't bloody or gory enough and that's why he didn't make it out there. Just as well. He's too nice a person, and too fine an En-

glish teacher, for that sort of wild life. Why, there's hardly
a one of them out there in Tinseltown who isn't on drugs.
You just have to read the headlines in the newspapers to
know that."

Mildred paused for a quick breath, not quick enough for
Noah to get a word in edgewise. "Where was I? Oh yes,
anyway when I spoke to Thad just a few minutes ago on the
phone, he implied, quite rudely as I said, that you'd...well,
that you'd absconded with Chloe—those were his words,
not mine—and if I wished to speak to her, I should phone
you."

"And you wish to speak to her?" Noah prodded with a
faint smile.

"Why, yes. Harvey asked me to get ahold of her, you
see."

"At this hour? It's past midnight." Noah caught Chloe's
eye. She gave him a questioning look. He held up a hand
for her to hold on for a minute as Mildred broke into her
explanation.

"Yes, well, when you're investigating murder, Noah, you
can't always have the luxury of doing all of your investigating at convenient hours. Being the wife of a police chief
isn't really all that different from being the wife of a doctor,
when you come to think of it. And now that Chloe has
agreed to help Harvey in his investigation—"

"What?"

"Oh dear, didn't she tell you? I suppose I thought that
the two of you were...Harvey seems to think...I do wish
my husband didn't jump to conclusions. Not that he does
that professionally, mind you. No, if you ask me I think he
tends to be a little too cautious in that regard. Don't get me
wrong, Noah, I have no doubt that Harvey will get to the
bottom of this ugly business. He won't rest until he does.
That is why he's crawling about in the bushes, in the dark

of night, out at the old Grange Hall at this very moment, looking for Devil worshippers. And that is why he asked me to track down Chloe and have her join him out there."

"That's crazy. Why Chloe, for heaven's sake?"

"Is Chloe there or not, Noah?" Mildred could get directly to the point when she needed to.

Noah hesitated, but then, finally, with a disgruntled look, he handed the phone over to Chloe.

She listened to Mildred quietly for a minute. "Yes," she answered. "Officer George Denk. Just past the Ryder Bridge. I'll meet him there."

Chloe hung up. Noah, his expression stern, was standing practically on top of her, arms folded cross his chest.

She smiled faintly. "Will you come with me, Noah?"

He scowled. "I was coming whether you asked me or not."

Her smiled deepened. "I know."

On the drive over to the Ryder Bridge to meet Officer Denk Noah argued vehemently with Chloe about getting more deeply enmeshed in the troubling and dangerous affairs of the town of Thornhill. But Chloe remained resolute.

"Then give me one good reason why you're doing it," Noah challenged.

Chloe didn't answer immediately. "Because you can't just bury old ghosts, Noah. You must exorcise them."

"You can't mean Amanda Emory, Chloe. That was a hallucination. You said so yourself."

"I wasn't talking about Amanda. I was talking metaphorically. Seven years ago I left Thornhill with a pile of unresolved feelings. I thought I could bury them. I couldn't."

"That was different."

"Different circumstances. But all the same people," she said quietly.

Noah glanced over at her. "I wonder what would have happened if you hadn't taken off then."

Chloe's eyelids fluttered closed. "I've wondered that myself," she admitted.

"Chloe—"

"Don't say anything, Noah."

"Let me just ask you one thing, Chloe. Are you really prepared to look into the dark side of Thornhill?"

"I'm prepared to get to the truth."

"Even if the truth means airing a lot of unnecessary dirty laundry? Because when you start digging into a community, Chloe, that's what usually happens. And some innocent people could get hurt in the process."

"Like Lara?"

He laughed dryly. "Innocent's not exactly the word I'd use for Lara. But whatever her crimes, Chloe, I don't think they involve murder." He hesitated. "At least not yet. But if she continues on this downward slide I'm scared that she might even be capable of that."

"I do marvel at your constancy, Noah," Chloe said coolly. "Lucky Lara. She stumbles, and all of her fine, and one or two not so fine, young men hover around her to make sure she doesn't hurt herself." As soon as the words were out, Chloe was ashamed. It wasn't Noah's fault that he was still in love with his ex-wife, no matter what her crimes. Wasn't Chloe, after all, still in love with him?

Noah said quietly, "When I said I was scared, I didn't mean I was scared for *Lara*. I meant I was scared for you."

Chloe was flustered. "Well, anyway, Harvey seems to have his eye on an entirely different suspect. Karin Niels. Lara told me Karin had a falling-out with Amanda a few months back and started up her own coven. Amanda, according to Lara, thought Karin's little group had taken on more sinister pursuits. If it's true, tonight being Halloween, it would seem a perfect time for Karin to hold a circle. Harvey must think so, too.''

"And are you supposed to offer your expert opinion of the event? Or does he intend to have you infiltrate and offer yourself up for sacrifice?''

"Like Dantes, Amanda's cat?''

"It's all a bunch of childish nonsense,'' Noah said. "Probably some nasty teenagers acting out. Why in heaven's name would Karin kill Amanda's cat?''

"Spite. Revenge. I don't know...''

"Plenty of people have a falling-out and don't go and kill their opponent's cherished pet. Karin Niels is a born actress. She simply thrives on attention and likes to play at being a sorceress. It makes her feel wild and dangerous and special. But killing animals or...worse, I find it very hard to believe Karin would be that vengeful.''

"Did you know that Lawrence Niels and Amanda were...involved?''

"Involved? I recall that Amanda dated Lawrence for a while. But that was before Karin came into the picture.''

So he didn't know about the affair post-Karin, Chloe mused.

"Actually, Amanda brought him to...our wedding,'' Noah went on. "That was a few months after his wife died. His first wife.''

"Ellen Niels.''

"Did you know her?'' Noah's voice registered surprise.

"I met her once at Amanda's,'' Chloe said. "Lara told me Lawrence and Amanda had an affair and Ellen found out and...killed herself. Killed herself with Amanda's atheme.'' Chloe felt a cold shiver that had nothing to do with the damp night air. "And then Amanda herself...''

"I hope you aren't thinking that Ellen's ghost possessed Amanda and got retribution, Chloe."

Chloe smiled thinly. "I really don't believe in ghosts, Noah. But I do believe that sometimes the most mundane and natural of events can prove more eerie and more amazing, even more improbable at times, than the supernatural."

"Amanda may have cared for Lawrence Niels but there was never any proof that Ellen Niels killed herself because her husband and Amanda were having an affair. I admit rumors were rife, but that's all they were...rumors."

"Maybe Amanda confided in Lara about her affair," Chloe suggested.

"Then Lara would have told me. She's never been one to keep confidences. She's also, unfortunately, quick to buy into ugly rumors. I guess she tends to think the worst of people. Guilty until proven innocent..."

Chloe gave him a curious look.

Noah could feel her eyes on him. He was uneasy. Why had he said that about Lara, he wondered? Did he really want Chloe to know about the times Lara had thought the worst of him? The accusations, the paranoia? The very fact that Lara had succumbed to her compulsion to cheat on him during their marriage made her believe that he, too, must have cheated. In a way, he had. If having fantasies about a lovely, vibrant auburn-haired young woman amounted to cheating.

Finally he glanced at Chloe, wondering if she really did have ESP, wondering if she had read his mind, wondering if she knew how many times he'd fantasized about holding her in his arms, making amends, making love to her.

They were crossing the Ryder Bridge. Up ahead was the old Grange, behind it the hill, where just a couple of nights ago Chloe had spotted that ghostly image. Instinctively

Chloe's gaze wandered to the hill as Noah slowed the car at the end of the bridge. Tonight the hill was bathed in moonlight. On this All Hallow Even, no terrifying image, no ethereal shadow in white, sprang into view. The ghosts and goblins were busy elsewhere. The hill loomed, barren and empty and seemingly without purpose.

Chloe breathed a sigh of relief. Yet when Noah gently, innocently touched her shoulder, she jumped.

He cast her a worried look, but merely said, "There's a police cruiser half-hidden in the bushes just up ahead."

"That must be Officer Denk," Chloe said in a voice that wasn't altogether steady.

"We can still turn back," Noah said, misconstruing her anxiety.

"No."

Without further protest, Noah pulled off the road, stopping about ten yards behind the darkened cruiser. The moment he stopped, a flash of light flooded the inside of the police car and then blinked off. A minute later, a tall, young officer cautiously approached the car, gun at the ready.

Chloe stepped out first and quickly introduced herself. Denk recognized Noah as he exited the car.

"Doc," Denk acknowledged.

Noah merely nodded.

Denk hesitated. "The chief gave me specific instructions to bring you to meet him, Ms. Hayes. I guess he assumed you'd be...alone."

"He assumed wrong," Noah said gruffly. "Let's go." His tone of voice sounded more like, *let's get this nonsense over with*.

"We should hurry, Officer Denk. I assume there's some sort of...meeting...going on at the Grange. They don't tend to last all that long. The chief won't be very happy if I show up too late."

Denk decided Chloe had a point. If the chief didn't want the Doc around, Denk figured the chief would handle it. As he led the way to where Harvey Mead was waiting, Denk asked Chloe, "Are you some kind of expert in this sort of thing?"

"Not exactly," Chloe murmured.

"I'm a church-going man myself, Ms. Hayes. I don't mind telling you that when the chief asked me to get a bit chummy with Karin Niels . . . well, I certainly didn't want folks around town getting the wrong kind of idea. I certainly wasn't about to go so far as to get myself invited to one of her shindigs. Like I told the chief, going to a Black Mass . . . well, that's where I draw the line. I mean, I did some reading up on these kinda things and . . . pardon me, Ms. Hayes . . . but I read that there were all sorts of . . . sexual perversions and worse, that go on. Anyway, the chief just wanted me to keep my eyes and ears open as to when she was planning her next meeting. We both figured on Halloween. And sure enough, she actually had the gall to suggest I join them. The chief figured she wanted to cover herself. I mean, if she invited a member of law enforcement, that would mean she wasn't doing anything that wasn't above board. Naturally, the chief said, she didn't think I'd actually go. And when I turned her down, she figured she was covered. But the chief and I came on down here earlier in the day and kinda set things up. You'll see."

Having said that, Denk put his index finger to his lips, and they approached the Grange. He guided Chloe and Noah around the side of the building.

Returning to the scene of the crime, Chloe thought, catching her breath. But no actual crime had been committed here, she reminded herself. It was only later . . . poor Alice Donovan. Poor, frightened Alice Donovan. Frightened with just cause.

A cold chill assaulted Chloe as she came up along the side of the Grange. Yes, it was true that no actual crime had been committed here the night she and Alice had been duped into coming. But Chloe was certain there had to have been a purpose in bringing them out here. And it couldn't have been merely to frighten them. Alice was already plenty frightened. And there were a lot of other ways to frighten Chloe. No, they'd been tricked into coming to the Grange that night for some far more sinister and diabolical reason. A cold, sick insight gripped Chloe. Whoever had lured her and Alice out here that night had actually intended to kill them both. Chloe suddenly felt certain of it. How ironic, Chloe thought, that only Mrs. Harris's nosiness had saved her. Lucy's nosiness and Thad Emory's crush on her.

"Are you okay?" Noah whispered to her as he put his arm around her shoulder.

She nodded.

Harvey Mead drew away from the wall of the building where he'd been watching the activity inside through a recently drilled peephole. He removed his headset as Denk led his two charges over. Denk was relieved that the chief didn't seem put out by the Doc's arrival. Quite the contrary. He rummaged in an equipment box to find an extra pair of headsets so that Noah as well as Chloe could hear the proceedings going on inside. Earlier that day, after securing the necessary court order, Denk and the chief had rigged the place with bugs. They'd drilled only two peepholes though, so Noah would not be able to watch the proceedings. As for Denk, his task accomplished, he was dispatched back to wait in the relative comfort of his patrol car and watch for anyone coming from or going to the Grange.

"How long have they been at it?" Chloe whispered her question to the chief. Not that she needed to whisper. It was unlikely any of the participants inside the Grange could have overheard them what with all the chanting and eerie chamber music filling the old hall.

"About twenty minutes." Harvey spoke in normal pitch. "I was afraid you'd miss it."

Noah smiled wryly. "We wouldn't miss it for the world, Harvey."

Harvey shrugged. "So far it's been pretty dull and innocuous. There are seven of them inside. First thing they did was shroud all the windows with black cloths, then they lit the candles, started chanting and dancing around."

"What? No ritual cat sacrifices? No sexual perversions going on?" Noah asked cynically.

Harvey smiled. "Not yet. Not that I'm hoping for anything like that, mind you."

Chloe put her headset on and pressed her eye to the peephole that allowed her a clear view of the candlelit *service*. She glanced over at Harvey after a minute. "Can you identify them? With the black hooded robes it's hard for me to recognize anyone. Except for the leader. I'm sure it's Karin Niels."

"Yes, that's Karin Niels, all right. I recognize her singing voice from church choir," Harvey said with a sly smile. "As for the others..." Harvey identified five of them—a local investment counselor, a realtor, the owner of the herb shop off Main Street, a retired businessman and an art dealer. He'd seen them all arrive. They hadn't donned their black hoods until later.

"That one on the far right came in late. Maybe ten minutes ago," Harvey went on. "I'd say a man from the way he walked. Not that it couldn't be a lady with a masculine way of carrying herself. Whichever, I can't make a positive ID."

Harvey offered Noah a look. He watched for a moment then shook his head, having no better luck than the police chief. "He's completely in shadow."

Chloe focused her attention on the black-robed figure at the far right. As she intensified her concentration, the noises of the night—the wind rustling the trees, the sounds of animals and crickets, the breathing of the two men beside her, even the chanting and the music inside the Grange—grew silent. It was as if Chloe's exterior world had been sucked free of sound and motion. Only her interior world pulsed.

Yes, a man. Definitely a man. A raw, potent masculine aura exuded from the black-robed figure. His breathing— she could hear his breathing. Familiar, unpleasant, making her skin crawl. The breathing undulated through her, wave after wave like a sexual assault, salacious, malodorous, repulsive.

And just then the man stepped forward, the high priestess of the Black Mass entreating him with outstretched hands. He took hold of a candle. The light illuminated his eyes.

A chill wind struck Chloe's soul. She shivered.

"It's Peter Mott," she whispered. And yet her voice sounded amplified to her, as if it was caught in an echo chamber.

Noah scowled. "Looks like the bastard is burning his candle at both ends."

Harvey hmmphed. "I swear, I don't know what any of them see in him. Even poor Alice Donovan..."

"Alice?" Noah asked sharply. "She was involved with Peter Mott?"

"Not involved exactly," Mead said in that laconic way of his that always held so much intent. "She was wild for him, but he wouldn't give the poor thing the time of day."

"Are you sure?" Noah persisted, catching Chloe's interest now.

"Why are you so surprised?" she asked Noah.

"It's just . . . Thad said . . . well, he didn't actually name names. But I thought he was telling me that Alice had a mad crush on Lawrence Niels. And not only Alice." He hesitated. "Amanda, too."

There was a leap of a pulse in Chloe's throat. "Amanda and Peter Mott. That explains a lot."

"What are you saying, Chloe?" Harvey urged.

"It's just that it's suddenly clear to me. I think Amanda might have been in love with Mott for years. Even back when I was in college. There was an . . . incident between me and Mott. I reported him to Amanda. She threatened to expose him if it ever happened again. But I wonder now if she was outraged not because a professor had made an indecent advance toward a student, but because she was jealous. That's why she made it clear to Mott if he bothered me again she'd destroy him. She was obsessed by jealousy. Jealousy," she repeated. Then she stared at Noah. "That night Amanda died. The argument with Lara. Lara called Amanda a jealous shrew. Now, it makes sense. Lara always did go after the men who were loved by those close to her, and then gloat over it . . ." Chloe stopped abruptly, suffused by embarrassment. She hadn't meant to be so personally revealing.

Even Harvey Mead seemed at a loss for words. His expression was oddly troubled. He pressed his eye to his peephole again. Chloe offered hers to Noah, deciding she'd rather just listen on her headset.

A minute later the chanting to Lucifer came to an abrupt end. Noah and Harvey observed Karin Niels raise a narrow stick skyward as the dark, breathing shapes surrounded her in a half circle. Chloe listened to Karin's intonation. "Thou art the light of the world, thou art the light of hell, mighty prince of sin . . . I know thee by all thy names, in all thy guises . . . This then is my sacrifice. Let it prove to thee my worth and grant me thine power and thine grace. The good spirits be damned . . ."

Chloe heard both Harvey and Noah draw breath. She noticed a sharp acrid smell. And Karin's voice came again, harsh and hollow. "Dust to dust, ashes to ashes . . ."

An inexplicable fear throbbed in Chloe's throat. She took in a deep breath. It burned. The air in her lungs was hot, fiery. The putrid smell in the air intensified. It, too, burned. A dreadful heat broke out inside of her, searing, blistering . . .

"Let me see," she hissed, shoving aside one of the men. She wasn't even sure whether it was Noah or Harvey.

A life-size waxen image lay in flames, stretched across the altar. As the wax melted in differing spots it made the figure appear almost lifelike. It seemed to writhe in pain as it was engulfed by flames.

Chloe stumbled backward with a horrified sob.

It was her, of course. The head of the figure had not yet been touched by the flames. It was a stunning likeness. . . .

Noah grabbed Chloe in his arms and held her tight, but she broke free, gasping for breath. Her skin still burned. The fire spread down her arms, her legs . . . the sickening scent of the burning wax smelled now like burning flesh.

Chloe ran. She was halfway across Ryder Bridge before Noah caught up with her.

THE SILVER MOONLIGHT filtered into the room, spilling uneven light over the bed. A pleasant heat spread through Chloe as she sipped the tea laced with a heaping tablespoon of honey. The sweetness took the sour taste from her mouth, soothed the nausea. When she finished the last drop, Noah took the cup from her hand and set it on the bedside table.

"Better?" he asked softly, smoothing back her tangled curls with an almost unbearably light touch.

"Much," she murmured.

"You've been through hell."

"I overreacted. Power of suggestion. And..." She hesitated. "My parents died in a car accident. Someone rear-ended them and the gas tank in their car exploded. The car went up in...flames." She lowered her lids. She didn't want him to see her tears.

He cupped her chin, lifting her face toward his. "I won't let anything bad happen to you, Chloe. We've both been through enough bad times." He, too, had tears in his eyes, but he made no effort to conceal them. "I was so confused, Chloe. I made such a mess of everything. I hurt you, I hurt Lara.

"Lara and I should never have gotten married." He smiled faintly. "I'd like to give you the excuse that she cast a spell over me. Maybe that would get me off the hook a little. But I deserve to be on that hook. I wanted to be needed. I was foolish and selfish enough to want a woman to believe I was her whole world. I deluded myself into believing that Lara saw me that way. And besides..." He stopped.

"Tell me," she whispered. "Tell me everything, Noah. Maybe the truth can set us free."

Their eyes held. "You used to terrify me, Chloe. I felt as though you could see into my soul—see the selfishness, the vanity, the fierce competitiveness, the jealousy, the avarice...."

"I saw the gentleness, the kindness, the dedication, the drive," she answered back.

"Can you ever forgive me, Chloe?" He searched her face, willing her to say yes. But she didn't.

"I don't honestly know yet, Noah."

The sorrow in his face hurt her, but her own hurt clung to her and she wasn't sure how to expunge it. Or if it could be expunged.

Noah rose from the bed. "Well, I should let you get some rest. If you need me, I'm just across the hall." He hesitated for a moment, then started for the door.

Chloe's next words stopped him. "I don't know about forgiveness, but I do know about need. I need you, Noah."

Slowly, tears streaming down the hollows of his cheeks, he turned to her.

Tears glistened in Chloe's eyes, too. "I've never needed you more than I need you tonight."

Chapter Eleven

Chloe felt a rush of longing as Noah folded her against him, her body stirring with pent-up desire. There was a newness and a familiarity all at once.

Silently, he put his hands to her face and gently brought her close, kissing her softly, sweetly. When their lips parted, they exchanged grateful smiles.

His mouth grazed her neck, her shoulder. With slow, sensual deliberation, he began to undress her. She lay very still, aware of her own accelerated heartbeat. It had been seven years. Would he still find her body beautiful? Would those captivating gray-green eyes of his still hold her in thrall? And the worst fear of all—would she pale in comparison to the delicately beautiful blond Lara?

Her anxiety heightened with each item of her clothing he dispensed with. But if Noah was aware of her attack of nerves, he gave no sign of it. He seemed, in fact, almost in a trance. A magic spell? Or was it merely the moonlight filtering into the room, spreading a warm, seductive glow?

Done with his task, Chloe's exposure complete, Noah propped himself up on one elbow and consumed her with his eyes. Chloe felt boneless, possessed, drowning in his gaze, burning in it. And yet wanting it, swept up in a need that was even greater than she'd realized.

"You're more beautiful than before. I didn't think that would be possible," he whispered, his warm breath caressing her skin.

Chloe thrilled to his words. And when, at last, his hands moved with light, deliberate strokes over her firm breasts, down her belly, sculpting her with his fingers, she felt ecstatic, transported.

Her eyes never left his face as she helped him undress. There was such tenderness in his face, such pride and longing. An almost mystical allure. How often over the years had she pictured this face in her mind, never quite able to conjure it up clearly? The edges had always blurred. Now they were sharply defined, vivid and so intense she felt overwhelmed.

As he stood to rid himself of his trousers and boxer shorts, Chloe studied him. His body was still a marvel of firm muscle and proud carriage, his movements fluid and graceful. The seven years had done him no disservice at all.

The bed dipped as he stretched out beside her.

"Do you know that you're smiling?"

Chloe's smile deepened. "Am I?"

"I've missed that smile of yours. When you were in school you were usually so intense and serious, it always used to astound me to see a smile suddenly appear on your face. And what a smile. So radiant, so pure and true. It seemed to come from some secret core of you, some bright point of light within."

Ever so delicately, he traced the curve of her lips with his finger. "There's such mystery and delight in your smile, Chloe. It always draws me to you, but I never seem able to get close enough to inhabit the mystery, become a part of it."

She touched his cheek. Her smile wobbled on her lips. "It isn't a mystery, Noah. My smile isn't so much who I am, but what we become together."

"Chloe," her name broke from his lips as he drew her warm, naked body against his.

Chloe's arms threaded underneath his, pulling him closer, closer, bringing his mouth back to hers where she welcomed it greedily, thankfully. At last, a feeling of safety and security enveloped her. Noah, only Noah, warmed her. He heated her. And she welcomed the heat. She came alive wherever his fingers caressed, wherever his lips pressed. Here again with Noah, maybe she could lay the ghosts to rest, if only for a brief moment. It was enough.

Seven years, and they remembered each other's desires as if they'd made love last night. And all the nights before. They knew where to kiss and fondle to pleasure each other. Chloe kneaded Noah's shoulders, his spine, his buttocks. She remembered how sensitive he was. Her hands cruised wantonly up along the insides of his thighs and she thrilled to the moan of pleasure that erupted from deep within him. She took him in her hands. He was already hard as she stroked him.

His mouth moved to her breast. With his tongue he drew circles around her taut nipples, his hand sliding down to the core of her, where his fingers matched the motion of his tongue, until she could barely breathe.

They rolled. She rose up over him, felt the trembling race through her muscles. She gazed down at him, drinking him in.

"Chloe," he whispered. And she heard it like music. He reached up for her, twining his fingers in her wild auburn curls. He drew her closer until his tongue could trail down to her breasts. His hands slipped under her buttocks, lifting her, guiding her, until he was inside her at last. They both gasped loudly, unashamedly.

It had never been so good for either of them. Neither could catch their breath, their lovemaking fiery and abandoned. Spirals of ever increasing pleasure swirled through them, linking them together. Neither of them wanted it to end, but they couldn't fight against their soaring desire. Release was their only recourse, and when it came in an explosive ribbon of blinding color, the world spun, the moon tipped out of orbit. Afterward Chloe smiled at him. Her smile filled the stillness, the darkness, Noah's soul.

THE JARRING RING of the phone woke Noah. Blindly, he reached out in search of it. He knocked something over. He squinted. A teacup. Empty. He found the receiver.

"Noah?"

He blinked several times. The voice on the other end sounded astonishingly like Chloe. But that wasn't possible. Chloe was lying next to him....

He turned to check. The space beside him was empty. He was fully awake now. He clenched the receiver until his knuckles turned white with strain. "Chloe? Where are you? When did you leave? Why did you leave?"

"Slow down, Noah. I can only answer one question at a time. I'm with Harvey Mead. At the police lab. We just found out the results of the cognac analysis. Thanks for passing the sample along to Harvey last night, I'd forgotten it entirely. There *were* traces of hyoscine... And Harvey told me you're the one who discovered that Alice was poisoned with a variety of hemlock. He said to tell you they found more of the hemlock among Amanda's herbs."

"Right," Noah said tightly.

"Noah, I'm sorry I took off the way I did. I woke up very early. Your appointment book was open at your desk in the bedroom. I saw that you didn't have to be at the hospital until noon. We...got to bed...late. And so I thought I'd let you sleep.''

Noah shut his eyes. ''You really are lousy at lying, Chloe.''

There was an overly long silence. ''It wasn't exactly a lie. You did need your sleep.''

''And you needed...?''

''Some distance,'' she admitted, and then hurriedly went on. ''Harvey's bringing Karin Niels in for questioning. I'm going to stay. Not that I'm all that keen for a face-off, but I want to hear directly from her why she felt it necessary to burn me in effigy. Lara's theory is that Karin sees me as the new witch in town and it's a battle of good versus evil. If that's true, I mean to set her straight. This witch business is getting entirely out of hand. Harvey thinks, and I agree, that at this point it could be obscuring real evidence.'' She hesitated. ''I phoned Lara a little while ago...to see how she was feeling. Thad did stay the night with her. She seemed...better...this morning. More in control. More focused.'' Chloe laughed softly. ''Thad got on the phone, too. But I cut him off. I wasn't in the mood for a...sermon.''

''Chloe...''

''It's just a few minutes past eleven. I tried to set your alarm clock radio, but I started to worry I might not have done it right, and you'd oversleep. That's why I called.'' A pause. ''Part of why, anyway.''

Despite his anger at her flight, he had to smile. ''What's the other part?''

''I just wanted you to know that last night...'' She grappled for the right way to express her feeling about what last night had meant to her. But everything that came to mind seemed so trite and clichéd. And there was nothing trite or clichéd about what making love with Noah last night had meant to her. "I don't think I can put it into words, Noah. All I can tell you is...I haven't stopped smiling since."

"I was hoping to see that smile when I woke up this morning. Will I...get another chance?"

There was a long silence. "Sorry Noah. Harvey needs to talk to me. I guess I'd better hang up now."

"Wait. Chloe?"

"Yes, Noah?"

"Even if you are a lousy liar...I love you."

Silence.

"Did you hear what I said, Chloe?"

"Yes." Her reply was a bare whisper.

"One more thing, Chloe."

"I really..." She sighed. "What, Noah?"

"You were even smiling in your sleep. I just wanted you to know that."

KARIN AND LAWRENCE NIELS entered Harvey's office with a bristling caution. Chloe could sense the thin, taut wire of tension between the pair and guessed that it was close to the breaking point. The couple did their best to conceal their agitation with their matched veneers of cool, supercilious unapproachability.

On close inspection, Chloe observed that Karin Niels was one of those women whose very presence demanded and got notice. It wasn't that she was exactly beautiful—if taken bit by bit, nothing about her approached perfection—but she had a distinct aura of beauty which was perhaps more compelling. Her best feature was her skin which was as finely textured as a ripened peach. Dressed today in an elegant, exquisitely cut apricot suit finished off with a silk polka-dot ascot, she looked far more like a devotee of the good life than she did a devotee of Satan.

Lawrence Niels, the trim, handsome, sixty-six-year-old bank president, wore a custom-tailored, navy, double-breasted jacket with a crest on the breast pocket, gray slacks, and a Palm Beach tan. He looked, thought Chloe, just like the type of man people would willingly, even eagerly, entrust their money to; a man who radiated confidence and authority. However, Chloe observed, at the moment that confidence and authority was being sorely tested. She detected a tightly controlled nervousness and underlying insecurity that Niels was taking great pains to hide.

Harvey made the introductions. Lawrence Niels took Chloe's hand, not so much shaking it as pressing it in a paternal, confident fashion. The gesture lacked conviction. Chloe wondered if he knew about his wife's recent pyrotechnics down at the old Grange, or whether he was anxious about something else altogether.

As for Karin Niels, unlike yesterday's evil-eye glance, today she batted her eyes innocently at both the chief and Chloe. "What seems to be the trouble, Harvey?"

Before Karin had finished the sentence, Lawrence reached out to clasp his wife's arm. "Please dear, let me handle this matter."

Karin smiled demurely. "I'm sure there's really nothing to handle, darling."

Lawrence gave his wife a sharp look. Then immediately he turned to the chief. "I don't understand why you deemed it necessary, Harvey, to call my wife to your office. It would have caused you little inconvenience to drop by the house if you had something to discuss with her. Frankly I see this maneuver as nothing more than intimidation." His tone was haughty and superior. But again

Chloe picked up that undercurrent of nervousness. No, more than nervousness. Fear.

Harvey smiled pleasantly. "It wasn't a maneuver, Mr. Niels," he said in typical laconic fashion. "It was a request. A request that your wife here has obviously chosen to honor." His smile moved over to Karin. "I appreciate your taking the time to drop in, Mrs. Niels."

"Of course, Chief. I have no reason not to comply with your request. You'll have to forgive my husband. It's just . . . well, you know how rumors get out of hand in this town. I'm sure that by the time the noon bells go off, everyone in Thornhill will know my presence has been requested by the police."

Lawrence Niels looked over at Chloe. "May I ask the reason for your presence, Miss Hayes, before we go any further?"

Karin Niels smiled provocatively as she answered her husband. "Why, don't you know, darling? Miss Hayes is a renowned psychic. I gather the chief feels she can add a unique element to his investigations."

"As you already mentioned, Mrs. Niels," Chloe responded with a smile deliberately aimed at matching her adversary's, "rumors get out of hand in this town. To set the record straight, I'm here because I want to know why you bear me such ill feelings." Chloe's voice was cool and calm, and her smile didn't waver.

"Ill feelings?" Karin's finely shaped eyebrow lifted. "Why I don't even know you, Miss Hayes."

Chloe shot Harvey a surreptitious look and he gave her a subtle nod okaying her direct approach. Chloe's gaze fixed on Karin's face. "Then what were you doing, last night, burning an effigy of me?"

"What?" Lawrence Niels exclaimed. "Psychic, is it? Psychotic is more like it."

Harvey shrugged. "We have it on good authority that at midnight last night your wife conducted a Black Mass. And that part of the ceremony involved laying a life-size waxen figure on an altar and setting it aflame. We further have it, again on good authority, that this figure bore an extremely credible likeness to Miss Hayes here."

"My wife, Chief, was in bed with me last night at twelve o'clock," Lawrence Niels declared. Although he addressed Harvey, the bank president's gaze was fixed on Chloe, his eyes as bright and hard as sapphires.

Karin pressed her lips together. Chloe saw a flicker of rage in the woman's dark brown eyes. Karin said, "That's right, Chief. So, whoever your stooge is, he doesn't know what he's talking about." Karin's fingers with their professionally manicured nails were fidgeting with her ascot.

Harvey telegraphed a look to Chloe. She caught it and then switched her gaze to Karin. She studied her quietly for a couple of moments, watchful, assessing, deliberating, ignoring Lawrence Niels's presence in the room. A twitch that had started at the right corner of Karin's mouth was joined by one at the left corner.

Chloe said, "I spent some time with Peter Mott last night." At Chloe's mention of Mott's name, the effect on husband and wife was electric. Karin turned beet red with rage, completely obliterating the peachy tint to her complexion. Lawrence's complexion dipped to the opposite extreme.

Chloe hadn't said anything that wasn't true. She had seen Peter Mott last night. Over at the Emory house. But both Karin and Lawrence had jumped to the conclusion that Chloe had seen him after the Black Mass. After the pyrotechnics. From the look on Karin's face, it was clear she had no doubt that it had been Peter Mott who'd squealed.

Lawrence's gaze shot to his wife, weighted with emotion. And that emotion, Chloe noted with surprise, was hate. "You damn fool. You swore you weren't seeing Mott anymore."

"Shut up, Larry," Karin shouted, her fury no longer in check. "You don't understand. You never understood me. The only thing you care about or think about is your precious career, your reputation, your position in this dumb little town. Peter's the only man I ever met in this hole-in-the-wall who's got even a touch of class."

"Class? Right. Mott's just dripping in class. He's dripped it over half the women in this town. Including, it appears, Miss Hayes here."

Karin slapped her husband across the face. It wasn't a love pat.

Harvey saw the rage and humiliation in Niels's eyes and felt sorry for the man. He also saw that Niels was preparing to reciprocate Karin's blow in kind, and hurriedly stepped in. "Let's try to stay calm. I didn't mean to start anything here. I'm just trying to do my job." He zeroed in on Karin. "Last night, you did conduct a Black Mass, isn't that right, Mrs. Niels?"

Karin gave Harvey a cold look, but nodded.

"And you did set fire..."

"Yes," she snapped, cutting him off. "It did no damage, so I don't see why..."

Now it was Harvey's turn to cut Karin off. "I'll repeat Miss Hayes's question, Mrs. Niels. Why do you bear Miss Hayes here such ill will?"

She gave Chloe a supercilious smile. "It was nothing personal."

Lawrence Niels's jaw tensed. "She's right, you know, Miss Hayes. I think I can explain the...situation."

Karin glared at her husband. "I can explain perfectly well, myself. The 'sacrifice' as it were, was purely for a cathartic effect. Several members of my little... group... were concerned that you, Miss Hayes, might... interfere... with the smooth operation of our... program."

"Program?" Chloe queried sarcastically. "You mean devil worship."

Lawrence Niels snorted. "Oh come now. Karin just likes being the center of attention. These nonsensical little midnight gatherings are nothing more than theatrical performances. They haven't done anyone any harm." He shot Karin a narrow look. "You did tell me though, that those little gatherings were growing tedious and you were looking for some new interests."

"Did I?" Karin replied dryly.

Lawrence quickly looked away. "Is that all you have to ask my wife, Chief?" He deliberately ignored Chloe.

"I have a couple more points, actually," Harvey said. "First of all, Mrs. Niels, I'd like to assume these little private circles of yours have run their course and that in the future, you'll confine yourself to more... innocent gatherings. Which brings me to my second point. Milly happened to mention to me that you said something at the last Improvement Society meeting about Amanda Emory being distraught about something. What was it she was upset about?"

Karin's eyes narrowed. "Defection, Chief. That's what she was upset about."

Harvey looked puzzled, but Chloe slowly nodded. "You mean Amanda was upset that Peter Mott was thinking of leaving her circle and joining your group instead."

Karin's smile didn't touch her eyes. "Amanda was rather a fool when it came to men. I know it isn't nice to speak ill of the dead, but Amanda did act like a schoolgirl where Peter was concerned."

"Just how upset would you say she was?" Harvey prodded.

"You mean, was she upset enough about Peter to commit suicide?" Karin asked.

"If it was suicide," Chloe injected soberly.

Karin gave an involuntary gasp. "If you're trying to imply that Peter had anything to do with...murder, no. I know Peter. I know him better than anyone." And with that she stormed out of the office.

Lawrence Niels stared at the door his wife had slammed. Gone now was any hint of his authoritative, confident air.

"I sometimes wonder what I ever saw in her," Lawrence muttered. Slowly he looked first at Harvey and then at Chloe. "I can't seem to make a go of this marriage business." He smiled wearily and seemed about to make his own exit when Harvey interrupted.

"Where did you think your wife was at midnight, last night, Mr. Niels?" the chief asked.

Lawrence Niels hesitated. "I went to bed early last night. I took a sleeping pill. Lately I've had trouble sleeping, you see."

"Then you didn't realize your wife had gone?" Harvey prodded.

"Realize? No. I already told you that."

Harvey sighed. "Mr. Niels, I'm going to ask you something that's strictly routine. On the night of Amanda Emory's death—"

Niels didn't give Harvey a chance to finish. "My wife and I were out of town that night. In Boston at a bankers' convention. The Hilton Hotel. I've got the hotel receipt, if you want proof."

"Not at the moment," Harvey replied amicably. "Just trying to sort things out."

"Was it murder, Harvey?" Lawrence asked nervously.

"Let's just say, foul play hasn't been ruled out." He paused. "If it was murder, what do you think about Mott as a suspect?"

Lawrence Niels laughed dryly. "I wouldn't know. And, under the circumstances, I'm probably the wrong person to put in a good word for the professor." He smiled wearily. "Not that I think Mott really means anything to Karin. It's more a matter of conquest for her. And now that Mott and Lara Emory are involved, Karin's feeling a bit miffed."

Lawrence kept looking off into the distance. "I don't know why she behaves the way she does. All I do know is that my wife is willful and quite heartless."

Chloe moved closer to him. "Why do you stay with her then?" she asked softly.

Lawrence Niels's bluer than blue eyes bored into Chloe's. "Did you ever love someone you knew wasn't good for you, Miss Hayes? Did you ever love someone and hate them at the same time?"

Chloe started to tremble. Niels didn't notice. He was already heading out the office door. Harvey noticed though. And he gave her a pitying look.

"IT WASN'T VERY sporting of you to run out on me last night."

Chloe looked up from the book she was reading to see Thad Emory sitting across from her at the large library table.

She flushed. "If I ran out on anyone, it was your sister. And she didn't seem to be in any shape to care. Or to notice, for that matter."

Thad smiled. "You're right on both accounts. I, however, did notice. And I did care. I never even got to have a dance with you."

"I wasn't in much of a dancing mood last night."

"What kind of a mood were you in?" Now it was Thad's turn to flush. "I'm sorry, Chloe. That was uncalled for. And none of my business."

"You're right on both accounts."

He smiled boyishly and then checked his watch. "Look. It's almost six. Can I make up for my crassness by buying you dinner?"

Chloe hesitated. Would Noah expect that they'd be having dinner together tonight? Dinner and ...? She hadn't heard from Noah all day. Not since the phone call she'd made to him this morning from Harvey's office. He'd sounded irritated that she'd gone off as she had. But he'd told her on the phone that he loved her. Did he think that under the circumstances an avowal was required? Or had he meant it for the moment and later reconsidered? Maybe he was simply giving her the space she'd told him she needed. She did need the space. The question was, did she want it?

"Sure. Dinner sounds great."

Thad's look said he had a pretty good idea of what had gone through her mind before accepting his invitation. But the look also said that the important thing was that she had accepted.

THE MUSIC WAS SOFT and sounded faintly alien. The lighting was dim, candles on madras tablecloths. The red paneling added to a feeling of intimacy. The air was redolent with the scents of cardamom and curry.

"It's hard to believe this used to be the hardware store," Chloe said with a smile as Thad helped her into her seat.

"Jake's lost its lease and a bank was going to move in, but then a group of women in town who'd taken a series of Indian cooking classes decided to get their husbands to buy the building for them and open an Indian restaurant. They just opened a few weeks ago. I haven't tried it yet, so I can't promise how authentic it's going to be."

"I'm sure it will be great. Anyway, however good it is, I'm just glad this place didn't become another bank. Half the businesses on Main Street seem to be banks these days. When I was a student here there was just the Savings and Loan and New Hampshire National."

"Speaking of the Savings and Loan, I hear you met Lawrence Niels today."

"Okay, let me see. You have a friend who has a friend who has a brother who goes bowling with a guy who's a cop. And that cop happened to see me going into Harvey's office and then either he or one of his buddies, who later told him, saw the banker and his wife go in . . ."

Thad chuckled. "It's not always that roundabout. My secretary's brother is the desk sergeant at the station house. I'm afraid, Chloe, that you're fast becoming a celebrity here in Thornhill and you know how celebrities live in fishbowls."

"Just think how lucky you are that you didn't make it out in Hollywood or that would have been your fate as well."

A funny look altered Thad's usually pleasant demeanor. "Maybe some of us can handle that sort of fate."

"You are happy teaching at Dorchester, aren't you, Thad? I hear your students think you're fabulous."

"What do you think?"

Chloe laughed awkwardly. "I meant they say you're a fabulous teacher."

"I know. I was just fishing for a more personal compliment. I guess maybe my problem is I don't give up on anything I want, even when the odds are stacked against me. They are, aren't they, Chloe? Noah's still holding all the cards. He merely has to snap his fingers—"

"That's enough, Thad," Chloe said sharply just as the waitress, dressed in a colorful silk sari, approached the table. Chloe, still agitated, perfunctorily ordered the first dinner plate on the menu, no longer interested in the cuisine. She was regretting having accepted Thad's dinner invitation. Thad ordered the same as Chloe, obviously interested only in getting rid of the waitress.

"I know I'm likely to end up with a plate of curry in my lap, but I have to speak frankly to you, Chloe. All I can say in my defense is that I care about you very much. I saw what Noah's cruelty and callousness did to you once before. And while you may be the psychic, I think in this instance I can better see the writing on the wall."

Chloe sat very stiffly in her chair, her hands clasped in her lap. "And what exactly do you see written there, Thad?"

"Heartbreak," he whispered.

Chloe felt her pulse start to race. Hadn't she caught flashes of the same writing?

"Noah's still in love with Lara," he went on softly. "He didn't want the divorce. He did everything in his power to prevent it."

Chloe's throat was raw. She grabbed her water glass.

"Chloe, listen to me. He's no different now than he was seven years ago. All Lara has to do is snap her fingers and he'll come running. She's done it before and the guy tripped over himself getting back to her."

"Stop it, Thad."

"It's the truth, Chloe. And I think you know it. He's using you, damn it. He's using you to get back at Lara. He'd do anything to get back at her. If he can't have her, I believe he means to destroy her. Lara swore to me, in absolute confidence, that she believes Noah has been drugging her."

Chloe froze. "Why Noah?"

Thad's eyes narrowed. "Then you believe it, too. Drugs would certainly explain Lara's weird behavior and mood swings. I've never seen her like this."

"Grief can do that to people," Chloe said defensively, even though she, too, believed drugs played a part. She simply refused to believe in Noah as the culprit.

"I don't think it's simple grief over Mother's death," Thad said. He sighed. "Mother was afraid of him."

Chloe stared at Thad, dumbfounded. "Afraid of Noah?"

"Noah blamed her for turning Lara against him."

Chloe shivered. She remembered Lara making a reference to the same thing. "Why would Amanda turn Lara against Noah?" she demanded.

"She didn't really. Oh, she may have told Lara on occasion that she didn't think the marriage would last. And the more she got to know Noah, the less she liked him. Mother never was one to hide her feelings. But, that wasn't why Lara divorced Noah. She just grew weary of his possessiveness, his need to dominate her, his...mental cruelty. But when she confronted Noah and told him she wanted a divorce he flew into a rage. My mother and I were both present. Lara had deliberately asked us to come over for support. She was afraid Noah would go wild. And he did. He turned on Mother, blaming her, calling her a spiteful, meddlesome witch. He had to blame someone. And he couldn't blame Lara. He's never been able to blame Lara for anything.''

Chloe felt a wave of nausea. "Why...blame...Amanda? Why not...blame Peter Mott?''

"He didn't know about Peter until after the divorce.'' Thad leaned closer. "It was awful that night. He threatened Mother. He said if she kept up her meddling, one day she'd pay the price.'' He stared hard at Chloe. "And she has. The ultimate price.''

"Thad, you can't be thinking Noah was in any way involved in your mother's suicide.''

"Was it suicide? I know about the autopsy. Harvey Mead showed me the report showing hyoscine in mother's blood. Yes, strictly speaking, the atheme was plunged into her heart by her own hand. But who's to say someone didn't guide that hand? She could have been so drugged she never even knew what was happening.'' Thad's shoulders sagged and he gave Chloe a sad, weary smile. "I said as much to Mead and I had the feeling he'd already been thinking along the same lines. Not that he's likely to ever prove it. Of course, Alice Donovan's death was sloppier. The murderer was in more of a hurry. Or more of a panic, most likely.''

"Even if your theory is true, it still doesn't mean Noah—''

"Killed my mother? Killed Alice Donovan?'' Thad finished for her.

The candle on their table flickered and went out. Chloe felt as if a cold, clammy hand was pressing into her chest. *"Beware, Chloe. The devil wears many guises..."* The words reverberated within her head.

"Just before my mother died, Chloe, Lara, in one of her weaker moments, considered a reconciliation with Noah. She was confused, unsure of what to do. Mother did a tarot reading for her. Based on that reading, Lara decided to leave well enough alone.'' Thad reached out across the darkened table and took Chloe's hand. ''A man can be driven to heinous acts in the name of love, Chloe. And when a man loves a woman the way Noah loves Lara . . .''

Chapter Twelve

It wasn't quite nine when Chloe managed a weary good-night to Thad at the front door of Lucy Harris's. He was still all apologies. "If I'd had any idea that Lara and Noah were going to show up at the restaurant..."

"Please, Thad. It's not...your fault." No, it was Chloe's fault. Her fault alone. She should have known better. And they say you don't make the same mistake twice.

She felt drained and exhausted as she opened the front door.

"Ah, Chloe," Lucy Harris greeted her in the hall. "There's someone come to see you," she said right out. Then, on closer inspection, she asked, "Are you all right, Chloe? You don't look at all well."

"Allergies," Chloe muttered. "Who's here to see me, Mrs. Harris?"

The small, spry figure of Mildred Mead popped out of the parlor, peering at Chloe over her wire-rimmed spectacles. "Have I come at a bad time?" she asked solicitously.

A bad time? You could definitely say that. "I'm not feeling too well. Stomach," Chloe mumbled clutching her gut.

"Indian food. It'll do it to you if you're not used to it. The spices. I know just the thing. Bicarbonate..."

Of course, she knows where and what I ate for dinner. Anger broke through Chloe's torpor. "I don't need bicarbonate," she shouted at Mildred. "And I can't stand this damn fishbowl of a town. I should never have come back here. I should never have gotten involved. I'm choking on the treachery and corruption and deceit smothering this place. Smothering me," she screamed, fleeing up the stairs to her room.

Lucy Harris made a tsking sound. "Indian food?" She gazed at the police chief's wife. "How *did* you know she'd eaten Indian food by the way?"

Mildred smiled. "Paula Dubois saw her at the new Indian restaurant on Main Street."

"Paula's involved in the restaurant? I thought it was Janet Murray, Robin Shaw and Lynn McKensey."

"Paula's doing their desserts. Just temporarily. Carol Olman was going to be the pastry chef, but now that she's dating Lynn McKensey's ex she thought it would be awkward. Anyway, Paula can always be counted on in a pinch. But it's really too much for her. She's got more than enough to manage what with her catering business and her daughter. And ever since Amanda's passing, she's been in a terrible state. Which is why I came over to see Chloe. Paula saw her at the restaurant and wanted to speak to her, but she felt awkward about it. Well, you know how timid Paula can be. Although I must say the success of her catering business has done wonders for her self-confidence."

"No small thanks to you, Mildred Mead. You've been a godsend to that child. I hear her little girl, Jessie, calls you Nanny. If that isn't the sweetest." Lucy gave Mildred a conspiratorial look. "Who do you think little Jessie looks like?"

Mildred's eyes sparkled. "Like Paula, I'd say."

"Oh Mildred. You know what I mean."

"Yes, I know what you mean, Lucy Harris. And I have always had my suspicions."

"I knew you did."

"But I'm not going to say what they are. Just this morning Harvey warned me to be very careful about speaking or writing about any matters that might stir up more scandal in Thornhill. There's plenty enough brewing in this town as it is. We wouldn't want Thornhill to get a reputation as another Peyton Place, now, would we?"

Lucy wasn't paying any attention. "I wonder if Paula would confide in Chloe about Jessie's father. If she did, I hope Chloe would have the good sense to encourage her to confront him and demand he accept his responsibility. I think it would do Paula a world of good."

"Right now, that isn't Paula's chief worry, Lucy." Mildred sighed. "If only she hadn't gone to that coven of Amanda's that night."

"Did she see anything?" Lucy asked eagerly.

"Harvey questioned her and the others in detail, and got nowhere. There was Paula and poor Alice, a couple of Amanda's students, Peter Mott, and Gordy Beal from the French department there. Her regulars. Lara didn't attend that night supposedly because of a headache, although Paula is convinced Lara and Amanda had a falling-out earlier that day."

Mildred flushed. "Oh dear, I probably shouldn't have said that. Hearsay. Only hearsay."

"I won't breathe a word." Lucy tried to affect a casual tone. "What were they fighting about?"

"I don't know," Mildred said a little too quickly.

Lucy's mouth twitched. "We both have our suspicions though, don't we?"

Mildred pushed her glasses higher up on her nose. "If you ask me, I think Amanda and Lara were both being made fools of. The rest of us in this town know that Peter Mott has only one genuine interest. And that's himself."

"I couldn't agree more. But do you think he was involved in this ugly business? Do you think Amanda killed herself over a broken heart?"

"The question is, if Alice's murder is connected to Amanda's death, it raises some very sticky questions about precisely how Amanda died."

"But I thought it had definitely been ruled a suicide." Lucy giggled nervously. "Of course, what if she was being blackmailed? Someone might have driven her to suicide. Maybe on that very night Amanda had a confrontation with the blackmailer and then, in despair, killed herself as her only way out." She took a breath. "And maybe Alice stayed behind and overheard Amanda and the blackmailer. That would explain..."

"According to the others, the whole group left together."

"Yes, but Alice might have forgotten something and gone back." Lucy gripped Mildred's arm. "Or she might have spotted Mott going back and followed him. Well, it was plain as day that Alice was crazy in love with Mott. Why, I think she must have taken more of her so-called love potions than cups of her beloved English tea."

"Well," Mildred said, "there are plenty of logical theories about this business. And some not so logical. Take Paula. She's got herself convinced that both Amanda's death and Alice's are connected to supernatural skulduggery. She's afraid it's some black-magic plot to kill off Amanda's whole coven because they were into good deeds and wanted to draw down only the good and pure powers. Paula says the only thing that will save her is psychic protection." Mildred sighed as she glanced up the staircase.

"And she feels Chloe Hayes is the only one who can provide that."

"Fiddlesticks. Chloe Hayes is no more a psychic than I am," Lucy declared. "Of course, the other night when she went off I did have this . . . premonition of danger."

"A powerful premonition, at that," declared Mildred with a sparkle in her eyes. "Why, you even had a vision of just where she'd gone. How else would you have known she was at the Grange?"

Lucy cleared her throat and didn't quite meet Mildred's sparkling gaze. Instead she took a turn looking up the stairs. "You might want to come back tomorrow to speak to Chloe, Mildred. She is in a state. I blame it wholly on Noah Bright. I don't think they're suited. I really don't."

"You just disapprove because they spent the night together."

"I am not that provincial, Mildred Mead. And how do you know she spent the night with him?"

"Really, Lucy. I told you when I first came over that she didn't end up spending the night at Lara's as she'd planned."

"Well, if she did spend the night with Noah, I don't think that was a very wise move at all."

"You may be right," Mildred mused. "Paula not only saw Chloe at the restaurant having dinner with Thad Emory. She also saw Lara Emory and Noah Bright at another table."

Lucy Harris's small mouth shaped itself into a round O. "No wonder Chloe is so upset," Lucy murmured. "Don't tell me Lara and Noah are getting back together?"

Mildred couldn't resist editorializing. "Now talk about an unwise move. That was a disastrous marriage from the start. Everyone in town knew that. Including the two of them." Mildred checked her watch. It was just twenty minutes past nine. "I did promise Paula I'd plead her cause with Chloe this evening." Again her eyes went to the stairs. "Perhaps I'll give her a little while to calm down a bit, though. You wouldn't happen to have any decaf about, Lucy?"

A CHILL CLUNG to Chloe's bed-sitting-room. Odd, since Mrs. Harris was not one to stint on heat. She crossed the room and checked the windows. They were tightly shut and there was no breeze sneaking in along the cracks. Gingerly, she tapped her palm to the steam radiator in the corner. Hot.

Chloe sighed. Inner agitation and despair chilling the soul. That had to be it. She flashed on the image of Lara and Noah entering the restaurant, hand in hand. Noah's hand, the hand that only last night had incited passion like a riot in her blood...

"He's still in love with Lara.... Heartbreak... He didn't want the divorce.... He blamed Amanda.... He threatened Amanda.... Was it a suicide...?"

Thad's words kept echoing in her mind. At first they masked the sound. But little by little she grew aware of it. A faint hum. No, more like a buzz. An insect buzzing by her ear. Only it wasn't really so close. It was coming from across the room.

Her eyes fell on the closet. Yes, it was coming from there. Inside the closet. Emanating from there, but filling the room more and more. And the texture of the sound was changing. Not so much a buzz now. A low rumble. Punctuated by dashes of silence. Like someone with a bad chest cold trying to get more breath into his lungs.

Chloe felt her skin crawl with terror. The strained breathing sound from the closet grew louder, curling around her like a thick membrane. The walls of the room seemed to be sweating. Perspiration trickled down her spine. Her own breathing grew labored, her gaze locked now on the closet.

She knew someone was in there.

Was she moving toward the closet door or was it somehow advancing toward her? The chill she was feeling evaporated. She felt hot and clammy now, the space between her and the door narrowing with each ragged breath she took.

Her hand lifted inexorably to the knob. "Please..." The sibilant pleading whine of her voice sounded almost like the hiss of a cat.

Like Dantes.

The knob of the closet door was like ice. Then fire. Somehow her hand clung to it. But pulling it open...that was something else altogether. She couldn't move a muscle. She was in limbo. And the breathing behind the door was coming in sharp, rapid spurts now.

MILDRED AND LUCY sat at the pine table in Lucy's cozy kitchen with its potbellied stove, bluebell motif wallpaper, calico curtains and delicious aroma of fresh-brewed decaffeinated coffee. Along with the coffee Lucy set out a plate of fresh-baked chocolate-chip cookies.

"You know, Mildred, we could be off on the wrong track focusing on Peter Mott. Not that I trust the man. I don't, but still we may be barking up the wrong tree."

"And which tree should we be barking up?" Mildred asked, pouring a generous amount of cream into her coffee.

"Well, I just recalled something about Lawrence Niels. Something I heard a while back."

"Niels? What did you hear about him, Lucy?"

"First, keep in mind what you said about Paula being worried that Amanda's whole group is in danger. She may be right."

"Evil spirits? The devil and his disciples? Well, then you wouldn't be barking up Lawrence Niels's tree, you'd be barking up his wife's tree. She's the one who's dabbling in black magic supposedly. Although, personally, I think she just took it up as a diversion. And to compete with Amanda. Jealousy and spitefulness. That's all it is."

"Oh, I agree, absolutely. I don't think that silly woman can cast any evil spells. No, as I said, we should look to the husband."

"You think he cast an evil spell?" Mildred teased.

"No. But I think he may have embarked upon a witch-hunt. It just so happens Niels told Jim Durham, the loan officer at the bank, that if he had his way he'd string up the whole lot of them. Meaning Amanda and her group. Niels, it seems, was beside himself after his wife joined up with the coven. And when she went off to start her own, he might have blamed Amanda for instigating the whole thing. Niels has a reputation to uphold. And his wife isn't helping it any. Her reputation seems to grow more scandalous each day."

"How did you hear about this threat Niels made to Jim Durham?" If Mildred was going to propose Lawrence Niels as another suspect to her husband, she wanted to be sure her source was valid.

"I play bridge with Marilyn, his wife. She said that Jim said Lawrence Niels was trying to get a group of well-heeled folks in town to put pressure on the college to throw Amanda out on her ear if she didn't stop her so-called scholarly coven meetings."

"Amanda had tenure. She couldn't be thrown out."

"Exactly," Lucy said. "What if, in desperation, Lawrence put some pressure on Amanda, began anonymously persecuting her? What if he drove her to suicide? What if he then made up his mind to get rid of the whole lot? One by one, starting with Alice Donovan?''

Just as Mildred was about to try her hand at poking holes in Lucy's latest theory, the doorbell rang. Lucy shrugged and rose to answer it. "I suppose we both know who that's likely to be."

THE BREATHING SEEPED into her bones. Slowly, inexorably, the doorknob started to turn, though Chloe felt certain her hand wasn't doing the turning. No, someone— something—some force inside the closet was manipulating the knob.

Even as she trembled, Chloe was held by a strange fascination.

The closet door emitted a creaking whine as it inched open. Chloe's skin prickled and tightened, the hairs on the back of her neck stood up, her pulse rate quickened.

The breathing sound continued, but it had evened out, softened, mellowed. Chloe's hand fell away from the knob. She stepped back. The door opened wider.

The light inside the closet was brilliant, blinding. Chloe shielded her eyes. She had no idea how long it took to get used to the brightness, but within the light a filmy form began to solidify. Slowly, it took on form and substance. And scent. The familiar scent of roses. Strong, cloying...

A pale hand extended from a billowy, white sleeve, palm outstretched. And in the hand a dagger...the atheme...

Chloe sank to her knees.

She didn't know how much time passed like that. She was only dimly aware of someone coming to stand beside her, holding her, grounding her.

It was Noah.

And Lara be damned, Chloe fell thankfully into his arms.

NOAH INSISTED Chloe go for a walk with him. Chloe didn't argue. She was desperate to get away from her room...that closet...the haunting vision.

It was close to ten o'clock. Lucy, accompanied by Mildred, was just stepping into the front hall to lock up as Chloe and Noah ducked out the door. The two women shared knowing looks.

Noah took Chloe's hand as they started down the street. A breeze slid through Chloe's loose hair, but the evening was surprisingly mild for the first of November. They walked for several blocks ending up at the pond. They started walking around it.

"Do you want to tell me what happened back there?" Noah asked softly.

Chloe felt limp. The vision had drained all of her energy. "Nothing. It was nothing."

"You saw something again, didn't you?"

"You must be thinking I'm deranged," she muttered. Then she laughed harshly. "Maybe I am."

"No." He went to put his arm around her, but she jerked away.

"I'm not that crazy, Noah."

"Chloe, just because you saw me with Lara tonight..."

"Forget it, Noah."

"She called me. Asked me to have dinner with her. She—"

"She just has to snap her fingers. Snap and you come running. You know the only thing I regret, Noah. I just regret that she was too drugged to snap last night before...before..." Despair and shame drowned her voice and she couldn't go on.

She tried to keep walking but he pulled her to a stop, pulled her into his arms. "She showed up at the hospital, claiming she had something important to tell me. Insisted on telling me over dinner. As soon as we walked into the restaurant she grabbed my hand. Damn it, I think she must have spotted you and wanted to make you think . . . well, exactly what you thought."

"Please let me go," Chloe said tightly.

"No. Not again. I'm not going to let Lara come between us again."

Chloe gave him a hostile glare. "What was it she had to tell you that was so important?"

Noah's mouth twitched. "She knew about the drugged cognac."

For a moment Chloe's fury took a back seat to her curiosity. "She admitted doctoring it?" If she had, that would mean she'd lied to Thad about Noah drugging her.

Noah's jaw tightened. "No. She didn't do it."

"Then . . . who?"

He didn't answer immediately. "She thinks it was . . . her brother."

"Thad?" Oh, that was just perfect. She tells Thad Noah's drugging her. Then tells Noah Thad's the one. If Noah wasn't just making it up. "Why would Thad . . . ?"

"She says it's because he wants her to sell the house. More than that. She insists he wants to get his hands on Amanda's whole estate. If he can convince the courts that Lara isn't psychologically fit to manage her half of the estate, he could be granted executorship."

"I think Lara really is out of her mind." But then Chloe had an altogether different thought. "Maybe Thad would have a case, at that."

"I'm not saying Lara is right about Thad, Chloe. To be honest, Lara always could lie like a champ. Anyway, what she told me isn't important right now. What's important is that you know that I meant what I said to you on the phone this morning. I love you."

His gray-green eyes held her, tugged at her, drew her in. To protect herself, she closed her eyes. Tears seeped through her lashes.

"And I know you love me, too, Chloe."

She felt a lump in her throat. "I don't think we should see each other anymore, Noah."

"That's not really what you want."

Her eyelids fluttered open. "What, are you a psychic, too? How do you know what I want?"

"You showed me last night," he whispered.

"She'll always be between us, Noah. I just can't... exorcise her. We're inexorably linked...the three of us." She looked up at the sky. Clouds were playing tag with the moon.

He took hold of her chin, tilted it back down to earth...to him. "That's not the whole story. There's something more. Something you're not telling me."

A dry smile curved her lips. "Maybe you really are psychic, Noah." She hesitated. "Thad said some things tonight, too."

"About Lara?"

It was hard for Chloe to continue. "About you. About you and Lara. And you and...Amanda."

"What about me and Amanda?" he asked with such bewilderment Chloe found herself breathing a fraction easier.

"He said you blamed Amanda for your breakup with Lara."

"What?"

"And that when Lara told you she wanted a divorce you flew into a rage and turned on Amanda who was at your house along with Thad. You called her a spiteful, meddle-some witch. You threatened her. You said one day...she would...pay the price."

The last thing Chloe expected was the relieved smile on Noah's face. "So that's why you don't want to see me any-more? Oh Chloe, sure I got a little worked up when Lara asked for the divorce. And I did blow off some steam in Amanda's direction. But I don't honestly remember call-ing her a meddlesome old witch. Then again, I might have. She said some pretty nasty things herself. Told me if I were more of a man maybe her daughter wouldn't have felt the need to look elsewhere for gratification. It's only now that I realize just why Amanda was so mad. She probably fig-ured that if I had satisfied her daughter enough, maybe Lara wouldn't have gone after Mott."

"You knew Lara was having an affair with Peter Mott? Thad thought you didn't find out until after the divorce."

"Are you kidding? Lara did everything in the book to make sure I knew. She wanted to prove to me that some-one wanted her. And I think, deep down she had some cockeyed notion that it would spark my jealousy, make me try to win her back, change my mind."

"Change your mind about what?"

"About wanting a divorce."

"You were the one who wanted the divorce?"

"Let's say I got the ball rolling. But no way was Lara going to have the whole town of Thornhill know I was the one who wanted out. When I didn't try to win her back af-ter her affair with Mott, she filed for the divorce herself. Which was fine with me. Just as long as we ended it." He met Chloe's gaze evenly. "I don't know if you can under-stand this, but I don't hold any of it against Lara. It's just the way she is. I guess, more than anything else, I feel sorry for her. She's never going to really experience what it is to love and . . . be loved."

"Maybe I do understand," she whispered.

He smiled and took her hand. "Shall we walk some more?"

She shook her head.

"Then I'll take you back to Lucy's."

Chloe stiffened. "No. I . . . I don't want to go back there tonight."

His eyes bored into hers. "Because you saw something in the closet?"

She tried to look away, but he took hold of her chin.

"Tell me, Chloe. Did you see something?"

Breathless, she nodded. "Do you think I'm deranged?"

A faint smile. "Maybe we're both deranged."

"What . . . do you . . . mean?"

"For a moment . . . I saw something, too."

"What? What did you see?"

He hesitated, his eyes locking with hers. "A flash. I saw a flash of silver."

The silver blade of Amanda's atheme, Chloe thought with a shudder.

Chapter Thirteen

It was close to 11:00 p.m. when Harvey Mead tracked Chloe down at Noah's house. When she spoke to him over the phone she wanted to tell him it wasn't what he was thinking. She was spending the night in his spare bedroom. It was all open and aboveboard.

But Harvey had more important things on his mind that night than who was sleeping with whom.

"I hate to keep doing this to you, Chloe, but I need your help again."

"Where are you, Harvey?"

He gave her the address, and this time he asked her to bring Noah and suggested Noah bring his medical bag. She said they'd be there in fifteen minutes.

Noah drove and Chloe sat silently beside him, the weight of all that still remained unspoken between them dividing them like an invisible wedge. When they turned the corner onto Arlen Street the house and driveway were lit up at number seven. Harvey's cruiser was parked behind a shiny, new, white station wagon. Letters were emblazoned in hot pink on both sides of the car: Pies to Go-Go.

As Chloe and Noah started up the walk to the front door of Paula Dubois's ranch-style home, the air seemed charged.

Harvey had the door open. He managed a faint smile, but it didn't alter the somber expression that occupied the rest of his face.

"Thanks for coming so quickly," he said, taking Chloe's arm, guiding her inside, nodding to Noah who followed behind.

"Paula's in the bedroom. She's okay... I think. More scared than anything else."

"What happened?" Chloe asked.

"Denk found her about a half hour ago. She was in her car, parked in the alleyway behind the new Indian restaurant on Main Street. She had her high beams on, or he might not have spotted her. He went over, saw her behind the wheel. Doors were all locked, motor still running. He said her eyes were wide open, but when he tried to get her attention... nothing. She didn't even blink, didn't move a muscle. Like she was in some sort of catatonic state. He gave up trying to rouse her and jimmied the lock to get in."

"Why didn't he take her to the hospital?" Noah asked, dropping his jacket over the back of a chair.

"That's just it. As soon as he got the door open, and shut the engine off, she just... snapped out of it. She was scared and confused, didn't even remember getting into her car. All she wanted to do was get home and make sure her little girl was all right." Harvey looked at Chloe. "Jessie. She's six years old. Cute as a button. Millie and I are kind of surrogate grandparents."

"Is... Jessie all right?" Chloe asked.

"Tucked in her bed snug as a bug in a rug. Baby-sitter said it was a perfectly ordinary night. No calls, no visitors. I had Denk drive the sitter home."

"I better go in and have a look at Paula," Noah said.

"Yeah. Second door on the right." Harvey pointed down the hall. Noah headed to the bedroom while Harvey escorted Chloe into a small but tidy living room. The Early-American-style furnishings looked as if they'd been bought as an ensemble right out of a furniture show room.

Despite Harvey's claim that all was relatively well, the air still held a strained sense of anticipation. Chloe sat down on the couch and looked up at Harvey who was standing by the brick-faced fireplace.

He cleared his throat. "Paula's likely to give Noah a hard time. Actually she only wants to see you. That was why Millie stopped by at Lucy's place. To speak to you on Paula's behalf, sort of. Paula's shy. But I guess Millie never got the opportunity. She told me you weren't...feeling too well and then she saw you duck out of Lucy's place with Noah."

"Why does Paula want to talk to me? I don't think I've ever even met her."

Harvey had difficulty making eye contact. That wasn't like Harvey at all.

"I guess she wants your help."

"What kind of help can I give her?"

A flush crept up over Harvey's collar. "Psychic help, she calls it. I'm afraid Paula's all carried away with fears and superstitions. I know I shouldn't speak ill of the dead, and I'm not saying Amanda wasn't a fine woman in...many ways, but she really shouldn't have encouraged a girl like Paula. Too innocent, too vulnerable, too...gullible."

"You said Paula has a daughter. Jessie."

"Yes, that's right. Sweetest little girl—"

"And a husband?"

Harvey gave her a shrewd glance. "I can tell by the look in your eye, Chloe, that you already know the answer to that one."

She smiled. "A hunch."

Harvey nodded and went on to tell Chloe a bit about Paula's background, her teenaged pregnancy, the scandal, her refusal to identify the father, and how Mildred had taken Paula under her wing after the girl's parents had thrown her out.

"Did you say Paula's daughter was six years old?" Chloe asked after Harvey finished.

"Yes. She'll be seven in December. December seventeenth."

Chloe stared at the Currier & Ives print on the wall, but she wasn't really seeing it. "That means Paula would have conceived in March. Seven years ago. My senior year at Dorchester."

Harvey saw something flicker in Chloe's eyes. "Paula was a senior in high school at the time. But, actually, you probably saw her over at the college now and again. She had an after-school job in the anthropology department. Filing and such. That's how she got to know Amanda. Not that she was involved in any of Amanda's... extracurricular activities back then. But Amanda always did have a way of drawing people to her."

Chloe started. "Yes, sometimes the wrong people."

Harvey got that sad look in his eyes again. And Chloe knew that he was mourning the loss of a love he had never quite gotten over. It wasn't something he would talk about again. Instead he said, "Paula's a good girl. Smart, pretty, a fine mother to Jessie." He stared down at Chloe. "I wish I knew what happened to her tonight out behind the restaurant. Why did she go into that trancelike state? Is she in danger?" He hesitated. "She swears she knows nothing about... Amanda. Or Alice. Nothing that should put her in any jeopardy."

"Maybe she's trying...to protect someone," Chloe whispered. A hunch. A powerfully strong hunch. The moment she said the words she felt a sharp jab of certainty in her chest.

Harvey saw the flicker of conviction in Chloe's eyes. Anguish washed over his face. He gave Chloe a pleading look. "If that's true, I'm afraid Paula's not about to confide in the chief of police. But maybe you can get somewhere with her. You've got to find out who she's protecting, Chloe. Before... it's too late."

Chloe was staring ahead, but Harvey's voice was fading. Another voice was taking its place, crowding out his words in her head. A realization. It grasped at her. It prickled her skin. Her breathing came in short, shallow gasps.

Harvey gave her a worried look. "What's the matter, Chloe?" he asked anxiously. But Chloe didn't hear him. He reached out to her, but her muscles were rigid, unresponsive to his touch. Chloe was feeling vibrations, murmurings. Her hand moved to her chest, her expression pained. Harvey was afraid she might be having a heart attack or something. He was about to call out to Noah, when Chloe lowered her hand, her features smoothing out. She stared directly at the chief.

"It's Jessie's father," Chloe whispered. "Paula is protecting Jessie's father. Don't ask me why I know. Tell yourself it's just one of my... hunches. Paula has reasons to suspect he's involved in the deaths of Amanda Emory and Alice Donovan. And she's terrified that... he won't stop there." She gazed bleakly at Harvey, unable to say how she knew, only that she did. She could feel his presence in this house. He'd been here. Recently. Chloe could feel his shadow like a thick shroud filling the room. Jessie's father. Paula's lover. Amanda's... murderer.

Before Harvey had the opportunity to question Chloe further, Noah came back into the room. He caught Harvey's eye first and then he looked at Chloe. Their eyes met and held. Noah's expression was tense, questioning.

"She wants to see you," he told Chloe in a low voice.

"Is she okay?" Harvey asked, the anxious surrogate father.

"Physically, yes." He paused, his eyes narrowing. "My opinion is that something scared Paula half to death. She was...frozen with terror, but as to why... She wouldn't give me a clue. I was afraid to push too hard. She's in a very fragile state. There's no telling what could happen to her if she felt pressured."

Harvey nodded morosely. "I swear," he muttered, "I'm beginning to think half this town has been bewitched. I've never seen so many people acting so weird—" He stopped. "No offense intended." The apology was directed at Chloe.

She managed a weak smile. "None taken." She kept the smile on as she passed Noah, but he wasn't fooled. He was too good at picking up on her moods, her desires, her fears.

Chloe hesitated at Paula's closed bedroom door. Finally she knocked softly.

A childlike voice bade her come in.

Paula Dubois was sitting cross-legged on her bed, still dressed in jeans and an overlarge sweatshirt, emblazoned like her station wagon with hot-pink Pies to Go-Go lettering, a winged apple-pie logo beneath.

Chloe did recognize Paula from her student days at Dorchester. She recalled having seen her on several occasions over at the anthropology department although she hadn't even known her name back then. Today, at twenty-four, Paula looked much like Chloe remembered her at seventeen. She was small-boned with delicate features, dark eyes, and flawless skin. Her striking ash blond hair was pulled back in an unstylish and haphazard ponytail, but it did nothing to detract from her natural loveliness. What did detract was the absent way she was pulling out tufts from her wool blanket and the look of hopelessness in her eyes.

When she listlessly lifted her head and saw Chloe at the open door of her room, however, her ennui instantly disappeared. It was as though she was suddenly charged with energy.

With surprisingly robust movements, Paula bolted off the bed and rushed over to Chloe. "Oh, you've come. You've come. You've got to help me."

Up close, Chloe could see the faint sprinkle of freckles on Paula's cheeks and across the bridge of her nose. And she could see the fear written in her dark green eyes.

"Can you tell me what happened tonight, Paula?" Chloe asked softly, taking the younger woman by the arm and guiding her back over to the bed where they sat down together.

Paula's face was drained of color, making her freckles more vivid. She twirled the bottom of her ponytail around her index finger. She'd been doing it for a while. The ponytail ended in a tight corkscrew curl. "It was...awful," she muttered. Her eyes darted to the window, as if she suspected someone was watching. How she'd ever know, though, was a mystery, since the shades were tightly drawn.

Chloe took Paula's trembling hand. She sandwiched it between her two palms. Paula closed her eyes, her long, dark lashes shadowing her cheeks.

Chloe studied Paula in profile, listening to the younger woman's nervous breathing. Her own breathing slowed. "You found something in your car, didn't you, Paula?"

A sharp intake of breath. "I knew you would know." And then she started to cry.

"It was a doll, wasn't it?"

She sobbed in earnest now, unable to speak.

"It's all right, Paula. It's all right. You're safe now," Chloe soothed in a low, melodious voice.

"I don't understand why...why..." But Paula couldn't go on. She broke into sobs again.

Chloe continued holding Paula's hand. "Why didn't you show the doll to Harvey?"

Paula shook her head as she kept sobbing.

"Is the doll still in your car?"

Again Paula shook her head.

Chloe looked around the small bedroom. She saw a brown canvas tote bag on top of a pine dresser.

Paula clutched at Chloe as she followed her gaze. "No. No. I don't want to see it again."

Gently, but firmly, Chloe extricated herself from Paula's grasp. She rose from the bed and crossed the room. When she reached into the tote she heard Paula's sharp cry of terror behind her.

It wasn't an image done in Paula's likeness. It was nothing like the gruesome bit of work Chloe had found in her car the other morning. This was an ordinary doll. A child's doll. A dainty porcelain-faced doll with pretty blond hair, ruby-red lips, pink cheeks, a red and white gingham dress overlaid by a starched white eyelet apron. Delicate white slippers and perfect white ankle socks adorned the feet. It was a beautifully crafted doll. Flawless. Except for one glaring imperfection. The eyes were missing. And they hadn't simply fallen out or been pried out. They'd been burned out, mutilated...

Slowly, Chloe turned back to Paula. "This belongs to your little girl. It's... Jessie's doll, isn't it?"

"He wouldn't hurt her. He wouldn't..." A new bout of tears.

Chloe wisely tucked the doll out of sight behind Paula's tote before returning to the younger woman's side. When she left the room she would take the doll with her. For Harvey. It was going to shake him up, too.

Chloe knelt before Paula, who sat on the edge of the bed slumped over, head in her hands, shoulders heaving.

"Who would hurt Jessie, Paula? Who did that to Jessie's doll? Who are you afraid of?"

No response.

"I can't help you if you don't tell me, Paula."

This elicited a response. Paula's head jerked up, her eyes, red and puffy from crying, searched Chloe's face with a beseeching look. "Yes, you can. I know you can. You can protect Jessie and me. You have the skill, the power. You know about psychic attacks. You had one yourself..."

"What are you talking about?"

"Amanda told me. She told me how you almost died seven years ago. She found you on the path to the glen, unconscious. She told me how you were able to fight off the attack, that you had a special skill, a power..."

"She didn't know," Chloe murmured, more to herself than to Paula. "I never told her about the vision, the atheme... How could she know?"

But Paula wasn't listening. "There are rituals. Amanda spoke of them. Rituals to ward off attacks. That night she died...that terrible night...if only she'd realized what danger she was in. If only she hadn't been so sure she could reason with him."

Chloe gripped Paula's shoulders. "Who, Paula? Who did Amanda believe she could reason with?"

"No. No. I don't know. I don't know. Please..."

"Did you see them together that night? Did you see him murder Amanda?"

"No. No. I didn't see anything. I swear."

"But he believes you did, Paula. That's why he's trying to scare you. He thinks you do know. The only way you can protect yourself is by telling me..."

"No. He'll hurt Jessie. He'll hurt my baby. You won't be able to stop him. You don't know him." Paula's whole body was trembling. She was approaching hysteria.

"It's his child, too. He wouldn't hurt his own child," Chloe argued gently, trying to reason with her.

But Paula was past reason. The glitter in her eyes was feverish. Her breathing was so uneven now, it caught in her throat in sharp gasps. "Oh, you don't understand," she wailed. And then all of the young woman's features shut down. Chloe could see Paula disappearing into herself.

She shook the terrified young woman gently. "It's okay, Paula. I truly understand. I will help you. You must listen to what I say now. Are you listening?"

For a long while there was no response, and Chloe feared she had, indeed, pushed the young woman over the edge. But finally Paula managed to faintly whisper, "Yes."

Chloe sighed with relief. She had forged a connection. "I will tell you how to ward off a psychic attack. The secret is strength, Paula. Not physical strength, but emotional tenacity. A mental refusal to submit to fear and persecution. That tenacity creates the protective shield around you. It keeps you from feeling defenseless. That's what you've been feeling. That's what I felt...when it happened to me. But then I refused to succumb."

Paula was listening intently now. Chloe was relieved to see life return to the young woman's features. And while she, herself, was still grappling with the truth or fiction of psychic assaults, what she was telling Paula did make sense to her. Whether it was psychic attacks, the power of suggestion, hallucinations, or delusions, the only way Chloe could imagine to fend them off was by sheer will. A fervent refusal to be intimidated. A willful channeling of strength, vitality, power with singleminded determination.

It took no psychic ability on Chloe's part to see the shadow of disappointment in Paula's face. Harvey had said she was superstitious and gullible. Would it be wrong to give her something more tangible that would encourage her to believe in her own ability to be strong? But what? And then Chloe realized that she had the perfect thing.

"Listen to me, Paula. I'm going to give you a special charm to wear around your neck. It's an ankh. Do you know what that is?"

"It's . . . Egyptian. The symbol of life. A hieroglyph."

"That's right. I have one in my purse, out in the hall. I'll go get it and be right back."

Paula nodded and Chloe rushed out to the hall and grabbed up her handbag from the hall table. Noah heard her footsteps and popped out of the living room, but she waved him off.

Once back in Paula's bedroom, Chloe riffled through her bag. She hoped she still had the ankh. She'd picked it up weeks ago on a visit to the Boston Museum of Fine Arts. She'd meant to use it as a Christmas gift for one of her colleagues. She could always order another one. If only she hadn't stuck it somewhere else. No, there it was. Still in its tiny plastic bag. She took it out of the plastic before removing it from her purse.

Placing the ankh in the palm of her right hand, she extended it to Paula. "If you wear this ankh on a chain around your neck, it will help you harness and guide your own energy to block off any malignant forces that are threatening you. But you must understand that your own will is the source of your power. Do you understand, Paula?"

"Yes. Oh, yes, I understand."

Chloe took Paula's hand and placed the ankh in the young woman's palm. Then she closed Paula's fingers around it.

A newfound calm flooded the woman's face. Chloe touched Paula's cheek gently. "You'd better get some sleep. You must be exhausted."

The calm disappeared as quickly as it had come. "Stay with me. Oh please. Just tonight. I can't bear to be alone. Not tonight. Please."

Chloe hesitated. The choice was to spend the night here with Paula or go back with Noah. Maybe staying with Paula made more sense.

Noah didn't think so at all. "You can't play guardian angel for this entire town, Chloe. First Lara, now Paula. Besides..." His eyes fell to the mutilated doll Harvey had stuck into a plastic bag. "If you stay, so will I."

"No. We'll be fine here, Noah," Chloe insisted. "You've got to be at the hospital first thing in the morning. You'll be lucky to get six hours sleep as it is. Go home, Noah."

"I'll post a couple of my men outside the house, Noah," Harvey said. "We'll make sure there are no... disturbances."

Chloe walked Noah to the front door while Harvey strolled into the kitchen to make himself a cup of coffee and ostensibly wait for the arrival of his men. But Chloe knew that wasn't Harvey's only reason for lingering behind. He wanted to hear about the conversation she'd had with Paula, a conversation Chloe'd been reluctant to discuss in front of Noah. She told herself it was because what Paula had told her was strictly police business. She probably shouldn't even have shown Harvey the doll while Noah was still in the house. Why had she? Had she wanted to see Noah's reaction? Was it possible, even now, she didn't trust him? *"Beware. The devil wears many guises."* But Noah.

No, it couldn't be Noah. Paula's secret lover? A murderer? No...

"I'm not happy about this, Chloe," Noah was saying at the door. "I'm going to worry all night no matter what. I don't know why I can't stay here and worry with you."

Chloe gave Noah a distracted look. Something was tugging at the back of her mind, but she couldn't quite put her finger on it. Something Paula had said? Something she remembered from the past?

"Chloe?"

"Good night, Noah. I'll speak to you tomorrow," she heard herself say.

Noah lowered his head to kiss her, but Chloe drew back. He straightened up, gave her one last heartfelt look and left.

Harvey was sipping his coffee at the kitchen table. "Water's hot. I wasn't sure if you wanted a cup."

"I don't drink coffee."

"There should be some tea."

"That's okay. I don't want anything." She sat down at the table across from the chief. "I checked in on Paula. She's fast asleep." Chloe had also noticed that Paula had already found a small chain and was wearing the ankh around her neck.

Harvey waited.

"She's mortally afraid to tell me who the father is," Chloe said wearily. "I think she's convinced he's somehow equipped with...supernatural powers."

"Poor girl," Harvey murmured sorrowfully. "Well, maybe after a good night's sleep, she'll realize she's got to speak up."

Chloe hesitated. "She did say something that might help."

"What?"

A tight pressure rose up inside of Chloe. Something flashed before her eyes. Blurred. Too faint to make out. "Whoever murdered Amanda...was someone Amanda thought she could reason with."

Harvey frowned. "Well, Amanda was the type who thought she could reason with just about anyone."

Chloe shut her eyes. Flash. Flash. Clearer now. Silver. A flash of silver. The dagger. The atheme. The answer lay in the sacramental atheme.

"Where is the murder weapon?" Chloe suddenly asked. They both knew that the atheme was, indeed, a murder weapon. Amanda hadn't killed herself: someone she'd hoped she could reason with had guided the drugged woman's hand.

"I have the dagger locked in my office safe," Harvey said quietly.

"Could I come over tomorrow and have another look at it?"

Their eyes met. Chloe knew Harvey was remembering the disturbing response she'd had to the atheme when she'd seen it last. But he nodded.

She watched Harvey drink his coffee. "If only Paula would tell us who the father is," Chloe mused.

"Well, that's not to say he's the one, you know. You say Paula confessed she didn't actually see him put that doll in her car. And that she swore she didn't actually see him with Amanda that night."

"Yes, that's what she says."

Harvey stared at her over the rim of his mug. "But you've got a hunch she did see him that night."

"Yes," Chloe said quietly. She got up. "Maybe I will make myself a cup of tea." She rubbed her neck, her shoulders. Her legs felt stiff as planks and she had a sour taste in her mouth. "Someone had better stay with Paula and her little girl until . . ." she knew she didn't have to finish the sentence.

Harvey nodded, and Chloe turned the fire on under the kettle to reheat the water. Her eyes fixed on the bluish flame. Like the flame, a memory burned in her mind.

The kettle whistled.

"Chloe? Chloe, your water's boiling. What's the matter?" Harvey was beside her, removing the kettle from the flame.

"Chloe?" He touched her shoulder.

"I just remembered something," she said quietly.

"What's that?" Harvey could hear the portent in her voice.

"It was the spring of my senior year at Dorchester. I had an appointment to see Peter Mott in his office. To go over a paper, ostensibly. But, instead he tried to make a . . . move on me. I ran out. I was very upset. That's probably why I forgot . . ."

"Forgot what?" Harvey prodded gently.

"Who Mott was with when I entered his office." Chloe stared at the chief. "He was with Paula Dubois."

Harvey considered that for a moment, but said, "Well, that's not so unusual. She was clerking for him and the other professors in the department."

"I didn't think it was unusual at the time, either." She hesitated, her eyes fixed on Harvey. "Except for one thing. Paula's shirt was . . . buttoned wrong. Like she'd had to do it up in a hurry after I'd knocked."

Chapter Fourteen

"Proof, Chloe. That's what's missing here," Harvey muttered. "And even if we knew for a fact that Mott was Jessie's daddy, what reason would he have for wanting to get rid of Amanda? Or Alice? What was his motive?"

Chloe pursed her lips. "Noah told me there might have been something suspicious and possibly underhanded about one of Mott's land deals. What if Amanda found out that Mott had pulled something dirty? Or what if Paula had confided in her that Mott was the father? Amanda might have threatened to expose him."

Harvey's face reddened. "But you're forgetting something Chloe. Amanda supposedly was in love with Mott."

"And Mott supposedly was in love with Lara." Chloe started pacing Paula's small kitchen. "Maybe Amanda felt if she couldn't have him herself, she'd make sure no one else would want him, either."

Harvey nodded slowly. "I suppose it's possible. Paula might have confided in Amanda. Maybe Amanda confronted Mott. They could have had an argument out there in the glen. Maybe Amanda still had the atheme in her hand and they got into a struggle. Paula might have seen it happening."

"And Lara," Chloe murmured.

"What? What about Lara?"

Something had just hit Chloe. A piece of the puzzle. "Paula may not be the only one protecting the murderer, Harvey. That night, Lara didn't go to the gathering in the glen. But afterward, what if she went out to the glen to meet Mott? What if she found him having an argument with her mother? What if...?" Chloe's mouth went dry. She looked at Harvey. "Yes. That could be what happened. It would certainly explain why she's been behaving so strangely. The strain would be terrible. The guilt. Feeling so torn between her mother and the man she loved." But even as Chloe was fitting together the pieces of the puzzle, something felt forced.

Harvey saw it on her face. "Spit it out, Chloe."

She frowned. "Somehow, I just didn't think Lara was really in love with Peter Mott. At least...not enough in love with him to let him get away with murdering her mother."

Harvey shrugged. "You never really know about love. Let's not forget Alice Donovan. Rumor was she was gaga over Mott, too."

Chloe stared at Harvey. "What if Alice sneaked back to the glen that night, as well? If she saw Mott heading back to talk with Amanda, Alice might have been curious."

"You think all three women, Lara, Paula and Alice, were actual witnesses?"

"They may not have all seen the actual struggle, but they might have seen Mott fleeing from the scene and put two and two together."

Harvey made himself a second cup of instant coffee. No sense worrying about the caffeine. He was already too wired up to sleep tonight. "It's making more and more sense, Chloe. Look at it this way. Mott had three women on his hands. There's Lara. He's supposedly in love with her. Then there's Paula. He figures he can scare her half to death by threatening to do harm to his child. And then there's Alice. She proved simply too big a risk. He might have thought for a while that he could hold her in check since he must have known she was in love with him. But he couldn't very well play on her affections without raising Lara's ire. No, poor Alice simply had to go...."

Harvey kept on talking, but Chloe was filtering out his words. A part of her said Mott was their man. He fit the profile. He had the means and possible motive. There was only one problem. He wasn't the only one who fit. She could play out the same scenario...only change the name. What if Mott wasn't the father of Paula's daughter? Who was to say, just because Mott had made an advance on Paula in his office that day seven years ago, that he'd actually fathered her child? What if Paula had had an affair with someone else at the time? And what if Lara Emory wasn't in love with Peter Mott at all? What if she was only using him to get back at her ex-husband for wanting the divorce? What if Lara was still in love with Noah? And what if, seven years ago, Noah and Paula—

"Chloe? You've got one of those looks on your face."

Harvey's voice dragged her from her disturbing ruminations. She stared dully at the chief. "I was just thinking...."

"You feeling one of your hunches?"

She felt sick inside. "No. More like one of my hunches isn't feeling...right."

THE NEXT MORNING Paula, despite the ankh, was in a bad state. Mildred arrived early to look after her and Jessie. When Harvey showed up to see about questioning Paula again, Mildred declared the young woman was in no shape to talk. If Paula was going to admit what she knew, it was going to take time and patience. Harvey put a man outside the house, just in case Jessie's so-called daddy made another visit.

Chloe was running out of time and patience. She decided what she had to do. She had to talk to Lara. One thing she felt certain of, Lara knew a lot more than she was telling. And Chloe felt a desperate need to know what it was. She felt a desperate need to feel convinced that Noah was in no way involved in this vile affair.

Paula, grateful to Chloe for the ankh and for staying with her for the night, offered Chloe the use of her station wagon for the day. Chloe decided to drive out to the Emory house without phoning first. She didn't want to give Lara a chance to make an excuse not to see her.

In the early-morning sunshine, the Emory house looked sad and withered. Chloe wondered if Lara really did plan to live here permanently or if she would sell. Even if it did mean splitting the proceeds with Thad, it would give Lara a chance for a fresh start. But Chloe knew that Lara would need to do more than to sell her house to get that fresh start. She would have to come clean. She would have to send a man she loved to prison for murder.

Chloe rang the doorbell. No one answered. She peered in the glass panel of the door. It didn't look as if anyone was home. She walked around to the side of the house. Lara's car wasn't parked in front of the garage. Chloe stared at the closed garage doors, remembering Lara telling her she never parked the car in the garage because there was too much junk in there.

Still, maybe Lara had cleaned it out and pulled her car inside. Might as well check, Chloe decided.

There was a row of glass panels on the old-fashioned garage doors. They were large wooden double doors that opened out from the center. Chloe had to stand on tiptoe to peer in. She tried one side, but the windows proved too gray and dirty for her to see into. She went to the other door, pressed her hand against the glass as she tried to see inside. The pane gave way, falling inward, shattering as it hit the hard cement floor of the garage.

Hot fear leaped into Chloe, its source unfathomable. Nervously, she peered inside the garage through the opening she'd inadvertently made. Lara's car wasn't there. Now that she could see into the space, Chloe saw only what Lara had said was there. Piles of old furniture, cardboard boxes, outdated lawn and garden equipment, a couple of old bikes.

But the fear didn't abate. Chloe tried to swallow away the lump in her throat without success. Her hand moved inexorably to the door handle, even as her body drew instinctively away from the garage door.

This is ridiculous, she thought. Just open the door, look inside to satisfy yourself that there's nothing to be afraid of, and stop letting these inexplicable terrors get the best of you, she ordered herself.

It wasn't easy to follow her own command, but she dredged up her courage and pulled the right side door handle. Part of her hoped to find it locked.

To Chloe's consternation, it gave way easily, albeit creakily. She stood at the open door, unable to make her legs move. There was a repulsive smell. It oozed out of the broken-down furniture, the cardboard boxes, the walls themselves. Chloe tried to tell herself it was just the smell of mildew and rot. But it was stronger. More vile.

The garage had a great dead soundlessness about it. Only the beat of the pulse in Chloe's own ears offered any relief from it. And it wasn't enough. Fear licked at her, wet, cloying, mingling with the sharp, awful odor in the air.

Was it the autumn wind gusting against her back that nudged her inside? Was it some unconscious decision to prove she had control over her fears that brought movement to her legs? Was some unseen force bidding her enter?

There was an open box of papers against one wall, another stack of them on top of a box beside it. Had Lara been packing them away? Or looking for something inside? Fighting to master her fear, Chloe's curiosity drew her over to the box.

It was just as she was looking at the papers—she saw they were the pages of a screenplay—that she heard the faint sound. Behind her. Cutting through the silence like a knife. A shadow blocked the crack of sunlight from the opening she'd left in the garage door.

As she turned and saw who was there, she let out a high-pitched cry. It was Peter Mott.

"Are you crazy, Chloe? Put down that damn pitchfork."

"Just back up, Peter. Back away from the door," Chloe warned, jabbing the air with her makeshift weapon.

"Okay, okay. Just relax," he said, stepping away from the garage door and onto the driveway. "For goodness sake, Chloe, you'd think I was going to attack you or something."

"You tried it once before," she hissed, urging Mott back further until she felt it was safe to step out of the garage without him making a grab for her.

"I thought you were a burglar. I came here to see Lara and I saw her car wasn't here and the garage door was open. I thought she was being robbed."

"Where is she? Where is Lara?" she asked warily.

"I just told you, I thought she was here. I came up to have breakfast with her."

"You didn't think I was a burglar."

Mott screwed up his face. "Okay, since you're the psychic, what did I think?"

"You thought it was Paula in the garage."

A muscle jumped in his jaw.

"You saw the Pies to Go-Go wagon parked out front. Paula's car."

"Okay. Maybe I did think it was Paula," he admitted.

She stepped around him, giving herself a wide berth, keeping the pitchfork aimed at him.

"And what were you planning to do if you found her in the garage?" Chloe demanded.

Mott merely shrugged. "Find out why she was snooping around Lara's property. Come to think of it, why were you, Chloe?"

"I don't see that that's any of your business."

"Well, I don't know about that. It's going to be my business soon enough."

"What does that mean?"

"It means I've asked Lara to marry me."

"When?"

"I proposed to Lara a few days before Amanda . . . died. Lara said she had to think about it. And then, losing her mother, naturally, she didn't feel ready to make a decision. Anyway, last night, at around eight-thirty she phoned me and said yes."

"At eight-thirty?" That meant Lara'd made the call soon after having had dinner with Noah.

"So typical of Lara to decide on impulse. I wanted to come right over, but she put me off. Said she had one of her headaches. I came over here this morning so we could celebrate. Actually when I first spotted Paula's station wagon, I thought Lara might have asked her over to discuss catering the wedding. Then, when I saw Lara wasn't home, I wondered what the hell Paula was doing nosing around the garage."

Chloe was doing some wondering of her own. "Did Amanda know you'd asked Lara to marry you?"

Mott stiffened. "Why do you want to know?"

Chloe's hand tightened around the handle of the pitchfork. "Is that what you and Amanda fought about that night?"

Mott's jaw twitched. "What night?"

"The night she died," Chloe said in a low, tight voice.

"Look here, Chloe. If you're trying to blame Amanda's suicide on me, you're way off base. I may not have been Amanda's first choice for a son-in-law, but I assure you she never said anything like *"Over my dead body."* He gave a glib laugh.

Chloe let the *suicide* ride. "Wasn't Amanda in love with you, Peter?"

"I certainly didn't encourage it. And we certainly didn't fight about her feelings toward me or my asking her daughter to marry me. Not that night or any other night. Anyway, I seriously doubt Amanda would have taken her own life because of unrequited love. That wasn't her style."

"Really?" Then Chloe thought of another motive altogether. "Maybe you and Amanda fought about something else."

"Obviously you have some notion as to what that might have been," Mott intoned superciliously.

"Maybe she found out that you'd swindled that poor old farmer out of a piece of property that turned out to be worth a pretty penny to Dorchester College and the Savings and Loan."

Mott's jaw stiffened. Chloe was sure she'd touched a nerve. But he quickly recovered. "That land transaction was entirely open and aboveboard. Just a piece of good luck. If your theory wasn't so laughable, I could charge you with defamation of character." He glared at her. "Now, are you finished theorizing, Ms. Hayes?"

"No, as a matter of fact I'm not. I've got one more theory as to what you and Amanda might have fought about."

"Really, this is getting tiresome."

"I think it's possible that Paula Dubois confided in Amanda that you were Jessie's father. Maybe Amanda threatened to use that knowledge against you—"

"I hardly know Paula Dubois. And I most certainly am not the father of her child. I never had relations with the woman, so unless you think I impregnated her through some supernatural means, Ms. Hayes, you'll have to pin the paternity on someone else." Mott gave Chloe a sly smirk that made her skin crawl, but nonetheless she did believe him, at least about Paula Dubois.

"Now, Ms. Hayes, unless you intend to use that pitchfork on me, I think you'd better grab a broomstick instead and fly off."

"Yes, you'd like that, wouldn't you, Peter. How nicely it's all working out for you. Chairmanship, land developer, soon-to-be husband of a wealthy heiress and owner of thirty acres of prime property on Honeysuckle Hill. Lara told me you wanted to buy this place from her. But it's so much cleverer of you to get it this way. Just think, a savings of three hundred thousand dollars."

"I happen to love Lara." He gave Chloe a hard, cold stare.

He's good, Chloe thought. Doesn't even flinch. Doesn't even look threatened. That's what was troubling her. Could this be the same person who had felt so threatened by her presence in Thornhill that he lured her out to the Grange with a phony letter, placed that vile doll in her car, surreptitiously started a campaign against her in town so that people like Karin Niels felt compelled to burn her in effigy...

Chloe met Mott's unflinching gaze. There was definitely something crafty and repulsive about the man. A womanizer, a cheat, a manipulator. Yes, he was all of those things. But a murderer?

No, she thought. There was something dark and sinister about the man who murdered Amanda and Alice; there was a madness about him, a madness disguised... *"Beware, the devil comes in many guises."*

Chloe let the pitchfork drop to the ground. Mott made no move toward her. She wasn't surprised. He had no real reason to harm her. So what if she saw through him. If anything, he was probably proud of the very qualities she found so reprehensible about him.

"Listen," he called out to her, as she got back into the station wagon. "When you do see Paula, tell her Lara and I will be in touch with her about our wedding plans. Oh, and if you're still around, Chloe, do come watch us take our vows at the church. Or don't witches go to church?" He gave her a sly grin.

Chloe gunned the motor and shot out of the driveway, leaving Mott coughing from smoke and dust. It was the only bright spot in her otherwise depressing morning.

She didn't know her destination at first. All she knew was that she was looking for Lara. Lara was still the key. Chloe felt it in her gut. She felt something else, too. A new fear. Where would Lara have gone so early in the morning? And wouldn't she have guessed her new fiancé would come over first thing to celebrate? Wouldn't she have waited?

Or had Lara gone to a particular place to gloat? Thad's voice slid unbidden into her mind. *"She's still in love with Noah..."*

A car horn beeped behind her. Only then did Chloe become aware she'd brought the station wagon to a dead halt in the middle of a street. And then she gasped. It wasn't just any street. It was Maywood Street. Her car had stopped right beside number seven Maywood, the quaint Cape Cod style home of Dr. Noah Bright.

The driver in the car behind her beeped again, longer this time, and with trembling hands Chloe managed to steer her car over to the side of the road so the driver could pass.

The front door opened. Noah stood there, no doubt curious as to why someone was beeping so much outside.

From behind the wheel, Chloe watched Noah's puzzled expression as he saw the Pies to Go-Go station wagon. Then he saw who it was behind the wheel.

Their gazes met and locked. Shadows of broken emotions flickered across Noah's face.

I love you, she thought. *Surely, I couldn't love you if . . .*

He was walking toward her.

Her body tensed.

He opened the car door, extended his hand. Cool, firm, strong. A doctor's hand. A healer's hand. *Trust me,* the gesture said. Tentatively, nervously, she reached her hand out to his.

Their shadows shot across the walk as they went hand in hand into the house. Once inside, he didn't let her go. He pulled her to him and kissed her. An urgent, searing kiss, yet somehow pained and tender.

She'd never been kissed like that before.

When he released her, she was stunned to see tears in his eyes. Now there was no masking the pain in his features. Anguish, longing, despair, love. It was all there, written into the lines and curves of his face. He stood there before her exposed—a man without disguise. *I know this man. I understand this man. I believe in this man. I love this man.*

And then aloud, her voice echoed her thoughts. "I love you."

He cupped her face as though it were a priceless, fragile jewel.

It took a moment for him to find his voice. "When I left you last night...I saw...a look in your eyes. Distrust. Doubt." He ran his tongue across his dry lips. "Fear. You thought I might be...the one. And then, just a minute ago, when I first saw you, that look was still there. You thought..."

She pressed her lips to his to silence him. And then she was kissing him fiercely, greedily. It was Noah who drew back.

"What made you change your mind? What made you...?"

She smiled tremulously. "I'm psychic."

Noah didn't smile back. "No, that's not it."

"What is it, then?"

"You love me. They say love is blind. Aren't you afraid your feelings may be coloring your reason?"

She stepped back, shaken by his remark. But he reached out and gripped her shoulders.

"I don't want you to have any doubts about me, Chloe. I don't think I could ever again bear to see the look I saw in your eyes last night. But I'm afraid, until this madman is found, it remains a...possibility."

"He will be found. I feel like I'm so close, Noah."

"That scares me more than all the rest. Chloe, if anything happened to you..."

She wiped away the tears on his cheeks. "Nothing's going to happen to me, darling."

"Yes, I forgot, the invincible, unsinkable Chloe Hayes."

"No. Not invincible or unsinkable. It's just that I'll be damned if I'm going to let anything happen to me now...now that we've found each other again. Now that I'm not afraid to tell you how much I love you, how much I need you. Oh, I do need you, Noah. I need your passion, your tenderness, your comfort, your strengths, even your weaknesses. I needed you seven years ago, but I was too scared to admit it or to really let myself show it. If I had, maybe everything would have been different. I don't know. For so long, I blamed you for everything. And now that I see I was equally to blame, I—''

"Blame is such a useless emotion, Chloe. And we've wasted enough time, hurt long enough, cried long enough." He slid his hands up under her shirt, his palms against her cool, soft skin. "I wish we could stop wasting time, but I know that we're not going to be able to get on with our lives until this madman is found."

"Madman." She rolled the word over on her tongue. "I wonder..."

"I wish you'd leave this to Harvey," Noah implored.

"Maybe he isn't mad at all. What if, on that night, he got into an argument with Amanda over something she'd discovered about him, and she threatened to expose him? That would explain the note. She might have been writing it out there in the glen when he appeared. A note threatening to expose him, rather than the start of a suicide note. Maybe he saw what she was writing and they argued, possibly struggled. Maybe he didn't even mean to kill her."

"But the hyoscine. If he'd drugged her, he must have meant to...harm her."

Chloe frowned. "Maybe he only meant to put her in a more amenable frame of mind to listen to reason. And Amanda believed, in turn, she could reason with him successfully."

"But it didn't work."

"No," Chloe said sadly. "And to make it worse for him, three women here in Thornhill knew enough to pose a serious threat to his getting away with his crime. He silenced one of them. He's got Paula scared enough about the safety of her daughter to refuse to come forward. And then there's Lara." Chloe gripped Noah's sleeve. "Lara. She wasn't home this morning. I went up to see her."

"She might have gone into town for breakfast. Or spent the night with Mott."

"When you had dinner with her last night, did she tell you she'd decided to marry Peter Mott?"

"No, but I'm not surprised. I don't think Lara ever could stand the thought of being alone. And there's been something between them for a long time. Maybe it'll work out for them. I suppose stranger things have happened."

"She wasn't with Mott last night. I saw him this morning. He came up to the Emory house looking for her, too."

"Maybe she went over to her brother's place," Noah suggested.

A minute later, after a brief conversation with Thad, Noah hung up and shook his head. "He hasn't seen or heard from her. I just caught him on his way out the door, heading over to the college. He said he'd check at Red's to see if she was having breakfast over there. He'll call here to let me know if he finds her."

Chloe nodded. She saw the worry on Noah's face. This time she didn't feel threatened or jealous. She wouldn't have loved Noah as much as she did if he didn't feel compassion and concern, even for an ex-wife who had hurt and betrayed him.

Chloe started for the door.

"Where will you be going?" Noah asked anxiously.

"The police station. I'd better see Harvey," she said. There was something she had to see at the station. The atheme. Somehow, Chloe felt certain the atheme was the key.

"PLEASE, PLEASE don't hurt me," Lara whispered.

"Don't whine, Lara. You know how I hate it when you whine."

She stopped, afraid now even to breathe. *I know this man. This man won't hurt me. He's just reminding me who's boss. Okay, okay, I'm reminded.* She dared to take some deep breaths.

"You don't have to tie me up, you know. It's a silly game." She kept her voice low and seductive, kept her ears tuned for sounds. Maybe someone would find her, rescue her.

"You actually are a little crazy, Lara. I don't think anyone in Thornhill will be surprised."

"Surprised?" It came out as a squeak.

"That you'd take your own life, my sweet."

Tears blinded her. "No. No. Why? Why are you doing this to me?"

"You're just too unpredictable, my darling Lara. You simply can't be trusted."

"But, that's not true. I haven't betrayed you. I've done everything you asked. I told Harvey Mead Mother died because of the possession of her body by evil spirits. I did everything else you wanted me to do. I haven't made any mistakes. I told you I'd never breathe a word. I told you that night in the glen, I wouldn't give you away. She drove you to it."

His smile was dark and insidious. "At first I thought that damn drug would never take effect. And then, when it did, it was almost too easy to guide her hand. Why, I think she even half believed she *was* possessed by an evil spirit."

"But you really didn't mean it. She provoked you . . ."

"Don't you get it, yet, Lara. I wanted her dead. I was sick and tired of her threats, her endless disapproving looks. And then to make matters worse, Paula had to go and confide in her about my being the one who got her pregnant."

"Paula was such a little fool," Lara said earnestly. "She had to know she could never mean anything to you."

"One thing about you, darling Lara. You always did take my side."

"I still do. I love you. I've always loved you."

"I know. But, this is nothing personal, darling. It's simply a matter of expediency. And it fits into my future plans." His voice was smooth, as blank as a chalkless blackboard. His smile was grim and secretive and oh, so final.

For the first time Lara saw that there really was no reasoning with him. Her mother couldn't do it. Nor could she. And suddenly Lara knew that Chloe was her last and only hope.

"ARE YOU SURE about this, Chloe?" Harvey asked cautiously, his hand on the handle of the safe.

"Yes." Her voice rang against the walls of his office.

As he withdrew the bag holding the atheme, Chloe could hear the ragged intake of her own breath. But she willed a cool calm.

It lasted until Harvey retrieved the atheme from the bag and extended it to her. "It's okay to handle it now...if you want to."

Flash. Flash. Flash. She saw her hand taking hold of the hilt of the dagger. She could see the muscles in her forearm harden as she gripped it tightly. All of her awareness shrank to a small point that was the atheme. She stared at it. Memories fluttered against the edges of her mind. Seeing the atheme for the first time in Amanda's class. That awful hallucinatory experience on her way to the glen just before her graduation. And then that first day in Harvey's office when just the sight of the atheme had caused that inexplicable spell of panic. She felt panic again now, but she was more prepared for it, could keep it at bay.

She forced herself to take deep, steady breaths as she studied the atheme intently. Then she closed her eyes and let her fingers run lightly over the hilt with its carvings.

Flash. Flash. Flash. A flicker of silver now. Caught in a ray of light. Her eyes began to burn, a blurry smear of a vision slowly taking hold.

"No. Something's wrong," she whispered.

"Wrong? What's wrong?" Harvey asked, baffled.

"It doesn't have the power," she murmured.

"Power?" He recalled her reaction to the atheme the other day. She'd certainly felt its power then.

Chloe slowly opened her eyes. She saw by the expression on Harvey's face what had gone through his mind. She smiled faintly. "It wasn't the atheme itself that made me panic when you started to show it to me the other day. My reaction was connected to my last memory of seeing it, seven years ago."

She stared at the atheme in her hand. "Maybe if I hadn't had that reaction...if I'd actually taken hold of the atheme...I might have understood. I might have realized what it was all about."

"I'm afraid I don't follow you, Chloe."

"This isn't Amanda's sacred atheme," Chloe said with firm conviction. "It's a copy."

"I don't get it," Harvey said, scratching his head. "This here is the murder weapon, Chloe. No doubt about it."

"Amanda must have discovered he'd made a switch. That must have been what they were fighting about. He'd stolen her atheme and she was threatening to report the theft unless he gave it back."

"What's the big deal about the atheme? Isn't one of these daggers much like any other?"

"Amanda's atheme was very special."

"Isn't that just . . . superstition?"

"Maybe in part."

"What else?"

"It was also quite valuable."

"A dagger? How valuable?"

The color drained from Chloe's face. "Valuable enough . . . to commit murder over."

Harvey stared at Chloe. "You really think so? Damn. You mean, all this time, it was greed, pure and simple."

"Nothing simple about it," Chloe whispered, a new fear slowly, irrevocably spreading across her face. "We've got to find Lara, Harvey. We've got to find her before it's too late."

Chapter Fifteen

A dissonant clanging was stabbing at Chloe's head, a memory rubbing at her mind.

"You're sure Lara wasn't home," Harvey was asking her.

Chloe started to nod, but then realized she couldn't really be sure of that. "She didn't answer my ring or Mott's, and I just took it for granted..." A whisper. A rasp of fear.

"I think I'll take a drive up to the Emory house and have myself a look around." He slowly pushed his swivel chair back from his desk.

"Do you think...she could be there?" She had a difficult time getting the words past her throat.

The chief leaned forward in his chair, meeting her gaze. His expression didn't change, but his eyes did. They darkened, grew more intense. "Do you, Chloe?"

Did she? She closed her eyes letting all her senses turn inward. What came to her was a disturbing rush of jumbled thoughts, blurred images, warring emotions...fears. The turbulence within her was reflected in her features. She looked drawn, taut, tattered around the edges. A fierce, insistent pulse rapped at her temples. Strangely it was not only the pounding of her own fears, but someone else's terrors woven in.

She opened her eyes to see Harvey's quiet, watchful gaze. There was no clarity to her feelings, only a growing sense of helplessness and desolation. When clarity did come, would it be too late? For Lara? For others? For herself? She clasped her hands together, her whole body trembling. Instinct. Intuition. A hunch. Events crowding on events, linking, forming a picture that was too awful to envision.

Harvey rose, shuffled his feet. "I'd better take that ride. Maybe Lara just went out grocery shopping. Could be she's back home now."

Chloe leaped up. "I'm coming with you."

Harvey hesitated, and Chloe knew why. The chief was thinking that maybe if Lara was home, she might not be in any condition to answer doorbells.

"I won't fall apart on you, Harvey, I promise."

As he was trying to make up his mind whether to let her tag along, there was a knock on his office door.

Harvey's eyebrows raised a notch as he opened the door to find Noah on the other side.

"Any word on Lara?" Noah asked without preamble. His face was slightly flushed and his hair was tousled, as if he'd been running his fingers through it.

Harvey shook his head.

"Did you hear from Thad?" Chloe asked Noah anxiously.

"He called the house about fifteen minutes after you left. Lara wasn't at Red's. He checked all the other breakfast spots in town, even the college cafeteria. He told me he'd stop up at the anthropology department to see if maybe she was over at Mott's office. I told him to call into the station house if he had any news."

"How's Thad taking this?" Harvey asked.

Noah shrugged. "How would you take it if your sister was missing and some madman, who'd already killed two women, was on the loose?"

"Well," Harvey said in a calming voice, "we don't really know she's missing yet. All we know is we can't find her at the moment. Could be she took off grocery shopping or on an innocent little jaunt someplace... maybe even down to Boston for a little getaway."

Chloe grabbed onto the possibility. "You might be right, Harvey. She might have gone shopping for a wedding trousseau. Peter Mott told me this morning that they're getting married. Yes, I can see Lara rushing out first thing in the morning. Boston's over a two-hour drive from here, so it would make sense that she left early. And her car's gone."

Harvey shifted his weight. "I'll just nose around up at her house. Probably a waste of time, but..."

"I still want to go with you," Chloe insisted. For all her longing to believe that Lara really had gone for an innocent shopping jaunt, anxiety continued to flow through her. And there was something more. Something she tried in vain to dispel. A premonition. A premonition that still held her in a strong, murderous grasp.

Noah, whose ability to read her mind seemed to be ever sharpening, gave Chloe a tense look. "I'll meet you both up there. I just need to make a stop at the hospital first." His voice was gravelly, laced with fatigue and tension.

LARA ACHED all over from trying to struggle free of the ropes he'd used to tie her to the wooden chair. She'd made no progress. If anything she was in worse shape than before, her wrists and ankles raw from her fruitless effort. The room was stifling, even though she could hear the howl of the wind outside. Her throat was so dry. If only he'd given her some water to drink. If only he'd listened to her pleas.

She was scared. So scared she couldn't bear to think. If only... If only...

She started to cry, her mind hurling back to that fateful night. If only she'd taken her mother's concerns and fears more seriously. If only she hadn't defended him, told her mother how terrible she was to say such things about him. If only she hadn't gone down to the glen later that night, after all. If only she hadn't seen... what she had seen.

Her sobs were choking her. Could someone choke to death on their own tears? she wondered.

A sound of footsteps cut off her sobs. He was back. His steps were approaching the darkened room again. How long had he left her alone? Minutes, hours? She'd lost track of the time.

The door opened and he stepped inside.

He was a stranger now, someone she didn't know at all. Even his features looked different. Memories slid into her mind, memories of the two of them together. But now they seemed to be memories of another pair altogether. He was different then, and even she seemed to be a different person then. Silent tears ran down her cheeks.

"Don't cry, Lara." His voice was soft, almost tender now. Could it be that while he was gone he'd realized that what he was doing to her was wrong, evil, obscene?

"I don't know...why...you don't trust me...anymore," she whispered.

He studied her thoughtfully with cold, hard eyes. "I can't afford to take any chances, Lara. Things have gotten so much more complicated. I hadn't planned on these complications. Now, I have no other choice but to take care of them. Chloe's proving even more of an irritation than I'd anticipated. She doesn't scare off very easily. Not like seven years ago when she fled in such a panic.''

He sighed, shook his head, fixed his eyes on Lara without really seeing her. ''It doesn't matter. She's turned into quite an extraordinary woman. The problem is she may be just a little too extraordinary.''

''She is a psychic,'' Lara said emphatically. Her mind started to race. Maybe if she could manage to get him to focus his concerns on Chloe he'd leave her be. ''If Chloe stays here in Thornhill much longer, especially if you spend more time together, she'll sense it. She'll know it was you. And what will you do then? She's the one you should have tied up here. Not me. Chloe's the one you have to fear.''

''Shut up,'' he said sharply, any hint of tenderness eradicated. ''Don't worry your pretty little head about Chloe. I'm going to marry her.''

''What?''

''You heard me.''

''You're crazy. You really are crazy. She won't marry you. She doesn't trust you now.''

''Oh, but you're wrong, Lara. She does trust me. And I'll reinforce that trust. I've got that all nicely planned.''

''And me? What about . . . me?''

He gave a slow, insidious, devilish smile. ''I told you earlier. I've got plans for you, too, Lara dearest. Shall I give you the details?''

Lara listened, his words curling through her, paralyzing her . . . a devil's voice twisted with a calculated madness.

THE BLEAK, gray November morning seemed to close down over the cruiser as Harvey and Chloe headed up Landon Road to the Emory house. The wind had kicked up, a steady howl sneaking in through the windows of the car, a droning background sound for Harvey's intermittently squawking police radio.

As soon as the drive had begun, Chloe had been struck with an odd sensation, a feeling that there was something she wasn't remembering. The closer the cruiser got to the Emory house, the stronger the sensation. What was it? Something important. Something she'd discovered. The memory was like a butterfly, fluttering, elusive, taunting, impossible for her to grab.

Harvey pulled up in front of the Emory house. Before getting out, he looked over at Chloe.

"Why don't you stay put? If I find anything, I'll...come tell you."

Chloe started to protest but, realizing that Harvey was trying to protect her, she changed her mind. "Okay. I'll just walk around outside here."

Harvey patted her arm. "Good girl."

She watched him get out of the car and climb up to the porch. He walked over to the front door, rang the bell. Once. Twice. On the third ring, he kept his finger on the buzzer for a good thirty seconds. Nothing.

He tried the door. Locked. He looked back at Chloe. Shrugged. Scratched his head. Chloe knew that if he was to go by the book, he'd have to return to town and get a judge to issue him a warrant.

She watched him hesitate, then bend down and lift up the door mat. A key was taped to the bottom of the mat. Just a lucky guess, Chloe wondered, or did Harvey have prior knowledge? What was it Noah had said to her the other day? She remembered it was something like—you start nosing around in a small town like Thornhill and there's no telling what kind of dirt you'll dig up, how many innocent people's private affairs might be made public.

Chloe stepped out of the cruiser. With the wind had come a drizzle. She felt a prickling on the back of her neck. She told herself it was just raindrops, but she knew that wasn't it. It was a haunting, inside of her. Pressing, claustrophobic.

She considered returning to the shelter of the cruiser. But then she turned up the collar of her tweed wool blazer and wandered over to the side of the house, just to check once again that Lara's car hadn't returned.

When she was in sight of the garage, she stopped abruptly. As if nature had been timed to coincide with her arrival, a bolt of lightning split the sky overhead. The flash was followed, moments later, by a fierce rumble of thunder. A piercing, violent clap that raised the hairs on her arms.

Staring ahead at the garage, Chloe wiped the back of her hand across her face. Sweat mingled with raindrops on her skin. She shivered, her gaze fixed on the garage doors. They were closed. She distinctly remembered that she'd left one of the doors wide open when she'd scooted out of there, this morning. Had Mott closed it after she'd gone? Or had someone else been here?

She looked back to the house. Should she go find Harvey? Again, she felt that strange magnetic pull drawing her to the garage.

She started up the driveway. She'd just take a quick look into the garage. Peek in through the opening left by the window pane she'd knocked out earlier. If she noticed anything out of place, or different in any way, she'd go back for Harvey.

On first glance, the inside of the garage looked unchanged. And yet . . . there was a terrible pressure in her chest. And the smell, that vile, putrid smell was even stronger than before.

And then, with a suddenness that arrested her breath, she remembered what it was that had been eluding her memory. That cardboard box. The one with the pile of papers beside it; the manuscript on top. A screenplay. *Draw Down the Moon* by Thad Emory. *Draw down the moon . . .* That was a common phrase used by witches. Was that what his screenplay was about? She'd meant to look at it more closely, but she'd been distracted—more to the point, terrified—by Peter Mott's arrival, and her panic had made her forget all about the screenplay. Now that she'd remembered it, she couldn't for the life of her figure out why it had seemed so important.

Curiosity temporarily dislodged her fears. She opened the garage door, noticing immediately that the box was now closed, the papers that had been beside it were now piled on top of the closed carton.

Mott—or someone—had come inside after she'd left. The realization, like the stale, foul aroma in the garage, seeped into her. The contents of that box had held a fascination for someone besides her.

The box was on top of a stack of larger cartons all of which were pushed out about two feet from the rear wall of the garage. Chloe moved around the old furniture and garden equipment to get to it. Blinking against the dimness of the room, she touched objects on the way to the now closed carton, as if to ground herself. Outside, the drizzle had become a true rain which pounded down on the old cedar-shingled roof.

As soon as she got to the carton, Chloe felt the breath rush out of her. An invisible fist in her gut. Her hand was trembling badly as she set aside the pile of papers and opened the box.

The screenplay wasn't inside the box. Chloe's fingers curled around a thick stack of bank statements. She lifted them and then stared into the box. Slowly, like a blind person reading braille, she guided her fingers over the sheet of paper revealed beneath the pile of statements she'd set aside.

Faint indentations. She traced them timorously with her index finger. But she knew. She already knew. *The atheme.* This was where he'd hidden the real atheme. And then, this morning after she'd left, he must have come back for it.

She glanced down at the floor. First all she saw was a scattering of papers. On closer examination she saw that the pages were from Thad's screenplay, tossed aside. As she knelt down for a closer look, she saw . . . the tip of a shoe edging out from behind the cartons.

Chloe's whole body felt limp. She rocked back and forth on the balls of her feet. She held her breath against the stench. The awful stench. The stench of death. . . .

"Chloe? Chloe, you in here? Oh, there you are."

Noah's familiar voice broke through the eerie hush that permeated the room. Chloe let out the breath she'd been holding. "Noah . . ."

The raspy sound of her voice made Noah rush to her side. He took gentle hold of her as he, too, saw the tip of that shoe poking out from behind the cartons.

"Hold tight."

She nodded numbly.

Chloe's voice was a faint whisper. "Is he . . . dead?" But she already knew the answer before Noah nodded.

"Where's Harvey? In the house still?" Noah asked gently.

"Yes," she whispered.

"Come on, let's go find him."

Gladly Chloe let Noah lead her out of the garage. It was no longer raining. The sun had broken through the clouds. Chloe hardly noticed.

"Why Mott?" Noah mused. "Why kill Peter Mott?"

Chloe froze. "I think . . . it was my fault."

Noah turned to her with a stunned expression. "What?"

"When he saw me by that carton in the garage earlier this morning—"

"You're not making any sense, Chloe."

But she knew she was making all the sense in the world. "Something drew me into the garage this morning. When I walked inside, I saw that open carton . . . the papers . . . and . . ." She gave Noah a wild look. "I sensed the presence of the atheme. He'd hidden the atheme in the carton, under the papers, only I didn't realize it then. I don't think Peter had any idea about the atheme. It was just . . . curiosity. He was merely wondering why I was so interested in that carton. If only I'd known at the time the atheme was there. It was the screenplay that drew my interest. A screenplay of Thad's. The title, *Draw Down the Moon,* made me think it was a play about witchcraft. I wondered about it. I don't know why."

"And you think, after you left, Peter went to see what was in the carton, and . . ."

"Who knows if he even found the atheme?" Chloe said wearily. "I guess he simply picked up that screenplay and was looking at it when . . ." She shivered and Noah put his arm around her. "The murderer must have come back at that moment for the sacred dagger. He saw Peter by the carton and . . . killed him."

Noah's expression remained puzzled. "What I don't get is, how'd the atheme get there in the first place? Harvey had the murder weapon under lock and key at the station house."

"The murder weapon is still at the station house," Chloe said quietly. "It's an excellent copy of the real atheme which must have been stolen sometime before Amanda's

last...coven. She must have known. During the ceremony, when she raised the atheme skyward, she must have
sensed that it wasn't the real one.''

Noah looked skeptical. "You're not trying to tell me the
real dagger had true supernatural powers."

Chloe sighed. "For some people, certain objects
can...generate a force. Magic? Wishful thinking? The
power of suggestion? I don't know what to call it. I only
know that atheme was sacred to Amanda."

"And to the murderer, it seems," Noah reflected.

Chloe shook her head. "No. To the murderer, the
atheme is power of a different sort. Amanda once told
me—and apparently at least one other person—that, in
certain markets, her atheme could bring in a small fortune."

Noah's mouth dropped. Just then, Harvey stepped out
of the back door of the house and saw Noah and Chloe
standing in the driveway. He smiled at them and waved.
"The house is empty."

Unfortunately Noah and Chloe couldn't say the same
about the garage.

AN AMBULANCE from the hospital carted away Mott's
corpse on a stretcher. Harvey and the rest of the crime
team, finished their work and took their leave. Noah guided
Chloe to his car to drive her back to town.

"You better take me over to the station house," Chloe
said. "I left Paula's wagon there."

"Okay. You drive it back to Paula's. I'll follow you over,
and after you drop it off, we can go back to my place."

"Don't you have to be at the hospital?"

"We'll have some lunch first and then I'll head over to
the hospital." He hesitated. "We need to talk, Chloe. I
know this isn't the best time to discuss...us, but...my

head's been spinning since you came back into my life. How often do people get a second chance?"

"Noah..."

"Listen to me, Chloe. When this awful business is over, I don't want you to go back to Boston. I want you to stay here."

"Stay?" Chloe's voice caught.

Noah smiled tentatively. "Stay with me. Spend your life with me. Marry me, Chloe."

"Noah..."

"I know. Lousy timing. Seems my timing's always lousy. But I love you, Chloe. And I don't want to lose you again."

"It's all happened so quickly, Noah. My head's been spinning, too."

"Do you love me, Chloe?"

"Yes." No hesitation. No need to think it over. Tears filled her eyes. "Yes, I love you, Noah." Her eyes fixed on him.

"Okay," he whispered solemnly, meeting her gaze. "Okay, then we can talk about our future after...after we find...Lara. After this is...over."

At Noah's mention of Lara's name, Chloe felt a sharp stab of awareness. "Lara isn't dead," Chloe whispered. "I can feel her presence. But it's so weak. I'm scared for her, Noah. I don't know how much longer—"

"Chloe."

"I know it sounds crazy to you. Vibrations, emanations, premonitions."

He released one hand from the wheel and clasped her wrist. "No. I wish it sounded crazy. What scares me is...it doesn't."

Chloe closed her eyes. "Lara's in danger. I think he means to kill her."

Noah's grip on her wrist tightened. "Who, Chloe? Who is he?"

"I thought, this morning, it must be Mott. I thought he might have lied about proposing to Lara to throw us off the track." She stared at Noah's hand clasping her wrist. "But it wasn't Mott."

"No," Noah said softly. "It wasn't Mott."

At first Chloe was silent. But then, suddenly words tumbled out. "Noah, we've got to go back. We've got to go back to Amanda's garage." Her voice was shrill, her stomach cramping.

"You think the atheme's still there?"

"No. No, he took the atheme."

"Then . . . why go back? What's there?"

"Please, Noah. Just turn the car around. Hurry. Please hurry."

Chapter Sixteen

When they were just down the road from the Emory place, Chloe put her hand on Noah's arm. "Let's go the rest of the way on foot."

He shot her a puzzled look, but pulled the car over to the shoulder of the road and switched off the ignition. "You think he's gone back there again?"

"I don't know," Chloe whispered, uncertainty creeping into her voice. "It pays to play it safe."

Noah hesitated as she opened her car door. Then he leaned across the seat and flipped open the glove compartment. There was a gleaming snub-nosed revolver inside.

A gasp of alarm escaped Chloe's lips as Noah took the gun. He touched her cheek with his other palm. She leaned into the pressure of his hand

"Noah . . ." Her voice was plaintive.

He kissed her trembling lips. "I'm just playing it safe. For both our sakes."

A lump welled up in her throat, a profound desperation filling her. With a mix of longing and panic, she pulled him to her. Welcoming his tongue deep into her mouth, she kissed him fiercely.

It was Noah who ended the kiss, drawing her from him, holding her at arm's length, fixing her with his all-seeing eyes. "You know who the murderer is, don't you, Chloe?"

She hesitated, swallowing down the balloon of emotion. "I don't know for sure—"

"A hunch, though. A good hunch." He stroked her shoulder absently with his thumb.

"Yes," she murmured tremulously. "A hunch."

MILDRED MEAD had decided to do a report on the growing problem of beer drinking among Thornhill teenagers. As an angle for her story, she thought to head over to the gorge below the Ryder Bridge—a well-known teenage haunt—to count the number of empty beer cans lying among the rocks. There were plenty enough there for any number of stories, but Mildred never did get around to counting them. Something else caught her eye and made her forget about her newspaper article altogether. Scurrying up the rocks she got into her car and sped to the nearest phone booth.

LARA THOUGHT he'd been kind to give her some water to drink before leaving her again, but now she realized it had been anything but kindness. She understood now that he'd put something in the water.

She kept blinking, trying to get her vision to clear. But nothing came into focus. She felt dizzy, nauseated. And scared. So scared.

Her mind was fuzzy, too. She couldn't remember... Had she written that note—that suicide note? Think. Think. She remembered telling him she wouldn't do it. She remembered him telling her, never say won't. But had she done it? Or was he waiting for the new drug he'd used on her to take enough of an effect to get her cooperation? Time. How much time did she have left?

The room was swaying, the walls buckling. And now it wasn't Chloe's name she called.

"Momma. Oh, Momma." Her mother had powers. Her momma would show her a way out. "Please come to me, Momma."

She swallowed air in shallow breaths as she cried out for her mother. Little by little she detected a new scent in the air. The scent of roses....

So hard to see. Her eyes burned. Sleepy. Need to stay awake. "Momma?" A deeper breath. "Are you here, Momma?"

And then, slipping between the door and the jamb, like a bat, a filmy, white shadow appeared.

"My little girl. My baby."

"Momma? Is it really you, Momma?"

"Poor baby."

"He's bad, Momma. He's so bad." Tears flowed down Lara's cheeks.

"I know, baby. I should have known all along. There were signs. The scrawl of greed..."

"What can I do, Momma?" Lara whined. "He's going to kill me."

"My baby. My poor baby. You must fight him."

"How, Momma? How can I fight him. He's too strong for me. He keeps drugging me. I can't think straight. Don't let me die, Momma."

"Don't be afraid. He feeds off your fear. Be brave, my darling girl. Stay alert. Above all else, hold fast."

"I'm trying, Momma. I'm trying." But in her effort, she suddenly remembered. "Momma." Her voice was a plaintive wail. "I wrote it, Momma. I wrote the note. I remember now. He untied me...he dictated the note to me.

My...confession. My...suicide note. Oh Momma...it's too late. It's too late..."

"Be strong, my girl. He left you untied. Get up. Get up and get out of here. You can do it, my girl..."

"Yes, Momma. Yes..." Then her eyes rolled back in her head and she slumped over.

HARVEY MEAD braced himself against the wind as he watched the proceedings from the rocky promontory overlooking the gorge.

When the car Mildred Mead had found was rolled back upright, Denk gave his chief a thumbs up sign. The car was empty. A couple of minutes later, Denk climbed up the rocks and handed Harvey the papers he'd found in the glove compartment.

"It's the Emory girl's car, all right," Denk said. "The boys are going over it, but on quick inspection there's no sign of bloodstains inside. My guess is the car was empty when it hit the bottom."

Denk and Harvey Mead climbed up to the bridge and walked to its northern end.

"Look," Denk pointed to the tire marks in the dirt just past the bridge. "The car must have gone down over the rocks this way."

Harvey nodded. But his eyes weren't fixed on the tire marks in the dirt. He was looking up the road at the old Grange Hall...

THE WIND HAD kicked up again. So much for sunshine. The sky was bleak. The earlier soaking rain made the ground spongy beneath their feet. Chloe hugged her jacket to her feet, feeling a chill that was unrelated to the weather. Noah walked beside her, his hands shoved in the pockets of his raincoat. His right hand made contact with the cold steel of his snub-nosed revolver.

She looked over at him, started to say something, then changed her mind. Not until the garage was in sight, did she speak.

"I have to get something . . . in there." Curly strands of auburn hair fell across her cheeks.

Noah studied her. He thought her eyes looked haunted. "Okay," he said reluctantly. "I'll stand guard outside. Just in case . . ."

At the door of the garage, Chloe felt a surge of raw panic. But there was no turning back now. She'd chosen this path . . . or perhaps it had chosen her.

She pulled the garage door open, and even as fear drummed against her temples, she stepped inside. Without hesitation she made her way to the back of the garage.

They were still there. For a moment, all she could do was stare down at the scattered pages. Then slowly, she bent down to scoop up the screenplay. *Draw Down the Moon* by Thad Emory.

In the dim light, she began reading the first pages, a dark, gory horror story about a secret coven in a small college town. . . .

"Isn't it strange how fiction is often a harbinger of fact?"

At the sound of the familiar masculine voice, Chloe's head jerked around. He was standing in the doorway of the garage.

"It's all there," he said. "The whole sordid story. Witches' covens, mystical symbols of power, dark deeds, all perpetrated for mortal greed. My inspiration. It would make a great movie. Only now . . . well, there are enough such films around."

"Where's . . . ?" Before she could finish, he cut her off.

"I do love you, Chloe. I've loved you for such a long time." He smiled. "You're not surprised it's me, are you. It's been tripping around the edges of your unconscious for a while, but I was successful at keeping it at bay. I knew, though, that it was only a matter of time. You are good, Chloe. As good as Madam Witch always said you were."

It occurred to Chloe in a distant part of her brain that greed hadn't been his only driving force. No, there was something more that drove him to commit such heinous acts.

"Not to worry, darling. We'll get married right away. A wife can't be made to testify against her husband. I'll make you happy, Chloe. We can go anywhere, start a whole new life."

"No..." The emphatic rejection burst from her lips as she stared at Thad Emory in revulsion. Sweet, unassuming, ordinary Thad Emory. She remembered when he'd come to see her in Boston, before taking off for Hollywood. He'd seemed so awkward and earnest as he'd confessed his love and begged her to marry him. She'd tried to be kind, but in the end she'd told him she didn't love him. And for a moment, his bland, pleasant face had revealed black fury. Only for an instant, and then he'd got it under control. And he'd said, "Well, one day when I'm rich and famous, you'll regret this decision."

Now Thad made no effort to camouflage his dark rage. "Has Noah asked you to marry him already? The bastard. Thinks he can waltz back into your life as though nothing has happened. Well, he let you go once, and he'll have to let you go again. You will marry me, Chloe. Because, really, you have no other choice. Anyway, I've taken care of everything. It won't be as if you were marrying a criminal. Soon the police will find Lara and the suicide note she left, confessing to her crimes. I'll be home free, darling."

Thad started toward her. "We're home free."

"Where's Noah? What have you done to Noah? Tell me," Chloe pleaded. *Noah can't be dead. I'd know. I'd sense it. Or am I too frightened to sense anything but the portents of my own demise?*

"Doctors shouldn't carry guns around," Thad said laconically, pulling the snub-nosed revolver from his pocket. "Doctors aren't meant to kill. They're healers."

Tears cascaded from her eyes. "Noah," she screamed out.

"I'm afraid the doctor is . . . indisposed at the moment."

"You haven't—" She couldn't finish. It was too awful.

"You're the psychic, darling. Can't you still feel his presence?"

Yes, yes, she could. Faint. But, yes . . .

"Not for long, though." Thad flashed her a smile. "Don't look so grief stricken, darling. I've only knocked him out and put him away for safekeeping. If you're a good girl, I might even arrange a final reunion."

How could she ever have seen this cold-hearted, cold-blooded murderer as ordinary and unassuming? She wanted to scream at him, curse him, claw him. But her rage would only provoke him to strike back. She had to hold her fury in check, play for time.

"I don't understand, Thad. I've always thought of you as a warm, caring, loving man. I don't mean just your feelings for me . . . but for your mother . . . your sister." She almost gagged on her words.

"They weren't blood relatives, Chloe. That should count for something. Amanda was always reminding me of the fact I was adopted. Every time I did anything naughty, I could see that look in her eyes. *He isn't my son. He doesn't have my genes. He's tainted by bad blood.*"

"But Amanda treated you like her own. I know she loved you."

Thad snickered. His eyes had a feverish glint. "Did you know my real mother was a witch as well?"

"No. No, I didn't know." *Pretend interest. Keep him talking. Make him think that he can still win me over to his side.*

"Yes, it's true. She'd studied witchcraft with Amanda in graduate school. To hear Amanda tell it, my natural mother meant to use the *faith* for her own dark, sordid deeds. Unfortunately she didn't get many opportunities. She died in childbirth. Amanda told me how I was shuffled around for a few years, but she'd made a deathbed promise to my mother to keep an eye on me. Finally, when I was four, thinking she couldn't have any children of her own, Amanda decided to adopt me. The year I turned six, she gave birth to Lara. Her natural child. That was when I knew I would never really matter to her...."

As Chloe listened to Thad ramble on, she began to fill in all the blanks. She realized, as she stared at this warped man, that greed was only the icing on the motives that had driven him to murder. He had lived his life consumed with feelings of rejection, jealousy, hatred. And once he'd stolen that atheme, he had set a course in motion on which there was no turning back.

Thad needed no prodding to go on with his tale. He seemed pleased to talk. "When I went out to Hollywood, I thought I'd be able to begin again, start fresh, make it on my own. I'd show you all. That screenplay you've been reading? I wrote it in Hollywood. No one wanted it. Too tame. That's a laugh, isn't it?"

"I always thought you were a talented writer, Thad. What does Hollywood know?"

He laughed. "Amanda thought it was extraordinary. She found it a couple of weeks ago while she was cleaning out the garage. I'll never forget the funny look she gave me after she read it." An ugly smiled distorted his features. "You see, the script was about a witch who possessed a very valuable and powerful atheme. A young man comes along, pretends to be a believer, but is really just interested in stealing the atheme and making himself a fortune. When he does steal it, a dark, evil force is unleashed."

"You've been planning to steal the atheme since you returned from Hollywood?" Chloe asked, wondering why he'd waited all that time.

"No. That was the funny part. I never really thought the atheme was worth all that much. Oh, Amanda had alluded to its value over the years, but I always thought she meant its spiritual value. I didn't find out about its extraordinary monetary value until after Amanda read the script and gave me that strange look. Lara told me afterward that Amanda had once been offered close to a million bucks for it."

"So you turned fiction into fact," Chloe said in a low voice. And the theft had unleashed a dark evil force within Thad himself.

"I thought, at first, I'd get away with it. I had a terrific copy made. It cost me a pretty penny. Only, the minute Amanda took up the atheme, she knew. She knew it was a fake. I had worried about that. That's part of the reason I doctored that wine she always sipped during the ceremony."

"And the other ... part?" Chloe asked in a low voice.

"I figured if she did spot the fake she might want to ... cause trouble. And I really didn't want any trouble. I hid in the bushes and watched the proceedings that night. When the circle was over, Amanda stayed behind. I waited until everyone had left, or so I thought. Amanda was sitting in the center of her circle, writing something. I thought I could sneak off without her spotting me. I was wrong. She immediately accused me of stealing the atheme, and demanded its return or she'd turn me over to the authorities. She was pretty cogent at first, but· fairly soon the drug reached its peak. I did what had to be done.

"I really had no other choice, Chloe. The same for Alice Donovan. It turned out she'd come back to the glen for a sweater she'd left behind. I tried my best to put the fear of the devil into her, but in the end I decided it was better to be safe than sorry."

"And you decided the same about Peter Mott?"

"Well, I never really cared much for Mott. Sleazy character if you ask me. I wasn't thrilled that Lara had agreed to marry him. Of course, Mott was tickled pink to get his hands on prime Honeysuckle Hill property."

"But that wasn't why you killed him. He discovered the atheme. The real atheme. In the carton in the garage. Where you'd hidden it."

"Ah, yes. I see there's really no need for me to explain things to you, Chloe."

"But... but what about Paula? Did she see you that night, too?"

"Unfortunately. I ended up putting on a show for half the town it seems. Paula got all the way to her car and then remembered something she wanted to discuss with Amanda. Amanda was dead by the time she arrived back in the glen. And I was still tidying up. Oh, I gave her some song and dance about hearing Amanda crying out to the devil like she was possessed and then stabbing herself before I could stop her. Paula always was gullible. I warned her there'd be hell to pay if she got involved or involved me in any way. When I thought she might weaken, I reinforced my warning. I stopped by her place and snatched one of the kid's dolls."

"Your kid."

"I wouldn't have hurt the kid, Chloe. I'm not that kind of guy."

"Where's Lara, Thad? Does she know the truth, too? Is that why you've been keeping her drugged?"

"She came down to the glen to make it up with Amanda. They'd had a spat earlier that night." He paused. "It was too late to make it up with her. And now...it's too late for Lara. I have to tidy up all the loose ends. There's no other way."

"And Noah? Is he a loose end, too?" She could hardly get the question out.

Thad leaned so close to her now, she could feel his stale breath on her face. "That depends on you, Chloe. Noah was never the right man for you, darling. It's my love that has remained true and constant."

"Then why did you lure me out to the Grange with Alice that night? It was you who sent the notes. It was you who dressed up in that white robe and played ghost...."

"Ghost? You really have this thing about ghosts, Chloe. In a minute you'll have me believing in them, too. It wasn't me you saw on that hill. But I did send the notes. Forgive me, Chloe. But when you first showed up back in Thornhill I thought...well, I thought you'd sense what I had done and turn me in. And, then, of course, there was Alice. I figured I could kill two birds with one stone. Only I found out Lucy knew where you'd gone. She was carrying on so much about you being in some kind of danger and how she meant to send the police out for you that I scrapped my original plan."

"Instead, you decided to play the knight in shining armor," Chloe said sarcastically.

"A nice touch. It did throw you off my trail, admit it."

THE MEETING ROOM of the old Grange Hall was empty. There was a small office in the back of the building, off to the right of the low platform stage. Harvey Mead motioned to Denk to check it out.

"Door's locked," Denk informed him.

"Unlock it," snarled Harvey as he approached.

Denk stepped back, drew in a deep breath, raised his foot, and kicked the door in. Harvey stood beside him, gun in hand.

The office was empty. Harvey cursed under his breath. Denk was inside, looking around. There was a closet. Both men held their breath as Denk opened it. An old file cabinet, empty shelves. Harvey flashed his light along the walls, the floor...

"Well, well," Harvey muttered, bending.

Denk was looking over his shoulder. "Hey, a trap door. Must go down to the cellar."

"Good guess," Harvey muttered, pulling it open.

"Is she dead, Chief?" Denk asked nervously, moments later.

"Near enough," Harvey muttered. He was feeling Lara's faint pulse just below her ear.

It was Denk who spotted the note tucked in the pocket of Lara's shirt. He scanned it quickly. "Look at this, Chief. A suicide note."

"Suicide, my eye. Look at her wrists. She must have been tied up for hours. Our murderer's getting sloppy. Must be cracking up. Help me get her into the squad car. You drive her to the hospital. Use the siren. She might not make it if we have to wait for an ambulance."

"What are you gonna do, Chief?"

"Me. I'm gonna wait right here for the bastard to return. If my guess is right, his plan is to stick Lara back in her car and have it look like she drove herself into that gorge."

"Won't he be surprised when he shows up to find both the car and the girl missing?"

Harvey gave a dry laugh. "Yeah, maybe he'll think they dematerialized."

THAD GAVE CHLOE a curious look. "You really do believe in ghosts, don't you Chloe? There was the ghost on the hill. And then the other night at Amanda's house just before Noah and I arrived you mentioned something about seeing a ghost. I blame myself in a way."

Chloe gave him a puzzled look. "I don't understand."

"Well, maybe if I hadn't pulled that dumb stunt on you back in college..."

"What stunt?"

"That time right before your graduation. I saw you heading for the glen and I put on mother's robe and took up her atheme. I just wanted to scare you a little. I suppose I was angry that even though you and Noah had broken up, you still wouldn't give me the time of day."

"That was you...?"

"You really freaked me out in the end. You honestly thought I was a ghost. When I raised the atheme you went into shock, grabbed your chest like you were having a heart attack and passed out. I had to dump the costume and run back for Amanda, pretending I had no idea what happened. If I'd known that silly prank would chase you out of my life for seven years, I would never have done it. Ironic, isn't it, that I couldn't scare you off again when I really thought it in your own best interest not to stick around."

"You mean that doll you put in Alice's purse for me to find."

"Actually, I got it from Karin Niels. She made it to use in one of her nonsensical ceremonies. Down with the good witch. Long live the wicked witch. She didn't want to part with it, but she owed me a favor."

He gave Chloe a gloating look. "You remember Dantes, don't you, Chloe? I never could stand that cat. I was checking out one of Karin's circles down at the Grange one night when the cat wandered in. Karin's meager theatrics weren't lighting any sparks, so I decided to light some myself. What better way than a nifty sacrifice of the good witch's familiar?" He grinned, reaching out to stroke Chloe's hair.

Chloe snapped her head away, but Thad only laughed. "I bet you don't pull away when Noah touches you, do you, Chloe? Oh, maybe you did for a while. Noah was high on your list of suspects, wasn't he? I helped that along nicely, I thought. Especially that night at the Indian Restaurant. It was my idea, you know, that Lara drag Noah to the same restaurant. The look on your face when you saw them walk in together was priceless."

"I knew it couldn't be Noah," she said without thinking. As soon as she saw the look of disgust on Thad's face, fear bubbled in her chest.

He gave her a long, thoughtful look, his expression unreadable. "I don't know, Chloe," he said finally. "Maybe a happy ever after ending isn't in the cards for us. You're the psychic. What's your intuition?"

Chloe went numb. There was a sour taste in her mouth. The taste of death. Her own, Lara's . . . and Noah's.

Chapter Seventeen

Flash. Flash. Flash.

"Beautiful, isn't it, Chloe?" Thad crooned, stroking the hilt of the atheme as if it were a lover. The candlelight caught the silver double-edged blade, making it shimmer. Thad's sneering closed-lip smile spread across his face as he held the atheme up high, as if he was calling down a demented god.

In the dim light of Amanda Emory's basement, Chloe could see Noah's prone form tumbled on the floor. He was bound, as she was, hand and foot. His eyes were closed. A wound on the base of his skull was trickling blood, leaving a small, thickening puddle on the floor.

Thad lowered the atheme, kneeling before Chloe on the cold cement floor as she sat huddled against the wall. His eyes were slightly glazed as he ever so lightly touched the tip of the blade between her breasts.

He is the Devil, Chloe thought in despair. Then, in a rush she remembered the brief lesson in self-defense against evil forces she'd given Paula. *The secret is strength. An emotional tenacity. A mental refusal to submit to fear. That tenacity creates the protective shield* . . .

Her eyes glistened with determination as she glared at Thad. "You hide your doubt and fear, Thad, but I can see it. I can taste it. Your plan isn't working. Even now, it's coming apart. Amanda won't let you go, Thad. I *have* seen her. I've heard her. She must have retribution, Thad. It's the only way she can rest."

"You can't play your psychic games on me, Chloe. I don't believe that crap."

"Don't you?" She looked deep into his eyes, trying desperately to ignore the blade at her breast. "Haven't you felt her presence, Thad? Haven't you picked up her scent? The scent of roses, Thad. Amanda's scent." She let her eyelids flutter closed. "I can smell it now. I can feel her presence at this very moment." Slowly, she opened her eyes, casting her gaze beyond Thad. "She's with us."

He gave a dry laugh, but it took no special powers of perception for Chloe to hear the nervousness in his voice.

Slowly she returned her gaze to Thad. But not before she risked a surreptitious glance at Noah. A glance that filled her heart with jubilation. Noah's eyes were open. He'd even managed an encouraging smile.

"Go on," Thad said, suspicion mixing with alarm. "Tell me about your ghost, Chloe. I've still got some time. Amuse me, my dear."

"Time's already up, Thad. For you. She's turned you in, even now."

"Who? Amanda's ghost?" He gave a deprecating sneer. Or at least he tried. His mounting fear frustrated his attempt.

"No, Thad. Not Amanda's ghost."

"Who then? Lara? Impossible. By now, she's dead. She was practically dead when I left the Grange. All I have to do is go back to collect the body and dump it in her car down at the gorge. I've figured it all out. Lara won't betray me. Nor will you, Chloe."

Chloe hadn't meant Lara. She'd been referring to Paula Dubois, wanting him to think his terror tactics hadn't worked and she'd told Harvey all she knew. But as soon as Thad mentioned Lara's name, a vision of her flashed before Chloe's eyes.

"Lara isn't dead, Thad." Was she saying this just to make him nervous, or did she somehow really believe it? A hunch? "Harvey Mead found her in time. She's telling them how you made her write that note you told me about. How it was you—"

"No, I don't believe you," Thad spat out.

"And then there's Paula."

"I'll take care of her."

"Too late, Thad." Knowing her life and Noah's depended on it Chloe lied as convincingly as she could. "Paula's already confessed that you are the father of her child. She's told the police how she saw you that night . . ."

"Shut up."

"Just like Alice saw you . . ."

"Shut up, I said."

"And Lara." She gave him a demeaning glare. "You certainly did end up in the limelight, Thad. Only, I don't think you can handle the limelight as easily as you thought you could."

"Well, there's no audience now," Thad snickered. "There's no one here but your half-dead boyfriend."

Chloe fixed her gaze just over Thad's right shoulder. For several moments she deliberately kept silent. When she did speak, her voice was very low. "Are you certain of that, Thad? Are you so sure you don't believe in ghosts?" she whispered chillingly.

She saw the flicker of doubt in his face. Keeping the atheme pressed to her breast Thad gave a quick look around. "What are you trying to pull, Chloe?"

She faced him down like a duelist, her eyes fixed unblinkingly on him. "She's here, Thad. She can't rest. Not until...she has your soul. That's what she's come back for." She took her eyes off Thad for a moment and motioned to the basement window. "Look Thad. The moon. Amanda's drawing down the moon, calling on the gods and goddesses to help her."

"You're crazy," Thad snapped, but there was no hiding the building tension in his features.

"Breathe deeply, Thad. Can't you smell her perfume? Roses? The fragrant scent of roses. Yes, she's here. Didn't you know she'd come back for you, Thad? Way down in your gut, didn't you know?"

All the while Chloe spoke in a low, droning voice, she risked periodic glances in Noah's direction. He was fully conscious now. She could see the movement in his arms; knew he was working at the ropes that bound his wrists together behind his back. Maybe Thad had faltered; not bothered to tie him up tightly, thinking Noah wouldn't regain consciousness at all.

There was a flickering of light. Thad's eyes suddenly shot over to the small group of candles he had lit. One had gone out. "The wind..." he muttered.

"It isn't the wind, Thad," Chloe crooned. "She likes the darkness. The air is growing heavier now. And the scent of roses..."

Chloe could see by Thad's taut grimace that he could smell the rose scent. The power of suggestion? Perhaps. Was it working on her as well? For she could smell Amanda's scent, too.

"She isn't...here. I don't...see..." Thad's voice faltered, caught and stopped. Did he see her? The atheme dropped from his hand. His face was ashen, his breathing shallow. Tears began sliding down his cheeks, as he whispered in a very young, frightened voice, "No. She's not here. She's dead. I killed her. She can't come back. There's no such thing...as ghosts."

He staggered to his feet. His face was so white, it looked entirely drained of color. "No. No. Don't...don't come near me..." His eyes were dazed. He stumbled back, tripping over Chloe's foot. He landed hard on the concrete floor, but the pain of the fall was minor compared to the anguish cutting across his face. "No...please...I'm sorry," he whimpered, his whole body shaking. "Forgive me, Mother. Mother..." He shielded his eyes with his arm and began sobbing wildly. "Don't take me, Mother. Don't hurt me."

He clutched at his throat as he saw the hands descending toward his neck. He flailed and screamed, his voice a pitiful wail. "No, Moth...er," he cried, the last syllable soaring into a bloodcurdling yelp.

"You can't resist a psychic attack, Thad," Chloe whispered.

The hands reached for his neck. Thad began to choke. His mouth gaped open, his eyes bulged. He made a few pitiful rasping sounds...

"Noah," Chloe cried out fearfully. "Noah, help him."

Noah, who had managed to loosen the bonds around his ankles enough to stagger to his feet, lurched in Thad's direction.

Dropping to his knees beside the stricken man, Noah bent over him listening for a heartbeat. He heard nothing. He struggled to get his hands free.

Minutes later, as he felt the rope around his wrists begin to give way, he knew it was too late. Still, he administered CPR for several minutes hoping to get a pulse. Finally, he stopped, staring down at Thad Emory. Then he gave Chloe a haunted look. "He's dead. I...never saw...anything like it."

Chloe nodded slowly. "It was his own fear—first blinding him, then choking him."

"I think," Noah murmured, "he honestly believed it was Amanda's ghost."

Tears rolled down Chloe's cheeks as Noah untied her and then cradled her in his arms. She thought about what had just happened; she thought again about the vision in white on the hill behind the Grange, the blinding light in her closet; the ethereal voice whispering, *"Beware, the devil wears many guises."*

Chloe lifted her head and met Noah's gaze. "Maybe it *was* Amanda's ghost," she whispered. For only now was the scent of roses slowly dissipating....

Epilogue

It was a few days later when Mildred Mead sat drinking tea with Noah and Chloe in Noah's Maywood Street living room. Mildred was doing a piece on them as part of her What's What article for the *Tab's* early-December edition.

"I just got finished interviewing Val Thatcher over at North Country Realty for our real estate update section," Mildred remarked, "and she told me Lara had put the Emory place on the market."

"I think it's for the best," Chloe said softly.

Mildred nodded. "I couldn't agree more. She left for her European trip yesterday you know."

"Yes, we know," Noah said with a half-smile. "A trip will do her good. She's always wanted to travel."

Mildred hesitated. "Harvey told me she donated Amanda's atheme to a museum in New York. I think it would have been a bad omen for her to sell it...under the circumstances. Besides, with Thad gone—may he rest in peace—I wonder if he knew about his weak heart?" Her head tilted as she gave Noah an intent gaze. "It was a heart attack, wasn't it?"

Noah entwined his hand with Chloe's. He gave a tender squeeze. "Yes, Mildred. A heart attack."

Mildred shrugged. "Anyway, Lara's set for life financially even without selling the atheme. And I wouldn't be surprised if she didn't fall in love with a lord or a count or some such noble personage in her wanderings."

Noah, put his arm around Chloe and pressed her lightly to him. "I hope so," he said softly. "I hope one day she finds real love."

Chloe touched Noah's cheek. "So do I."

Mildred beamed at them, then remembered her *Tab* article. "So, what about the two of you? Is it just rumor, or are you, shall we say, informally engaged?"

"For the record?" Chloe quipped.

"If you'd prefer to tell me something off the record—" Mildred began, her eyes twinkling.

"For the record, Mildred, we're formally engaged," Noah cut in. "You can quote me on that," he added with a wink.

"Oh, I'm so happy. I always said the two of you made a perfect couple." Mildred gave a secret smile. "Well, of course, no couple is really perfect, but you know what I mean."

Noah grinned at Chloe. "Yes, we know. And we agree."

"When's the big day?" Mildred asked eagerly.

"Well, Christmas isn't far off," Chloe murmured. "And since all I want for Christmas—for life—is Noah, I think a Christmas wedding would be nice."

Noah kissed her tenderly on her lips. "That would be nice." His gray-green eyes shone with love.

"Perfect," Mildred said. Then she reached out and patted Chloe's hand. "And you're going to be a big success teaching at the college."

Chloe looked startled. "How did you know I'd be working at Dorchester? It was supposedly hush, hush, until I received written confirmation of my appointment from

Arnie Metcalf, the acting chairman of the anthropology department."

Mildred and Noah shared a smile. Then Noah pressed Chloe's hand to his lips. "Nothing's ever a secret for very long in a small town like this," he said with a devilish smile.

Everyone loves a spring wedding, and this April,
Harlequin cordially invites you to read the most
romantic wedding book of the year.

**ONE WEDDING—FOUR LOVE STORIES
FROM OUR MOST DISTINGUISHED
HARLEQUIN AUTHORS:**

BETHANY CAMPBELL
BARBARA DELINSKY
BOBBY HUTCHINSON
ANN McALLISTER

*The church is booked, the reception arranged and the
invitations mailed. All Diane Bauer and Nick Granatelli
have to do is walk down the aisle. Little do they realize that
the most cherished day of their lives will spark so many
romantic notions....*

Available wherever Harlequin books are sold.   HWED-1AR

Take 4 bestselling love stories FREE
Plus get a FREE surprise gift!

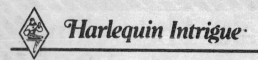